Copyright © 2024 by Marie Violet.

All rights reserved.

No part of this publication may be reproduced, distributed, or transmitted in any form or by any means, including photocopying, recording, or other electronic or mechanical methods, without the prior written permission of the publisher, except as permitted by U.S. copyright law. For permission requests, contact marievioletauthor@gmail.com.

The story, all names, characters, and incidents portrayed in this production are fictitious. No identification with actual persons (living or deceased), places, buildings, and products is intended or should be inferred.

First published in 2024.

ISBN: 978-1-0687650-1-8

WHISPERS OF THE NIGHT RAVENS
BOOK ONE

THE ARCHER & THE FLAME

MARIE VIOLET

Content Note

The Archer & The Flame is an adult fantasy romance story. It contains several mature themes including:

- Violence (including blood, gore and death) and strong language/profanity

- Explicit sexual content (including multiple open door romance scenes)

- Depiction of mental illness including panic attacks

- Loss of a parent/family member and grief

- Drowning

- Torture (mentioned)

- Emotional abuse (mentioned) and imprisonment

If you feel that there is something which should be added to the list, please let me know.

For anyone carrying the weight of the world on their shoulders.

Even the strong need a break sometimes.

A GUIDE TO THE TYPES OF
MAGIC FOUND IN IDRIX

COMMON MAGIC: USABLE BY ALL FAE

GLAMOURS
WARDS OF PROTECTION
BARGAINS

BLESSINGS: BESTOWED UPON THE CHOSEN FEW

FIRE
EARTH
WATER
AIR

ANCIENT MAGIC: ALL THAT REMAINS

ENCHANTED ARTEFACTS
MAGICAL BEASTS

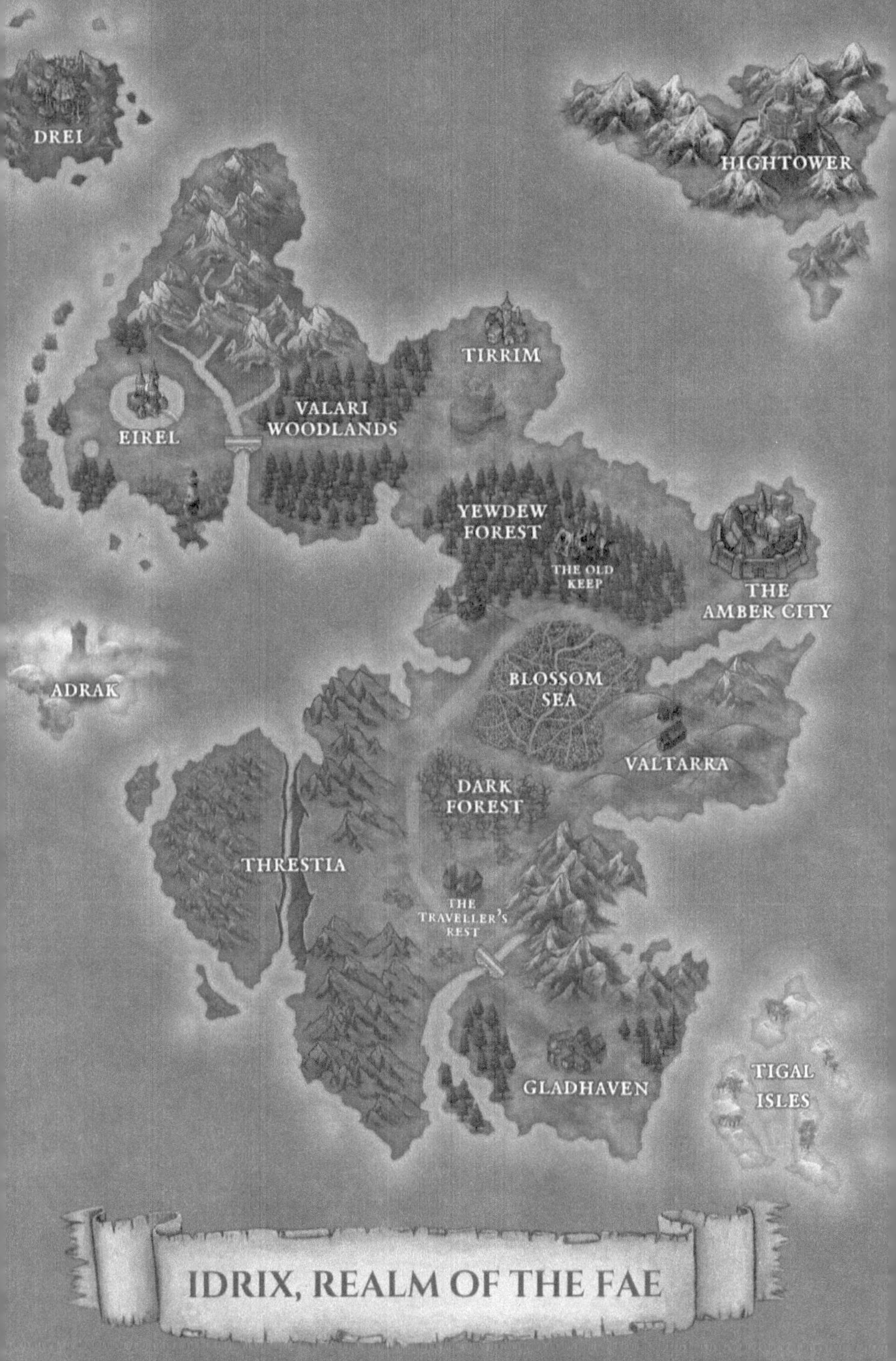

DREI
HIGHTOWER
TIRRIM
VALARI WOODLANDS
EIREL
YEWDEW FOREST
THE OLD KEEP
THE AMBER CITY
ADRAK
BLOSSOM SEA
VALTARRA
DARK FOREST
THRESTIA
THE TRAVELLER'S REST
GLADHAVEN
TIGAL ISLES
IDRIX, REALM OF THE FAE

Chapter 1

It was said that those who entered the gates of the Amber City were bestowed with the favour of the gods, a parting gift from the five deities that pooled their magic to birth Idrix thousands of years ago.

It was a convenient myth, spun up in a bid to attract hordes of admiring visitors, and judging by the fae battling to press their hands to the white stone as they passed, it was working.

I wasted no time with the frivolous tradition, not when I was counting down the hours until I could return to the peace and quiet of the forest. Here, in the bustling city, it felt like a distant memory. But I had orders to carry out, and I'd never failed a mission. I had no intention of starting now.

"Maps! Get your maps here! Need a navigator?" Hawkers swarmed me, eagerly thrusting scrolls of faded parchment at my chest. I batted them away with a knowing glare, unwilling to become another victim of their schemes. The maps were freely available from the Grand Library, taken and resold to unsuspecting travellers, and the navigators whose services they pedalled were inexperienced youths, more likely to lose you than provide direction.

At my dismissal, they lost interest and moved onto easier marks, of which there were many, but it was only the beginning of my trials.

The city was nothing short of spectacular. I strode through curved streets lined with white buildings, adorned with sculpted facades of intricate patterns and the famous amber stained-glass windows that gave the capital its name. A row of trees divided the footpath in two, but in the place of leaves hanging from the branches were orbs of ever-burning flame, ensuring darkness never blanketed the city. Beneath them, fae talked and laughed loudly, sipping from tiny, steaming goblets as they occupied wooden benches. Perched on a hill, overlooking it all, was the White Temple, the sacred monument where the Circle of the Enlightened carried out their divine judgements.

I didn't linger. Where once the city had stirred my curiosity, promising cultural delights found nowhere else in Idrix, I had long grown tired of it. Instead, I headed directly to my destination.

The busy marketplace at the heart of the city was my idea of hell. Too many sweltering bodies were packed under its glass roof, struggling against each other. The heavy scents of spiced pastries, roasting meats, and bubbling pots of wine battled for dominance, while the chatter of excited customers melded together into a grating noise. Strangers brushed against me, too close for comfort, my body tense at their unwelcome touch.

As with many buildings, the marketplace had been designed with appearances in mind over function. The masterfully decorated stalls, each encased in its own wooden structure, left a pitiful amount of room to walk between them. The poor design was a consequence of the capital's own making. Residents were hand-selected, invitations based on the size of their coin purse and their long list of accomplishments. Only the finest fae were worthy to reside where gods once walked, after all.

Unfortunately, that rarely included those with common sense.

It was a shame their inflated egos were just as large, looking down their noses at anyone who didn't meet their impossible standards. With my rough-cut silver hair, tattered clothing and bow slung over my shoulder, they made no effort to hide their sneers.

The sooner I left the city, the better.

I kept my elbows tucked in as I moved deeper inside, removing the temptation to jab the audacious fae pushing past me. Causing a commotion was a certain way to attract unwanted attention, and I knew better than to compromise myself like that. A scout of the Night Ravens was required to be stealthy above all else, blending into our surroundings to uncover the information we sought. Mere shadows that vanished once our orders had been fulfilled.

The occupants of the market were an impenetrable wall, an ever-moving obstacle standing between me and my target. The only way to move forward was to drag my body through any gap, no matter how narrow, ignoring the pressure against my ribcage and the queasy sensation it prompted. Yet there were those in the crowd that smiled, holding hands as they navigated the crush. Enjoying themselves. City folk scared me more than the dangerous creatures that roamed the Yewdew Forest.

When I reached the antiques merchant and the small haven of space his stall provided, I had to steady myself against the wall, breathing in the sweet air of freedom. Around me chaos reigned, the market becoming busier every moment. The next time Reuben required a scout to investigate it, I would tell him to look elsewhere.

"Are you well?" A young woman with hair as dark as the night sky and full, rounded cheeks asked. She was reassuringly steady, the embodiment of calm in the mayhem of the marketplace.

"I will be. I'm not used to the busyness," I answered. Was she asking out of true concern or searching for a weakness? If experience had taught me anything, it was that someone approaching usually had a hidden agenda. I stayed on alert, waiting for the stranger to reveal hers.

"Took me a while too. It's worth it though. There are real treasures here, if you know where to look." She smiled. "Good luck."

I couldn't figure out her angle. She'd asked nothing of me, my purse hadn't been relieved of coins, and there was no evidence of foul play. Had she been genuine? By the time I'd gathered myself enough to ask what she was doing there, she had already disappeared into the crowd.

The shelves of the antiques stall were crammed floor to ceiling with, from what my undiscerning gaze could tell, useless junk. There were dusty tomes, faded brass ornaments, and what looked to be someone's forgotten spectacles. But customers were rummaging through the wares, someone shrieking with delight as they unearthed a hidden gem.

Ignoring them, I approached the main counter, a white bar inlaid with amber detailing where the merchant was chatting jauntily with his patrons. He was well-built, a pristine teal cloak hanging from his shoulders, and an impressive ginger beard to match his bushy hair.

The moment he laid eyes on me, his smile vanished, his gaze drifting down my body and settling on my frayed sleeves. "There's nothing for you here."

I cleared my throat, removing a scroll from my pack and handing it to him. A red wax seal kept the thick parchment rolled up, the exceptional quality of the letter a vital part of selling my cover story. The supplies had come from Reuben's personal stores, and he'd instructed me to ensure a single crease didn't ruin the message's presentation. It had been easier said than done, but I was glad to see it had survived thus far.

"I'm here on behalf of my master. You're known as the finest purveyor of rarities on the mainland, and he won't settle for less." I laid the flattery on thick in the hope he'd be too busy preening at the compliment to read into the meaning. It wasn't a lie, at least not enough of one to prevent me from speaking it, but it wasn't exactly the truth either. Reuben was technically my master, as far as someone I would take orders from, and the merchant did have a reputation that preceded him.

He held the parchment gingerly, unconvinced by my efforts, peering around me as if to move onto his next customer.

I tried again, unwilling to give up without a fight. There was a reason I'd gained notoriety within the Night Ravens for being stubborn to a fault. "That's a letter detailing his requirements. He insisted I came directly to you."

He shrugged, after a long moment breaking the seal and unfurling the scroll. I waited with bated breath as he scanned the contents, nodding and humming to himself. Reuben had always been skilled with words, wielding them as others wielded magic. I didn't share the ability, to my frustration.

"Do you think I've built my reputation for excellence by being easily swayed by some pretty words? Your master should come here himself if he wants to talk business, instead of wasting my time with some lackey." He tore the parchment in half, letting the fragments flutter to the ground. "Guards!"

This was about to become complicated. Two men clad in the amber robes of the city guard burst in, grabbing my arms as they attempted to strong-arm me out of the market.

"She's outstayed her welcome. Escort her from the premises and make sure she never returns." He shifted his focus to the next customer in line, a handsome youth with an elaborate cloak.

It was time for my last resort. I would attract the notice of every thief in the surrounding area, but I had no other choice. There wouldn't be another chance to inspect his wares, not without a new scout assigned and weeks of preparation. By then, it could be too late.

"Wait. Look in my pack before you banish me. My master suspected you would doubt the legitimacy of his interest, so he sent me with proof of funds."

He hesitated. The guards dragged me away, but I put up no fight, watching him waver with a glimmer of anticipation. Pleading my case would be no help at this point; he needed to decide for himself. It was a delicate dance, and one misstep would cause him to lose interest.

We'd made it all the way back to the threshold of the stall, far enough for doubt to finally set in, when he spoke. "Check her pack."

I released a breath as the guards let me go, rifling through my pack with little regard for my belongings, evidently deeming there was little of value contained within. When they unearthed the sizable pouch, filled to the brim with silver coins, they handed it to the shocked merchant.

"A deposit should your reputation be justified," I said.

He picked a coin from the top of the pile, examining it in the amber light of the glass roof. Satisfied, he waved away the guards. "Your services are no longer needed."

They left the stall without a word, their blank expressions revealing nothing about his abrupt change of mind. It was unlikely to be the strangest course of events they'd witnessed while protecting the Amber City and its entitled residents.

He turned to me, becoming an entirely different man. "I hope there are no hard feelings. You can't be too careful with who to trust in these unsettling times." He laughed, as if we were sharing a private joke.

I brushed myself down, tilting my chin up in the haughty way I'd seen the residents do. "Indeed."

He murmured a few words into his assistant's ear, beckoning me to his side.

"Come with me," he said, pulling aside a curtain behind the counter and revealing an unremarkable wooden door. Opening it partway, he slipped inside. I followed closely behind.

Where I'd expected a storeroom with additional stock, the small room was bare except for a small table with a heavy chest resting on it. He placed my coin pouch next to the chest, keeping it within reach.

"Your master made a wise choice to seek me out. I have a talent for finding enchanted relics and persuading fae to part with them. It makes for an impressive collection, if I do say so myself."

I held back an eye roll, playing the part of a dedicated lackey, as he'd deemed me.

He retrieved an old key from his pocket, unlocking the chest with a loud click and exposing its valuable contents. Resting on a velvet-lined tray, equally spaced apart, were three artefacts.

The first was a thin dagger, the hilt carved from black stone and the tip impossibly sharp. Scratches marked the blade, but that didn't spoil its beauty. A goblet of ice came next, tendrils of fog spilling from its rim. It was so finely cut that its surface sparkled in the dim light like a gemstone. The third and final object was an elegant hand mirror, the glass held in place by hundreds of tiny butterflies, their wings fluttering in tandem.

They were extraordinary.

He grinned smugly at my reaction. "Beautiful pieces, aren't they?"

"May I?" I asked. I used my words sparingly, preferring to let him lead the conversation. Most fae found silence awkward and felt compelled to break it, usually by talking without thought. By holding my tongue, I could learn a great deal, sometimes things my target hadn't intended to share.

"Certainly. Examine them to your heart's content so you may send word to your master of their worth."

I picked up the dagger carefully, avoiding placing my fingers anywhere near its sharp tip. "What does it do?"

His finger twitched almost too quick to notice, but I did, filing away the information. "It belonged to the Prince of Shadows in Gladhaven's undercity, the prized dagger that he used to seize control of the misfits and miscreants to build his empire. According to my source, it's sharp enough to cut through anything."

"And this one?" The goblet was painful to hold, but I didn't let my discomfort show. He wasn't the type to respond well to weakness. Instead, I gritted my teeth and tolerated the pain.

"It passed through many owners over the years, and even I do not know it's true origin, but it is believed to indicate the presence of poison to its bearer."

"And the mirror?" It tickled as I held it. My reflection betrayed none of its secrets, simply showing my usual appearance. The determined gleam in my blue eyes, the sharp line of my jaw, and my silver hair as I tucked it behind the point of my ear.

"Smuggled out from Eirel. I went to great trouble to procure it on the assurance that it would show glimpses of the holder's future."

"And does it?" I couldn't resist the question.

His finger twitched again, and I worried I'd pushed him too far, but he answered. "It hasn't revealed the future to me yet, but I trust my source."

"I see. I believe I have everything I need." Everything I needed for my mission, at least.

I had to admire it. The ruse was meticulously crafted to draw attention where it was wanted, from his initial reluctance, to the artistry of the velvet-lined chest and his precisely chosen words. Any ordinary fae would be taken in.

But I was no ordinary fae.

My training with the Night Ravens had been exhaustive. I'd studied the history and characteristics of magic for years, from the elemental Blessings a rare few were gifted, through to the elusive artefacts that were all that remained of Idrix's ancient magic. I could spot an enchanted object immediately, but there wasn't a spark in the vicinity.

The glamour was impressive, a flawless example of the fae ability to mask something, or someone's, true appearance. But I knew what to look for. Almost invisible to the naked eye, a tiny flicker in the illusion was the confirmation I needed.

Fake. It was all fake. From the beating of the butterflies' wings to the ache in my fingers as I'd held the goblet.

Yet another dead end

"I take it your master will be satisfied?" The merchant's hand flexed towards my coins. I snatched them up before he could reach them.

"You have a collection that many would envy, but nothing that would suit his requirements at present." I kept my voice level, giving nothing away. "Should that change, we know where to find you."

"Another useless time waster," he muttered under his breath.

As frustrating as it was to walk away from the swindle knowing others would fall for it, my orders were to investigate, not intervene. And the last thing the Night Ravens needed was to make our presence known in the capital of all places.

"Thank you for your time," I said instead.

I made a swift exit from the antiques stall before the merchant decided to call for the guards again. Pushing through the crowd, I had hoped to leave behind the suffocation of the marketplace before I found trouble, but the day had more in store for me. A sharp pain was my only warning before I was relieved of my coin purse by quick hands.

As I'd feared, the thieves had found me.

Chapter 2

"Shit."

My little finger throbbed insistently, but there was no time to deal with the injury when I had more pressing concerns. After a fleeting glance to ensure there was no lasting damage, I scanned my surroundings for signs of the thief. For a moment, I worried they'd slipped away, consumed by the sea of faces.

Then I saw him.

A child burst through the market, fighting against the surge of oncoming fae and moving with an urgency at odds with those around him. I hurried after him, making rushed apologies to those I collided with in my haste to chase him through the crowd.

Once in the fresh air and open space of the city, he picked up speed, running like his life depended on it. I pressed on, pursuing him with every drop of energy I had. My lungs burned, each breath becoming more difficult than the last as I wove through the pristine streets in relentless pursuit.

I couldn't let this happen. Reuben had trusted me with the generous funds to boost the chances of my cover story being believed, a wise decision in the end, but we couldn't afford to lose them. That money was earmarked for vital supplies, and every member of the Night Ravens would suffer the consequences of my mistake.

It was my responsibility to make sure it wasn't lost to the capital.

The thief led me on a wild chase as he attempted to evade me, but he'd underestimated my desperation. I wouldn't let anything sabotage my position as a scout, no matter what it cost me.

We raced past the Grand Library before cutting through the Plaza of the Enlightened, curving around the enormous altar at its centre. Five statues possessing the gods' likenesses were buried in valuable offerings. The god of prosperity, Saru, and Ael, the goddess of magic, had the most ardent worshippers, but all had amassed piles of coins and jewels that glittered in the afternoon sunlight. It wasn't the only tribute we saw, but it was the largest by far.

Still, the boy ran, showing no signs of slowing.

My concern grew. I wasn't built for running long distances, thriving in situations where a more subtle approach was needed, but the pickpocket had forced me to pursue him across half the city and I didn't know if I could keep up for much longer.

He ducked into an alleyway and I followed close behind, smiling despite my breathlessness. We'd reached a dead end, an ivy-covered wall cutting us off from the rest of the capital. The boy skidded to a halt, his head darting wildly in every direction as he considered his next move.

I drew my bow in a bid to discourage him from doing anything reckless. My hand was sticky with blood, but I pushed through the stinging sensation to keep it levelled at him.

"I wouldn't do that if I were you," I said, a cold authority to my voice.

"Please. I need this." The boy's chin wobbled as he valiantly fought back tears. He was younger than I'd realised. Heartbreakingly young. Dirt plastered his distraught face, and his clothes were nothing more than rags.

I softened, remembering the disease that was hopelessness; how it robbed you of all the light in the world. "I need it too. Return the money and I'll let you go. I won't tell the guards, but only if you give it back now."

He met my gaze with a fierce determination that I had to respect, sizing me up to assess any chance of escape. I witnessed the moment the fight left him. He sank to the ground, holding out the pouch while he sobbed into the filthy sleeve of his shirt.

"Thank you," I said quietly, retrieving it from his tiny hand. My chest tightened, rage flooding me. He should be safe in a warm home, sheltered from the cruelty of life, not risking the wrath of the gods and the pretentious city fae, who were far less forgiving.

His broken spirit brought a memory to the surface unbidden, my cries for help left unanswered as the crushing realisation of my loss crashed into me. No one had cared, the burden mine alone to bear. I blinked it away, but the ache in my chest remained.

I did the only thing I could for him, pressing a silver coin into his palm, wincing at the sight of his marked skin. It was a poor substitute for what he'd attempted to steal from me, but it would provide a hot meal, at least. "Now, go."

He scarpered, leaving me alone in the alleyway, wondering if I'd only prolonged the inevitable. He might have stood a chance of success as a scout with the quick reflexes he'd displayed, but the dagger emblem seared into his skin was unmistakable. He was bound to the thieves' guild that caused the city guard so much strife. There would be too many questions raised by one of their young recruits going missing, and it wouldn't take long for whispers of a silver-haired woman with a bow reaching the wrong ears. Our chase through the streets must have been witnessed by hundreds of fae.

Scouts were forbidden from interfering beyond the scope of our mission. We were sent across Idrix to observe, record and report back. Whatever happened after that was out of our hands.

Clenching my teeth, I rinsed my injured finger with the unpleasantly warm water from my canteen. The wound stung in complaint as I dressed it with the cleanest of my rags. It would suffice until I healed, likely within a matter of hours, the shallow cut a minor inconvenience at most.

With the coin purse securely tucked into my pack, this time with a firm grip protecting it, I headed to my favourite place in the capital, an oasis of calm where I could steady myself before the journey back.

The glittering waters of the Sapphire Sea greeted me like an old friend. There was no land visible on the horizon with the coastline of Hightower just out of reach, but merchant ships dotted my view, their richly coloured sails contrasting the deep blue water in the golden afternoon light. I knew better than to wade in, staying behind the safety of the railing as I gazed out across the endless sea that had once been a huge part of my life, now tinged with a bitter sorrow.

It was a reminder of what was at stake, what adding to my tally of successful missions was all for. A reminder to not repeat the mistakes of the past.

I watched the bobbing waves until the air grew chilly with the retreat of the sun, goosebumps prickling my flesh. Taking a final look at the Sapphire Sea, not knowing how long it would be until I saw it again, I returned to the gates.

I blended into the throngs of fae exiting the Amber City, following them down steep stone steps and over a heavily guarded bridge to the grassy plains beyond. The guards paid us no mind, more concerned with who was entering, not leaving.

Here we passed the camps of those not fortunate enough to sleep within the walls, a second city that was smelly, messy and lively in a vast contrast to the perfection demanded of the capital's inner districts. Merchants travelled between tents, pedalling their wares. A huge fire pit attracted hundreds, its warmth providing sanctuary from the elements, and, most bizarrely of all, kegs of the famous Amber Ale floated towards a rowdy gathering, likely the efforts of an Air-Blessed fae hidden in the group. Not the wisest use of a rare gift, but certainly a bold one.

Instead of joining the masses on their way to Tirrim or climbing into a carriage to take the High Road south, I snuck away. My journey required a less trodden path, one that would swap the travellers complaining of their aching feet with more reclusive wildlife. There was nothing I wanted more in that moment. Doubling back to ensure I wasn't followed, I slipped into the welcoming arms of the Yewdew Forest.

And then I was blissfully alone.

Lush foliage brushed against my skin as I passed, a familiar breeze lifting the ends of my hair. I took a deep breath, letting the earthy scent flood my nose. Tension eased from my body with every step, my confidence blossoming the deeper I went.

Many Idrixians considered the forest dangerous, preferring to venture along the High Road and avoid it entirely. While navigating it carried some risks, they had been greatly exaggerated by tales the Night Ravens spun across Idrix during our missions, another layer of protection to conceal our existence.

In reality, there was nowhere I felt safer, the growing darkness posing no issues. I knew these woods better than the back of my hand; where the birds gathered, where the water was at its purest, and where to camp for the best vantage point. I could walk through it with my eyes closed.

I refilled my canteen at a stream along the way, draining it several times before my dry throat was satisfied. The events of the day had taken a toll, my body aching in places that usually didn't bother me. I hung my head in shame. It had been a close call with the thief, and before that I'd nearly failed to persuade the merchant to show me his artefacts. I had to be better than this. My mistakes weren't only my own, they affected everyone in the Night Ravens.

Nothing short of perfection was acceptable.

Unwrapping my makeshift bandage, I checked my finger, finding it healed save for a faint line where the cut had been. I hoped the scar would remain, reminding me of the cost of letting my guard down.

The last stretch of my walk was brutal in more ways than one. As I passed the familiar scenery of the woodland, I recalled everything I'd said and done during the day, analysing it in excruciating detail for ways I could improve. Obvious glamours were considered vulgar in the capital, a sign that someone couldn't afford the genuine article, but I should've taken more care to make a good first impression. It had been foolish to assume an attendant sent on behalf of their wealthy master wouldn't be held to the exacting standards of the city's residents. And I certainly shouldn't have let a young thief get the better of me. A frequent presence, the critical voice in my mind berated me over and over until numbness was all I had left.

By the time I stumbled into my favourite clearing, all I was capable of was collapsing on my bedroll. I laid on the thin material for several minutes before I was able to summon the energy to set up my camp. It was far from a pleasant experience. My arms protested as I gathered firewood, a heavy tiredness settling into my bones. Lighting my campfire took so much time that my teeth were chattering from the cold night when I finally succeeded.

To round off a wonderful evening, when unlacing my boots as I prepared for sleep, I discovered a hole. The soles had been thinning a long time, and I'd known this day would come, but I'd hoped they would hold on until the end of my mission. I let out a string of curses, the trees my only witness. All I could do was stuff the hole with large red-root leaves, but it would require a stroke of luck for the quick fix to last.

And as it turned out, luck wasn't on my side.

The next morning, a torrential downpour began, rain falling in an angry curtain that saturated the ground. I couldn't see more than a few feet in front of me, the forest becoming a grey haze. Each step trapped me in mud, my progress forward painfully slow. Which god had I angered to deserve such a miserable fate?

I finished my journey barefoot, my shoes hanging uselessly from one hand, trying not to cringe as my legs squelched into the sludge. My feet were so cold they stung, my skin blotchy red.

Setting my ruined boots down, I grasped for the barrier of the glamoured wards protecting the castle and its surroundings. The only indication of their presence was a small flicker where the invisible shields met the ground, otherwise the scenery was unremarkable.

Wards strong enough to hide the existence of something as large as the Old Keep required unmatched precision as well as power. The Night Raven's secretive founder was the only one capable of such a feat, though little was known about how they'd managed it.

A gentle warmth settled over me as the magic accepted me inside. Around me the scenery distorted, the canopy of trees vanishing, replaced by a ruined castle.

It must have once been an impressive fortress before it had withered away, reclaimed by nature. Four towers stood before me, one of which was little more than a few crumbling stones, joined by a curtain wall that had collapsed in several places. A large tree grew through the heart of the structure, its roots disturbing the foundations, yet it seemed to be the only thing holding it together. Moss covered every surface, and it was rare to find a crack that wasn't playing host to a plant of some kind.

Stone steps, crooked due to the shrubs that sprouted between them, led up to a surprisingly well-preserved gatehouse. Everything smelt damp and old, the scent heightened by the rainfall.

"You look terrible. I haven't seen rain like this in months," Sal said in greeting, leaning on a sword nearly as tall as her as she guarded the rusty portcullis. Her short, blonde hair was dripping with rainwater, but it didn't appear to bother her.

Despite being the Head of the Watch, she often took the front sentry position herself, preferring to be the first line of defence for the castle. Her intentions weren't necessarily selfless. Guarding the gatehouse meant she knew all the comings and goings of the Old Keep, bolstering her influence.

I held my stinking, sodden boots up to her, cringing as cold water trickled beneath my sleeve. "I'm due a visit to the supply cupboard."

She snorted, her eyes crinkling in the corners. "Good luck with that. You could show him the torched remains and Barrett would still lecture you on the importance of maintaining your equipment."

Sal was right. Barrett was a miserable bastard who would glare at you for daring to ask, whether it was warranted or not.

"I'm going to fight that particular battle after a long rest. I'll take all the luck I can get."

"You should hurry. Dinner's served and it's a full house tonight." Sal pulled a face. "It's stew, again." When you left the ruined castle as rarely as the sentries, a regular meal was guaranteed, but variety was not.

I looked down, grimacing at the state of my filthy feet. "I'll head over once I've bathed."

As I brushed past her, Sal clapped me on the shoulder so hard I stumbled, the most affectionate gesture the intimidating woman could offer. "Welcome back, scout."

Chapter 3

"Reuben's asking for you."

Already? Only an hour had passed since I'd returned to the Old Keep. Wet strands of silver hair clung to my forehead, still damp from my fleeting visit to the bathing pool before dinner. Usually, I was granted at least an evening to myself before receiving my next orders, but not tonight.

My half-eaten stew remained pleasantly warm, the rich meatiness of the broth making up for the lack of vegetables, or anything else of substance. I'd intended to savour the only meal I hadn't had to hunt myself all week. Evidently, that was no longer a possibility.

"Sorry, but he said it was urgent."

Pushing aside my growing irritation, I nodded at Selwyn. He was a young scout, freshly returned from his first mission, his wide eyes watching me warily as if I was a feral animal likely to bite. I was tempted to, with my brief taste of comfort so rudely interrupted, but the scout leader wouldn't summon me so hastily without good reason.

I had a complicated relationship with Reuben, but he'd always been straightforward with me. When he'd first recruited me nearly a century ago, I'd been a wild thing, lashing out indiscriminately without considering the consequences. He'd shown me a different path, one of patience and restraint, earning my begrudging respect over the years. However, I didn't need to like him to follow his orders, and Reuben enjoyed testing me. I never knew which side of him I was getting, the wise mentor supporting me in every endeavour, or the unrelenting leader who pushed me to my limits.

I wolfed down the rest of my meal, not wanting the limited rations to go to waste, huddling under my green cloak in search of a sliver of warmth. Even though the dining hall was crowded at this time of day, with little else passing for entertainment in the evenings, it was uncomfortably cold. Three long wooden tables divided the room, each flanked by a wonky bench on either side. Despite the best efforts of the Earth-Blessed steward who'd used his elemental magic to craft them, they were misshapen and sagged in the middle. Those who arrived late to mealtimes were often rewarded with the worst seat, struggling to reach the table from their low position. Luckily, I'd been spared from that fate.

No one looked my way as I exited the room, heading towards the east wing. The crumbling castle that served as headquarters for the Night Ravens, a secret order dedicated to the protection of Idrix, was just about suitable for habitation. Many rooms were exposed to the elements with large portions of the roof missing, others were so damp and rotten that spending any measure of time in them left you unable to breathe properly. The conditions improved every year. Even so, I dreaded returning. The cold, barren halls weren't the warmest welcome.

I hopped over a heap of rubble blocking the east stairwell, pressing my back against the wall to avoid the most damaged of the stairs. The early years were the worst. Now we had more than one dormitory, no longer required to sleep two to a bed without a scrap of personal space.

The downside of living in a secret fortress was that concealment was prized over comfort. And the Old Keep was all we had, its ancient protections keeping us hidden and safe for generations. There was deep magic in the old stones, at least if you listened to Sal once she'd had too much mead to drink.

I ventured to the upper level, avoiding the cracks in the stone without looking. For decades, I'd walked the path to Reuben's office for my orders, hoping that it would finally be the day where they meant something.

At first, I was blinded by naïve optimism, convinced that I would change the world. But the hundreds of scouting missions I'd undertaken since then had given me a strong dose of reality.

There had been the year I'd spent tailing the Lady of Hightower's suspicious handmaiden, though she was arrested for skimming profits from the crown forge before anyone could act on my intelligence. Then there was the time I'd broken into an academy in the Amber City to retrieve a dusty old book, and who could forget when I'd worked as a serving girl in one of Eirel's dingy taverns, listening to whispered conversations for confirmation that rumours of the lord's passing were indeed accurate.

It was far from the life I'd envisioned for myself, but choice was the luxury of the privileged. The rest of us made the best out of the hand we'd been dealt. And things could be far, far worse. With scouting, I had found something that I excelled at, kept a roof over my head and afforded me valuable protection.

I reached the heavy wooden door, one of the few remaining that hadn't fallen off its rusty hinges, knocking twice.

"Enter," Reuben said, his voice muffled by the door. It creaked shut behind me as I entered the office.

What remained of the castle's east wing had been turned into the heart of our scouting operations. Information that needed to be kept on hand was carefully filed away in the maze of interconnected chambers. Reuben's office itself was a trove of knowledge, the shelves crammed full of scrolls that could only be read with his permission. Flaming torches provided only a dim light, shadows flickering across the room.

Reuben's long, blond hair was neatly tied up, exposing the thin scar that marred it and the missing tip of his right ear, an eternal reminder of the foolishness of his youth, according to him. He never elaborated on how it had happened and I'd thought better of indulging my curiosity.

His icy gaze was unnerving in the way it assessed me as I approached. He hadn't visibly aged in the time I'd known him, but the dark creases under his eyes had deepened. Reuben rifled through a pile of parchment on his desk, dust scattering into the air. "Do you remember what I told you the day we met?"

How could I forget? It had felt like a pivotal moment back then.

I didn't hesitate with my answer, the words still clear after all this time. "You have two choices ahead of you. You can let this world beat you down and yield to it, or you can fight back."

He gave me the barest hint of a smile in acknowledgement, and I hated the surge of pride it provoked in my chest.

"Precisely. I'm afraid that choice will only grow more difficult." He examined me. "Anything to report from the Amber City?"

That's what he'd summoned me for? My confusion at his routine question was only brief before my training kicked in. "The rumours were just that, a merchant looking for easy pickings, nothing more. There was no evidence of the artefacts ever containing magic."

"As suspected, but we had to do our due diligence."

"There's something else." I hesitated. Admitting weakness in front of him felt like putting my shame on display, but there was no one else who could ease my conscience. No one else who could know the private details of my mission. "I had a run in with a recruit from the thieves' guild."

He straightened, scrutinising me with an unreadable look. "I'm assuming by the fact you didn't lead with that, you emerged unscathed?"

I deposited the pouch on the desk, still full of coins. "It's one silver lighter, if that's what you're asking."

"What did you do?" Reuben let out an exasperated sigh.

"You should have seen him. He was just a child."

"How many times have I told you? Do not draw unnecessary attention to yourself. We can't save everyone." His voice softened. "It wasn't your fault."

My lip quivered before I set my mouth in a firm line. "This isn't about that."

"Then don't let it cloud your judgement." He pulled a sheet from his stack of parchment, thrusting it at me. I took it wordlessly, scanning it for my next orders.

"We've known each other for many years now. I know you've grown frustrated with your missions of late." I opened my mouth to interject, but he held up a finger to silence me.

"Don't waste time attempting to deny it. That isn't why I asked for you tonight." He stood, circling the desk with slow, deliberate movements, keeping his head fixed in my direction. "Valuable information has come to light, and I need someone like you on it. Someone who can think on their feet. This won't be straightforward. In truth, I don't know what you'll face. But this is what you've been waiting for. An opportunity to prove yourself."

I tried to keep the excitement out of my voice. "What do you need me to do?"

"An old friend from across the Blossom Sea contacted me with concerning news. She was brief with the details, but it sounded like it could be a new danger, perhaps related to the curse. I need you to meet the informant and investigate."

I studied him carefully. Everything Reuben did was calculated, every word precisely chosen. The magical curse was the biggest threat to our survival, the reason the Night Ravens had been formed. I had my own reasons for wanting it broken for good. Reuben was luring me in with something irresistible. The question was, why?

"When do I leave?"

"At first light. You'll find the informant, a widow, running a bookshop in the village of Valtarra."

Valtarra. I retrieved my worn map from my pack, studying it. The edges were torn and fragile with frequent use and the ink faded, but it was still readable. I found Valtarra nestled in a group of villages south of the capital.

"I'm trusting you with this. There's no room for failure."

I swallowed my unease, grounding myself with a deep breath. "I understand."

"Report back to me as soon as you return, no detours. I don't care what I'm doing. This takes priority." Reuben resumed his position behind the desk. "That's all. I suggest you have an early night. You'll need it."

"That was my plan."

When I showed no signs of leaving, he looked up from his paperwork. "Speak your mind."

"You could have assigned this to Norwyn or Calliste." The experienced scouts were unmatched in their ability to uncover even the most secretive information. "Why me?"

Reuben leant back in his chair, observing me in silent thought, his face bathed in shadow.

"Calliste is on a long-term assignment, and Norwyn failed to return last week."

"He's missing?" He'd be the third scout this year who hadn't returned. While most of our orders bordered on mundane, there was always a risk that a mission could be your final one, but never so many.

"It wouldn't be the first time Norwyn has deviated from the plan for valid reasons. But I admit, I'm becoming concerned." Reuben noticed my discomfort. "Do you know why I recruited you?"

"I…" I found myself unable to answer. Back then, I'd assumed he'd pitied me, but I knew better now. Why had he made his offer?

"When I glimpsed you, I thought I was too late. You were sprawled in the long grass, bruised and broken, another victim of this world. But you hadn't given up. You were close, to be sure, and who could blame you? But you struggled to your feet and faced me, despite how much it pained you. Your persistence has always been an asset. I'm counting on it for this."

There was a lump in my throat, and I turned away from him to compose myself. "I won't let you down."

Not wanting to loiter, I walked towards the door.

"And Willow?"

I halted, the use of my name drawing my full attention. Reuben had resumed flicking through the stack of parchment. "Yes?" I said.

"Remember, no distractions. Come straight back with whatever you find out."

"Of course."

With a yawn, I left the office, but there was one last thing I needed to do before I could finally rest for the evening. I had to see a man about some boots.

Chapter 4

The mission began like any other, with the familiar trail of the Yewdew Forest and the thriving wildlife that called it home, but I was certain the similarities would end there.

My arm was steady as I lined up my shot, keeping the raglaw within range. A common sight, the plump birds provided a satisfying meal, sadly a rarity on my travels. Perched high in a dragontail tree, oblivious to my presence, it preened its obsidian feathers.

My arrow struck true, as they always did, the bird plummeting to the ground. I removed the shaft from its body, wiping the point on a filthy rag before returning it to my quiver. Arrows were a valuable commodity, and I couldn't afford to leave any behind. Not when I wouldn't receive more supplies for a while.

Retrieving my prize, I trudged through the mud of the clearing towards my modest camp, and the sack of plucked birds hung there, the result of my hunt. Knowing I could rely on my prowess with a bow to keep the hunger at bay, I'd declined provisions this time. Others weren't so lucky.

With the absence of the raglaw song echoing through the treetops, the forest had fallen into a hushed stillness. The afternoon light faded as the sun began its descent. Soon darkness would fall and bring with it a host of new challenges.

The defensive wards I'd woven around my camp let me pass without trouble, a warm caress on my skin greeting my return. It was simple magic, used in abundance by the fae, but I would take every advantage I could. Sometimes, the simplest measures proved to be the most effective.

Mercifully, the downpour I'd been caught in the previous day hadn't persisted. A campfire remained unlit where I'd assembled it earlier, beside a sturdy log covered in moss and the worn material of my bedroll. I dropped the bird I carried, my mind returning to the orders Reuben had given me. My brow furrowed. It didn't make sense. All I needed to do was meet the informant in Valtarra, find out what they knew, and report back to him. I'd spent days staking out dangerous woodlands and crept through bustling cities while evading notice, but a simple bookshop owner would be my toughest mission yet?

Still, I had no choice but to take it seriously. This was a golden opportunity, a stepping stone to prove myself capable of taking on the most difficult scouting assignments.

A chance to belong.

The raglaw was warm as I plucked its feathers a fistful at a time, depositing them in my pack with the others. If I was lucky, I could earn a few coppers in exchange. Sometimes that was the difference between sleeping outside and affording an inn.

All that remained for me to do was cook my dinner. I slumped on the log, holding my head in my hands. I despised this part. My bow felt like magic in my hand. Hunting prey was as easy as drawing a breath. But lighting a campfire? Near impossible.

Kneeling by the pile of firewood, I struck together two pieces of flint until they sparked. Or that was the theory. There was a technique to it, one I did not possess no matter how hard I practised. Instead, I relied on stubbornness, cursing all the while. With enough attempts, it would work eventually.

A shudder ran down my spine, tingling across my skin and making my hair stand on end. A warning. My wards had been breached. I was on my feet in an instant, pointing my bow at the intruder. We'd gone to great lengths with our stories, ensuring no one chose to travel through the forest without good reason. A stranger being this close to the Old Keep was suspicious at best, catastrophic at worst. My heart pounded, lodging itself in my throat.

I had to protect the Night Ravens.

"Having a little trouble there?" The voice was smug, taking far too much enjoyment in my struggle.

The stranger's approach allowed me to examine him more closely. He possessed a youthful charm, with twinkling green eyes full of mischief and dimples that showed when he grinned. Glossy brown hair fell onto his handsome face before he brushed it back. It would be endearing if that sort of thing affected me. I couldn't look past his polished appearance, the easy pride in his stature and his lack of supplies. He appeared to be nothing more than a liability, accidentally straying from the High Road with no concept of what he'd wandered into. Still, I remained on high alert, keeping my bow fixed on him.

The liability in question sauntered towards me, holding up his hands in surrender. "No need for violence."

"Come any closer and there will be," I said. His gaze darted to the bird resting next to the campfire, lingering too long for my liking. "I don't share. Leave now and I'll let you walk away with everything intact."

His lip curved up in a wry smile, if anything, encouraged by my hostility. "I'm Silas, and just who are you?"

I glared at him with enough venom to wither the most courageous heart. There would be no chance of him receiving an answer, no crack in my shield. He may not be an overt threat, but that didn't mean I wanted him anywhere near the Old Keep. Or me. "That's none of your business. Go away."

Silas' dimpled smile widened, my hand tightening on the bow in response. His reaction unnerved me. Usually, my hostility discouraged interest, leading others to believe I wasn't worth the bother, but my rage amused him. He could be dangerous, after all.

"Don't be so hasty. Perhaps we'll be useful to one another? You're struggling with your campfire. Luckily for you, that happens to be a strength of mine," Silas said. I kept my bow trained on him as he inched closer.

Too close. I wouldn't fall for that trick again.

I fired a warning shot into the ground just shy of his feet, hoping to scare him away before resorting to bloodshed. However, I wasn't afraid to escalate if he pushed me further.

To my dismay, he laughed, retrieving the arrow and examining it as if it was made of gold. "I meant what I said. I mean you no harm."

With an exhale, I released some of the tension in my body. We couldn't lie. The gods forbade it, their power rendering us incapable of speaking the words, but there was an art to phrasing things to hide a truth you didn't want to expose.

"How about a trade? I start your fire, and you share your food with me. Then it'll be like I was never here."

"I said I don't share." But even as I said it, my mind turned the offer over carefully, trying to find his angle.

I covered myself with my cloak more thoroughly, a cool breeze sending shivers through me as the sun bowed out of sight. I wore the basic clothing the Night Ravens had provided me with. A white shirt, frayed at the edges, brown trousers that itched, and a heavy green cloak with a hood. Easy enough to move in, but not the warmest of garments. The prospect of a roaring fire was enticing, but I hesitated, unsure if I could trust him, even with such a simple bargain.

"Well, in that case, I'll go. Enjoy your evening." Silas made a point of retreating so slowly he barely moved. He glanced back, checking I was watching him.

I considered his offer again. As long as I was careful with the terms and kept my guard up, I could benefit from his help.

I groaned, certain I would come to regret it.

"Wait." He stilled at my shout. "One bird, that's all, and you'll leave as soon as you've eaten. Or if I decide you've outstayed your welcome." It was specific enough to grant me protection should he be deceiving me.

"As you wish." He bounded over to my camp in a few paces. A thin string of light encircled my arm, mirrored on his, disappearing as the bargain bound us together.

This close, I could see the detailed embroidery of his doublet, intricate golden patterns woven into the green material. There was no telltale flickering, no obvious flaw to the illusion. He wore no glamour. It was genuine, hand-stitched and made to fit him like a glove. It must have cost a fortune.

He was important, whoever he was.

Silas extended an arm towards the unlit campfire. "Step back. This could get a little... heated."

I scowled at the instruction but obeyed. Flames, tendrils of scorching fire, flowed from his fingertips, igniting the firewood. I gasped.

All fae could use simple enchantments, like glamours and wards, but only the chosen few had Blessings, the ability to harness the elements - air, fire, water, and earth. I was already an adult by the time I'd met my first Blessed fae. In the Night Ravens, there were only a handful.

The fire's warmth soon reached me, the heat sinking deep into my bones. My shivers subsided at last. Silas sat on the mossy log, rolling his shoulders. I joined him, leaving a wider gap than necessary, unconvinced of his intentions. To my surprise, he smelt like the forest. It was a woody scent, punctuated by subtle notes of vanilla that only enhanced its soothing quality.

"I'm surprised you didn't try that earlier. Aren't you Fire-Blessed?" He cocked his head, assessing me. "No? With that temper? Gods, I'm usually better at this."

"What are you talking about?"

"Your Blessing." He said it like it was obvious. "You know, magic."

"I know what a Blessing is. I don't have one."

I skewered two birds, propping them over the open campfire. My mouth watered at the smell, providing a moment's distraction from my infuriating companion.

"Come on, you can tell me. We're friends now." He shuffled along the log to nudge my shoulder, unbothered when I shook him off. The flames danced and sizzled as juices from the cooking birds trickled onto them. "What's the big secret?"

I snapped, my limited patience depleted. "Would you fucking listen to me? I have no Blessing."

Silas reeled back like I'd punched him. Good. It was satisfying to wipe the smile from his face and gain the upper hand. Silence fell, only interrupted by the crackling of the campfire and the hiss of the meat as it cooked.

He frowned. "That's impossible. Everyone has magic."

It clicked. The casual arrogance, his fine clothing, the disbelief at my words. He was part of the nobility, sheltered from the world beyond his limited experience. "Everyone *you* know."

I awaited his rebuttal, but none came. He nodded, looking uncharacteristically serious for a moment before he masked it with an easy grin. "Good thing I now know you. What was your name again?"

I ignored him, turning the meat over slowly, careful not to burn my fingers. Silas leant back in deep thought. "You must be tough."

"Excuse me?"

"A Blessing isn't only about commanding an element, it's a way to prove you deserve respect. Where I'm from, we're pitted against one another to determine who is strongest. Lose, and you're treated worse than dirt. Without magic, you must be tough to have survived."

I busied myself with the skewers, though there was no need to interfere.

"You don't talk much, do you?"

"I think you're doing plenty of talking for the both of us. I only agreed to feed you. I don't owe you more than that," I said.

Silas shot me a dazzling smile. "You should count yourself lucky. Many have vied for the chance to dine with me."

If that was meant to impress me, he'd misjudged it. His popularity was no concern of mine. "Why don't you find one of them and leave me alone?"

"And miss an opportunity to find out more about my new friend?" he said, not missing a beat.

I bristled at his presumptuous familiarity. Was he always so forward with strangers? It only heightened my distrust of him. "We're not friends, and if you value your life, you'll stop trying to get to know me."

Silas let out a low whistle.

"I mean it. You cannot harm me, but I haven't made any such promises," I said.

"Have it your way." He shrugged, gazing around the camp with interest. "It's just you out here? No ferocious hunter to watch your back?"

I raised an eyebrow at him. "Who says I need one?"

"You're plenty ferocious. I'm not doubting that. Just working out if I should sleep with one eye open tonight."

"You should, but not because of my hunting partner," I said.

"So, there is someone? And you're sharing the same bedroll? Sounds cosy."

I didn't dignify that with a response, instead rescuing the raglaw meat before it charred.

"Here." I handed him a skewer. "Be careful, it's-"

"Hot!" Silas yelled before I could finish, yanking his canteen from his belt and gulping down the water. "It burns."

He truly was naïve to the world, possessing not a shred of common sense. I laughed, surprising myself as much as Silas. He snorted, the sounds of our laughter bringing life to the quiet forest.

"So that's what it takes. I'll be sure to injure myself more often if it earns a smile from you," he said.

I realised how close he was to me, so close I could feel the heat radiating off him. It became overwhelming. I withdrew back into myself, to safety.

"Finish eating, then leave as you agreed," I said, backing away. From the refuge of my bedroll, I hugged my knees to my chest.

"Did I do something wrong?"

I lifted my head, finding Silas' face anguished. "You are distracting me from my duties, and that's the last thing I need right now."

"So, you find me distracting?"

I scoffed. That's what he had gleaned from my words?

"Don't flatter yourself," I said. He didn't need his ego inflated any more than it was already. "I'm serious. You have a bargain to honour."

Breaking a bargain had unpredictable consequences, none of them pleasant, courtesy of the gods' displeasure. Some perished immediately, others were struck down with unimaginable illnesses or cursed with eternal misfortune. That was if you could break it. Usually, fate intervened to bind you to the terms.

Messing with bargains was a fool's game.

"Right," he muttered. "Has anyone told you how warm and welcoming you are?"

"It's worked for me so far." As he wiped his mouth and stood to leave, I offered him the only thing I was willing to, advice. "Be careful out there. Idrix is a dangerous place for those who are ill prepared."

Silas' bravado returned as a flame danced on his index finger. "I'm ready for anything it can throw at me."

Chapter 5

*T*he sea's wrath knew no bounds, crashing into me with such force that it stole my breath, my lungs flooding with water that burned.

I desperately reached out, grasping for a hand that I realised wouldn't be there. For it was too late, my soul shattered to the point of no return.

As the world became tinged with darkness, I closed my eyes and waited for the water to claim me.

Waking with the morning sun, I shivered beneath my blankets. My eyes were heavy with the fog of interrupted sleep, and it took a moment for my senses to return, reminding me where I was. The Yewdew Forest.

Safe.

I stretched, relieving the tightness in my shoulders from a night spent on the hard ground, my thin bedroll providing little in the way of support. My bunk back at the Old Keep with its lumpy straw mattress would've been an improvement.

The nightmare lingered at the edge of my consciousness, my heart pounding at its vividness. It didn't do to dwell on dreams, particularly those with a stubborn hold on the mind.

Raglaw chirped noisily with the day's start, but there was little point hunting more when I carried a healthy supply in my sack. Instead, I took the opportunity to forage some of the forest's bounty of berries and mushrooms while I could. Plenty of scouts had been caught out by a lack of provisions. Not every danger to our life was obvious.

Taking a familiar route, I set off at a steady pace. The forest's rich, earthy scent was like a balm for my nerves, my footsteps light as they crunched on dry leaves.

The sun shimmered through a canopy of trees, their branches shifting in the breeze, and there was a soft rustling in the undergrowth as small creatures scurried away from my approach. There was nowhere I'd rather be.

My thoughts strayed to what awaited me in Valtarra. It was unlike Reuben. His briefings were thorough, usually leaving no room for confusion or misinterpretation. Before I'd investigated the merchant in the Amber City we'd prepared for weeks, poring over old ledgers and records. It had taken me three attempts at proposing a plan before he'd approved. Yet this time, he hadn't asked.

It could be a good sign, an indication he trusted me to work independently without his oversight. It could even be a test, another chance to prove myself.

I hoped so.

A strange shape ahead of me made me stop short.

Silas' sleeping form blocked the trail, unmoving aside from the gentle rise and fall of his chest. He slept on his bare bedroll, the blanket still tightly rolled and tied to his pack as if he hadn't tried to set up his bedding. His campfire, also in the middle of the path, had extinguished overnight, which was unsurprising considering how damp his firewood was. If it weren't for his Blessing, I doubted it would have lit at all.

Most concerning of all, curled up against Silas' body was a stormfang pup, breathing softly as it slumbered. It was covered in grey fur, fluffy with youth, its long ears extended as it listened for threats even in sleep.

I froze. It was the only beast that could make me tremble in fear.

A dark part of me considered stepping over him and continuing on my way. I was hesitant to trust him with his true motives still unclear, but that didn't mean he deserved to die. It was reasonable to at least warn him of the danger he'd tangled himself up in.

I crept forward, balancing my weight to mask my approach. Nudging his shoulder with my boot as gently as I could, I hissed at him, "Silas, wake up."

He groaned to himself, but didn't stir.

I tried again. "Wake up, now. Your life depends on it."

That got his attention. His eyes fluttered open, a slow, lazy smile spreading across his face as he recognised me. "Well, good morning. This is a pleasant surprise. Didn't think I'd see you again."

He had stripped down to his shirt and trousers and his hair was tousled from sleep. His relaxed appearance was a stark contrast to the impeccably dressed man I'd met the previous day, yet it strangely suited him.

I crouched beside him, speaking in a low voice. "Whatever you do, don't move. There's a stormfang next to you."

His head turned towards the animal, and his brow furrowed. "The puppy?"

"The predator. Do you know how they hunt? They stun prey with their lightning before devouring them one bite at a time. I doubt there are many deaths more painful," I said.

"I appreciate your concern, but he's my friend, and he's just a baby! The poor thing limped towards my campfire last night with a thorn lodged in his paw, so I patched him up. Didn't realise he had stuck around afterwards." He gestured to the uneven hem of his shirt. A patch of material was missing, matching the bloodstained rag wrapped around the pup's leg. "See?"

"If the pup is here, its mother will be nearby. We need to leave, now." I shut my eyes, focusing on the sounds of the forest, checking for any indication we'd been discovered.

"Why? Look at him, he's harmless. And you've just rudely woken me. I require a moment."

"Aren't you listening? No one walks away from an encounter. If it sees us, we're as good as dead. They never forget a face."

"But I saved him," Silas said mournfully.

A bloodcurdling howl sounded in the distance, causing the hairs on my arm to stand on edge. We had to flee before it was too late.

"You're welcome to try to make a fully-grown stormfang see reason. I won't stay to witness your demise or the aftermath."

"You're serious?" He was wide awake now, appearing rattled at my reaction. "Have you seen one before?"

"Only once, from afar. I was able to escape before it saw me. I'll never forget it. That pup must be young because the adult was the size of a merchant's cart."

His eyes widened, darting to the stormfang. "What do we do?"

"First of all, stay calm."

"That's not helping!" He was breathing rapidly, the movement disturbing the animal.

"On the count of three, you're going to shuffle towards me, then you'll need to move as fast as you can. Grab your bedroll. I'll handle the rest."

"I could use my Blessing, face it head on." He turned pale at the prospect.

"It's too risky. We don't know how the lightning would react to your fire. You could wipe us all out. It's safer to run for it. Are you ready?"

He nodded, though it lacked conviction.

"On my count. Three, two, one."

Silas moved, jostling the pup. It rolled over, exposing its belly with its legs in the air. Sparks discharged from it. We flinched, skin tingling at the contact, but were otherwise unharmed. I breathed a sigh of relief.

Pulling Silas to his feet, I grabbed his pack and doublet, swinging them onto my shoulder. "Let's go, quickly."

I sprinted through the forest, dragging him behind me, my head snapping back to check that the adult stormfang wasn't following. I cursed my luck for needing to run again, though it had been much easier being the pursuer, not the prey.

Another howl sounded, this time from where we'd been moments before.

"Don't stop," I said. Silas' leg buckled, but he listened, pushing forward to close the gap between us.

I lost track of how much time passed. Only when the stormfang became little more than a muffled cry in the distance did we dare slow to a hurried walk.

I stopped suddenly, Silas crashing into the back of me. If it wasn't for our joined hands, he would've knocked me over. Clearing my throat, I withdrew my arm and neatly stacked his belongings against a tree.

If he was bothered by the gesture, he didn't comment. Instead, he sank to the ground, too winded to speak. I clutched my side, waiting for the sharp pain to subside where I'd pushed myself too hard.

His cheeks were red and sweat crowded his brow as he caught his breath. "Why did you help me?" he said, panting. "You couldn't wait to get rid of me yesterday."

I took a sip from my canteen, thankful for the immediate relief the water provided. His confusion was understandable, but I had no intention of explaining myself, especially since it could give him the wrong idea.

"Would you have preferred I'd left you to your grizzly fate?"

"Not at all. It's just…" he paused, finding the right words, "puzzling. But I am grateful, all the same."

"Don't get used to it."

"Wouldn't dream of it. Not with you keeping me on my toes." His jaw set in a hard line. "Do you demand anything in return?"

"Do I…" What?

"You saved my life. Where I'm from, that entitles you to ask something of me. Anything, with the exception of my life, of course." Then, as if I'd imagined the slip, the tension lifted. He directed an infuriating smirk at me. "I'm game for anything, if you are?"

"I don't need anything from you." I looked at him, properly this time, taking in his dishevelled appearance, his dry lips, the glazed look behind his eyes. "What are you even doing here? The forest is dangerous. It's no place for playing around."

"Is that what I'm doing? There was me thinking I was on an adventure." He stood, meeting me with a challenging stare.

"And you decided the Yewdew Forest would be a great location to visit?" My voice rose in disbelief. I thought we'd done enough to establish its reputation by now. I made a mental note to let Reuben know that more work was required.

"I never claimed to be good at it."

I stifled a laugh. "That's an understatement."

"Ouch, don't soften your words on my account." He obstructed the trail, sidestepping to prevent me from ducking around him. "Why? What makes you say that?"

"I don't know where to begin. You were literally sleeping on the path with inadequate shelter and no wards placed. You let a dangerous animal into your camp without hesitation, and you built your campfire with damp firewood. Did you not consider using your Blessing to dry it?" I looked pointedly at his lips. "When was the last time you had any water?"

He had the good sense to look sheepish. "With you, yesterday?"

I tossed my canteen to him. "Drink up, otherwise the creatures in this forest will be the least of your concerns."

His throat bobbed as he drank desperately, finishing every drop. I'd need to deviate from the trail to refill it from a stream before I left. One was nearby, thankfully, our run not steering me too far off course.

He returned my canteen. "Thank you. I had a stinking headache."

I turned to face him with a solemn expression. "Do you know what the most common cause of death is in the forest?"

"Stormfangs? Wait, no, I see where you're going with this. Is it dehydration?"

"Ignorance," I answered. This wasn't an easy way of life, especially for those who didn't know what they were doing. "Go home, Silas, before it's too late."

His smile faltered. I felt no guilt for the words. They could save him from a cruel fate if he was wise enough to heed them. He was evidently out of his depth on his so-called adventure.

I left him where he stood, meandering through the trees too quickly for him to follow. By the time I had reached the stream and returned to the path, he was gone.

He's not your problem, I muttered to myself, hoping he'd learned his lesson.

Chapter 6

When I emerged from the forest the next morning, I found myself in the enchanting Blossom Sea, named for its floral meadows that swayed in the wind like gentle waves lapping at the shore. I breathed in its sweet scent, letting my eyes adjust to the sunlight.

Flowers bloomed as far as the eye could see, specks of vivid colour that greatly contrasted the shady expanse of the forest. Every field spawned a flower of a unique shade and variety, each more striking than the last.

Enterprising fae traipsed from field to field, assembling bouquets to take to the city to sell, and despite it only being a few hours since sunrise, some were already visible in the distance hard at work. Even with the heavy footfall and the continuous picking they endured, the meadows never eroded, remaining a well-loved landmark for many in Idrix.

Finally, I was getting somewhere. I was one step closer to Valtarra, where the informant awaited my arrival. One step closer to learning what the hell this was all about.

Fae frolicked all over the fields, laughing in small groups. Children played, chasing each other through patches of flowers as tall as they were. I wondered how it felt to be so carefree.

My own childhood on the Tigal Isles was a lifetime ago, when my most pressing concern was finding someone to go head-to-head with during target practice, or sneaking back for second helpings of dinner. My heart ached at the memory, but there was no point dwelling in the past. There was nothing left there for me.

Drinking from my canteen, I studied my map, debating which of the winding paths would provide me with the quickest route to the village. With any luck, I would make it within a few days, swiftly adding another successful mission to my record.

Only then could I fulfil my duty. My eternal vow.

A twig snapped behind me. My bow was in my hand in an instant, locating the target.

"We have to stop meeting like this." Silas, the last fae I wanted to see, caught up with me.

I scowled, lowering my arm with barely concealed reluctance.

He looked remarkably intact considering how I'd left him in the Yewdew Forest. Aside from a few hairs out of place and a splattering of dirt on his doublet, he was back to his immaculate self. The speed of his improvement was impressive, not that I would tell him that.

"Are you following me?" I asked, fixing him with a lethal look that promised a painful death if he was. It was better than the alternative, at least, that he was staking out the Old Keep. For some reason, his interest lay firmly with me, and not the Night Ravens.

He scoffed. "Of course not. You made your thoughts on companionship abundantly clear. This is merely a wonderful coincidence."

"That's certainly one word for it." I had far stronger words in mind. Returning the bow to my shoulder, I glowered at him. All I wanted was a day of uninterrupted travel, but Silas clearly had other ideas.

"I'm glad you agree. So, what brings you to the famous Blossom Sea? Are you here for the scenery?" He gestured to the acres of blooming flowers. They'd taken my breath away when I'd first encountered them. It was my first glimpse of beauty on the Idrixian mainland after the horrors I'd endured, stirring hope that things would improve.

Today, they were an obstacle standing between me and my ambitions. A passing distraction, nothing more.

"That's none of your business," I said. I was growing tired of his attempts at conversation. We were just strangers crossing paths, if he was to be believed. I didn't need to divulge anything about my plans, nor should I.

Silas carried on as if he'd tuned out my hostility. "It's more beautiful than I imagined. The stories don't do it justice."

Now I was paying attention. "You've never seen it before? Not even from the High Road?"

Spanning the length of Idrix, connecting the Amber City with Gladhaven in the South, the road was the quickest, and most popular way to travel. It kissed the boundary of the Blossom Sea, elevated above the meadows, giving those who travelled along it a stunning view on their journey.

If Silas was seeing it for the first time, it meant he hadn't left the North until now.

Who was he?

"If you must know, I'm rather new to this adventuring thing," he continued, unaware of my scrutiny.

"Who'd have guessed?" I muttered under my breath, but my mind was whirring. He exuded confidence but lacked the condescending nature of the capital's residents. Perhaps a noble from Tirrim? Or there was Eirel, the mysterious Northern territory, but its gates were closed to everyone but a select few after the lord's passing.

It had taken me days to figure out how to evade the guards after my mission there, eventually escaping by hiding in the back of a stinking supply cart on its way to being restocked.

Silas conjured a perfect sphere of flame into his palm, juggling it between his hands absent-mindedly, not realising the skill and power he was casually demonstrating. "I'm secure enough in myself to be able to admit my weaknesses." He quirked an eyebrow at me. "You should try it sometime."

"And how do you know I won't use it against you?" I asked. There was no shortage of those who would take advantage of a naïve traveller, particularly one as unmistakably wealthy as Silas.

"I don't, but I have a good feeling about you." He shot me a dazzling grin, which didn't falter as his eyes met mine.

"Why do I get the sense you'd have a good feeling about everyone?"

A dark look crossed his face, so at odds with his usual cheery demeanour. "You'd be wrong."

"You don't know me. You could be wrong about me too."

His gaze held mine, unwavering. "No, I don't think so."

"We're strangers."

"Yet you still helped me. Twice. Without trickery or demanding reciprocity. I can't say the same for some of my other acquaintances."

Perhaps I'd misjudged him? But that was a risk I wasn't willing to take. A smiling face was capable of the cruellest deception. It was like my head had been doused with icy water, my senses sharpening. "I wouldn't get used to it. I also shot an arrow at you, don't forget."

"And missed me. I have no doubt that if you wanted to hurt me, you would've. Luckily for me, you chose to spare me."

I reached for my bow. "That's easily rectified."

It didn't discourage him. "And what if I did want to get on your good side? Do you like flowers?"

He attempted to hand me a hastily assembled bouquet he'd picked as we were walking.

I let them drop to the ground. "No."

"Perhaps I'll write you a poem," he said.

"Perhaps I *will* fire that arrow," I replied.

"Aha, that's it. Where's a fletcher when you need one?"

Far away, as luck would have it. Only the largest towns had enough trade to justify a fletcher permanently in residence.

"If you insist on following me, can you at least do it silently?"

I pointed out the nearest fae to us, a group of children playing in the fields. "Would you not be more comfortable over there? I'm sure they'd be more receptive to your presence."

He chuckled, a rich sound that was as annoyingly charming as the rest of him. "I've always been terrible at hide and seek. Besides, you're far more fascinating. I've never met anyone that's taken such an immediate dislike to me before. It's refreshing."

"I'm sure there are others who share my opinion. You obviously haven't been looking hard enough."

"Oh, so that's how it is?" Silas said.

Clearing my throat, I waited for him to pass me. "Goodbye. I'd say it was a pleasure, but I cannot lie."

"Just like that? Don't you think there's a reason we keep running into each other?" He was standing too close to me again.

I nudged him away. Silas stumbled before he could steady himself, provoking one of my rare smiles.

"I doubt it counts when you're deliberately finding ways for us to meet." I should have stopped the conversation there, left him talking to himself or, better yet, ditched him entirely. However, my curiosity won out. "Does this usually work for you? Following women around until you wear them down?"

Silas grinned, his eyes burning with mirth. "I've had no complaints."

My intuition flared, screaming at me to be cautious. Charm hid a multitude of sins. I'd fallen for it in the past, hope eclipsing caution, but I wouldn't make the same mistake twice. "Unfortunately for you, I have standards. You're wasting your time."

"We'll see," he replied, a casual arrogance in his voice.

"You doubt my resolve?"

"Not one bit. But I can tell when someone secretly likes me. You may deny yourself the truth, but your eyes don't lie."

Only my iron-clad restraint, honed by years of Reuben's patient tutelage, kept me from hitting him.

"The pollen must be affecting your eyesight. Let me set you straight. You are self-absorbed, irritating and lack any survival skills. You're nothing but a liability."

"Well, none of us are perfect. But you've certainly been paying attention." He winked. "I'm flattered."

I ignored him, a twitch in my brow the only sign of my frustration, instead unrolling my map and studying the terrain.

Taking a deep breath, I cleared my mind and returned my focus to the mission. Following any path that veered to the right would take me towards my destination. I set off at once, keen to regain any time I could. Silas hurried to keep up with me, brushing aside the flowers blocking his way.

"So, will you tell me your name yet?" he asked, breathless.

"No." Sweat beaded on my forehead, but I sustained my brutal pace. Perhaps he would grow tired and drop back if I kept it up. It was futile, based on the pep in his step, but I hoped all the same.

A tiny patch of white flowers growing between the path and the burnt-orange hillside brought a relieved smile to my face. Aurablooms. The perfect solution for my annoying problem.

Their delicate, miniature petals were more than just aesthetically pleasing. Young fae dared each other to pluck them, taking advantage of their strange power. Few followed through with the dare, too afraid it would expose their deepest fears, forever branding them a coward. Sweethearts lucky enough to have matching pink blooms were said to have a love destined to last for eternity. Successful couples stitched them above their heart on their wedding attire, blessing their union with the ultimate symbol of good fortune.

But aurablooms were far more useful than that. They reflected the emotions of the holder, their petals changing colour to signal what he or she was feeling. Sometimes they were glimpses of fleeting sensations, other times, your very soul was exposed for all to see.

Seeing as they grew only in the Blossom Sea, I doubted Silas was familiar with them. It presented me with a unique opportunity to uncover his true motives.

"There is something you can do to earn my trust." I pointed to the aurablooms, trying to appear nonchalant about it. "Pick one."

"I thought you weren't the flower type?" Silas asked.

"I'm not."

His twinkling eyes saw right through me. I held my tongue, not trusting myself to find the words to persuade him.

"Ah, I see. This is a test of some kind. Care to enlighten me?"

"And spoil the fun?"

A hint of a smile tugged at the corner of his mouth, and I knew I had him.

"Well, in that case, how can I resist?" Silas crouched, examining the patch of aurablooms. After careful consideration, he plucked the tallest flower within his reach. "If these are poisonous and bring about my premature death, I will haunt you for the rest of your days."

"Are you always so dramatic?" I kept my voice light but watched the aurabloom in his hand without blinking.

"I'm just getting started."

The petals shifted, each changing to a new colour. He laughed. "Nice trick, but a little anticlimactic, don't you think?"

I didn't answer, distracted as the colours settled. Interpreting the meaning behind them wasn't a precise endeavour, and some were a complete mystery, but there was no denying Silas had been holding back on me.

The first few petals held no surprises. There was a rich emerald symbolising the self-assured confidence that had been apparent from the moment we'd met, the sunshine yellow of his bright demeanour, and a bright purple that I couldn't place.

But then, there was the murky green of regret, a petal the colour of blood, a blush pink that I didn't want to consider too closely, and finally an icy blue I recognised well. Grief.

"Are you listening?" Silas said.

I snapped out of my focus, sifting through the new information as I faced him. I still didn't trust him, especially with the gravity of what the aurabloom had revealed, but he posed no immediate threat to my life. If he was deceiving me, he was doing a good job of hiding it. "Speak for yourself. I'm rather fond of them, as flowers go."

"Then you're in luck. I have a surprise for you." His hands were clasped behind his back.

"You're not as smooth as you think you are."

"You don't want my gift?" He pouted, exaggerating the gesture.

"I no longer have any need of it. Keep it if you want."

"I'll treasure it." He tucked the flower into the inside pocket of his doublet. "Have I proven myself to you yet?"

"A touch," I said.

"That's a start. I never could resist a challenge." Silas balanced a flame on his fingertip, extinguishing it with a single motion.

"Scared you'll lose the ability if you don't use it often enough?" I asked, more curious than teasing.

"Sorry, old habit. It comforts me." Flames licked across his palms, heat rising in the air between us.

It struck me that this was a rare opportunity to question someone with a Blessing, at least someone who would actually answer. It was information that could prove useful beyond my encounters with Silas, adding substantial depth to what I'd learned from my training with the Night Ravens.

"How old were you when it first manifested?" I asked.

"Seventeen. I nearly burned off my eyebrows. What a shame that would have been for the world."

"I didn't realise it could appear so late." While fae weren't born with Blessings, the ability usually developed before their tenth birthday. After then, you were deemed Unblessed, like the majority of Idrix.

"I was a late bloomer, if you can believe it. The dark sheep of my family. My mother tried to reassure me that it didn't matter how long it took, it would appear when the time was right, but I knew she was terrified for me." He grimaced. "Father told me in no uncertain terms that if I remained without a Blessing beyond my twentieth birthday, I would be cast out. That if it took that long to appear, it would be weak and pathetic, unworthy of my family name."

"He would do that?" I tasted bile in my throat.

"Perception is power, as he'd say. So, you can see why we were all relieved the day I gained my powers."

He ran his hands along the tall flowers growing beside the path. "At first, I thought I'd caught a fever. No one else in my family was Fire-Blessed, you see, so they were unfamiliar with my symptoms. The elements don't follow bloodlines, only the ability. I was burning up, unable to control it, until suddenly there was fire blazing from my hands. Now it's as if it's always been a part of me. I can't remember what life was like without it." He froze, realising who was standing next to him. "Gods, that was so insensitive of me. I'm not used to the whole no Blessing thing."

"You can't miss what you never had, although I suppose it would make lighting a campfire easier."

"Among other things. My favourite trick is when I meet someone rude. I raise the temperature ever so slightly to begin with so it's almost unnoticeable. They start to shuffle, maybe loosen their collar, but they can't bring themselves to complain, not when they see I'm unaffected. That would be admitting a weakness. By the time our business is concluded, they're sweating buckets."

"Nice to know you have such pressing concerns."

Silas shrugged. "When you're surrounded by ambitious and scheming fae, solely looking out for their own interests, the only way to tolerate it is to liven things up a bit."

"You can do that? Heat up a room? It isn't just the fire?" I asked. The books in the Old Keep hadn't covered that.

"The flame is just the physical embodiment of the magic. I surprise myself sometimes with what's possible, as long as my hands are free to wield it."

I straightened, the extent of his abilities making me realise the danger we were in. "Be cautious about who you reveal it to. You could make yourself a target if the wrong fae witnesses your power." Power was rarely just a blessing. It was also a curse.

Silas studied me with an intensity that made my skin prickle. "You're speaking from experience. Who are you exactly? You're an accomplished hunter, you knew what to do with the stormfang, and you keep checking your map despite knowing where you are."

He watched me expectantly as a wave of panic surged through me. I'd never needed a cover unless the plan had specifically called for it. Usually, my prickly demeanour was enough to discourage any curiosity. I wore the harsh words like armour, protecting me from hidden knives. It was easier than being selective with the truth, deceiving others without an outright lie.

Silas continued. "If you're here, you're travelling south and you don't strike me as the shopping type." Gladhaven was the only city to the south, a place where merchants unhauled the last of their stock before crossing the Sapphire Sea, resulting in irresistible bargains at its many markets.

I stiffened. It was vital that no one knew my movements. The information I hunted couldn't be traced back to me under any circumstances. An overconfident and loud-mouthed companion, too curious for their own good, was a liability.

My voice was quiet, laced with danger. "I'll only say this once. This may all be a game to you, a brief diversion, but there are real problems I need to take care of. Responsibilities." He had the sense to look nervous, more vulnerable than I'd seen him before. I needed to push the knife deeper, scare him away for good before he could ruin everything. "I know what you are. You're part of the nobility. You must be with such a strong Blessing. Well, guess what? It's time you grew up. Go back to your fancy house and easy life and chalk this up as an exciting adventure to tell your grandchildren about. Leave me alone so I can fix the mess fae like you inflict on fae like me."

"I-" He swallowed, not quite meeting my gaze. Better for him to be upset than cost me this information, or put himself at risk by being discovered by someone with cruel intentions. "Sorry. I was trying to get to know you. I'll go."

He sounded defeated. I considered apologising, to give him another chance, but I resisted. There was no time to be sentimental. Too much was at stake. And it was better to cut ties this way.

If he left now, he couldn't betray me later.

I watched him leave, not taking my eyes off him until he was only a speck in the distance. His shoulders were hunched, every step of his faltering. My guilt didn't lessen, but I buried it deep down until I was numb to it. I required a clear mind to meet the informant.

Chapter 7

The next day passed without event. It was a return to the familiar routine of my missions, crafting a plan as I crossed the blossoming fields.

Valtarra was a tiny village perched on the tallest hill bordering the Blossom Sea. It was the last place I expected to find a covert informant.

Given its size, it wouldn't expect visitors, particularly one with a weapon. If I kept my head down and didn't engage its inhabitants, they would likely keep to themselves, wanting to avoid trouble. My goal was to get in and out as quickly as possible, leaving no room for mishaps.

By the time I reached its entrance, three days after leaving the comfort of the Yewdew Forest, any remaining doubts had vanished.

Stone steps were expertly set into the hillside leading up to an arch decorated with fresh flowers from the nearby meadows. A gleaming sign proudly displayed the village's name, one of the villagers polishing it with vigour as I passed. With my worn clothing, splattered with dirt from my travels, I was noticeably out of place.

Unable to shake the feeling, I wrapped my cloak more tightly around myself. The judging looks the villagers cast my way weren't the disdain of the Amber City's residents, but cautious concern, as if by studying me from afar they could understand the reason for my visit.

I'd certainly travelled to less pleasant destinations during my time as a scout. We were the backbone of the Night Ravens, responsible for bringing news to the Old Keep. Sometimes, that meant sitting in the dirt for hours on end, hoping to overhear something of value. Sometimes, when luck evaded us, it was all for nothing.

I continued along the perfectly straight path, the cobbled stone neatly framed by colourful flowerbeds. Finding the informant wouldn't be difficult. The bookshop was at the heart of the village, one of a handful of buildings besides a row of charming cottages.

It seemed a strange shop to operate there, but as I approached, several young women emerged, clutching their new books and a picnic hamper. With its proximity to the Blossom Sea, it would do a roaring trade on the long summer days, where night was held at bay for all but a few hours.

A bell chimed as I opened the bookshop's cracked, peeling door, finding myself in a dark room with a low ceiling.

"Just a moment," someone said from the other side of the shop. It was a promising start.

I glanced around as I waited. The bookshop was an eclectic mess of parchment, old tomes and pamphlets, with no order to the chaos.

It was larger than I'd expected based on the outside, tall shelves dividing the long room into a series of aisles, which led to an open space in the middle, cluttered with odd pieces of furniture.

It felt like a different world to the pristine village. I loved it.

The lady who greeted me was just as chaotic, wearing a mismatch of clothing in clashing colours, her red hair wild and untamed. I masked my surprise. Was she the informant?

"How can I help you?" she asked, a beaming smile on her face.

I hesitated. Reuben had equipped me with a pass phrase to confirm I was speaking to the informant, but I could never be too cautious.

"This place is a breath of fresh air," I said, and she blushed at the compliment. "Have you been running it long? No offense, but you're not what I expected."

"You're not the first to say that. It's not every day you see a bookshop managed by someone so young, I suppose. It's a family business, owned by me and my mother, but I'm usually the one serving customers. Is there something in particular you're looking for?"

"I'm not sure just yet."

"In that case, browse until your heart's content. I'll be here if you need me." Her enthusiasm spilled into every word.

I chose a strategic position at the front of the shop, feigning interest in a heavy reference book and turning the page every so often. But my attention was firmly fixed on the door and who would walk through it. For a while, the odd patron came and went, but the bookshop remained quiet, mostly leaving me alone with the young girl.

When nearly an hour had passed, a different door opened, this one at the back of the shop. My head snapped towards the noise.

A woman loitered in the doorway. She was the opposite of the redhead, clothed plainly in dark colours that matched her black hair, neatly tied up. A widow. Her gaze landed on me, sweeping over my worn clothes and the bow I carried.

"Dorea, fetch us some tea, would you?" she said.

Dorea obeyed, rushing out of sight to make the tea, a symphony of banging and clattering causing me to be concerned at what shape the kitchen would be in afterwards. The black-haired woman crossed the shop floor, locking the door and flipping the sign in the window to closed, granting us relative privacy.

It had to be her, but I spoke the coded message to be sure.

"I'm enjoying the lighter days. It brings out the vibrancy of the flowers." I kept my voice casual, observing her for any signs of recognition. She nodded, her posture relaxed as she faced me.

"I prefer the rain. It does the flowers good," she said, completing the secret phrase. "I'm Cassandra. I'm the one who sent for you."

She beckoned me over to a small table squeezed into the middle of the room between piles of dusty books, before taking a seat herself. "You're here sooner than I expected. Sorry about the codes. Reuben always did enjoy his little games."

I couldn't picture them knowing each other. Reuben had kept to himself for as long as I'd known him.

"This is important. I came as soon as I could." I tried to release some of the tension from my body. It was essential that she trusted me and I was well aware of my tendency to make a terrible first impression. I would rather fight a pack of rabid wolves than socialise with strangers. I set my mouth in what I hoped was a friendly smile.

Dorea interrupted us, setting down the teapot so hard that hot tea spilled over the table. She squeaked, rushing to fetch a cloth, mopping up the spilt liquid as she apologised profusely. Her face had turned as red as her hair.

"It is no hardship. Sit with us," Cassandra said. She filled our cups with what remained in the teapot. "I do not know where to begin."

Dorea's wide eyes flitted between me and Cassandra. "What's going on, mother?"

"Our visitor wants to hear about your work last month."

All the colour drained from Dorea's face, including her blush from moments before. "I can't. I-"

"I know. But she needs to see for herself."

I frowned, not liking the direction this was heading in. Dorea was taking quick breaths, unable to sit still in her chair. Her mother was rubbing soothing circles on her back. It felt like I was intruding on a personal moment, and I wanted nothing more than to give them some privacy, but I'd travelled here for a reason.

"If I may," I said, seizing control of the situation. I picked up my cup of tea, knowing full well I wouldn't be drinking it. Although everything checked out so far, it wasn't worth the risk of ingesting something harmful if this was a trick of some kind. "Why don't I ask you a few questions to start with?"

Cassandra nodded. Dorea let out a nervous giggle while her mother comforted her.

"How did this all begin?" I feigned a polite sip of my tea, keeping my gaze on the table to avoid direct eye contact with either of them. Staying detached was the best way to proceed here. If my presence became too distracting, I could spook Dorea and miss an important detail.

"Times are changing and less fae are visiting the meadows every year. Too many thieves and swindlers taking advantage of the visitors. The bookshop isn't doing as well as it used to. Once we could comfortably support our family with the takings, now it's hard just to keep a roof over our head. When the offer came, it was like our prayers had been answered."

"What offer?"

"Researchers in the South. They wanted someone experienced to catalogue their findings. The details were vague, but they offered us more than the shop would make in six months. Dorea volunteered to do it. The travel would be hard on me, you see. I'm not as young as I used to be." Her hand balled into a fist on the table. "We should've turned it down."

"What was this research?" I asked to Dorea, wondering what this had to do with the Night Ravens.

She tried to answer, but all that came out of her mouth was a rasping sound. Her mother shushed her, clasping her arm.

My heart sank. I knew what that meant.

"They made her agree to a bargain," Cassandra explained. "She can't utter a word about anything to do with the project."

My teacup rattled as I put it down more hastily than I'd intended. Why would researchers need a bargain with Dorea? It was suspicious, but I needed more information before I could inform Reuben.

"What about the fae you worked for?" I said, trying to find a way around it. "Can you tell me anything about them?"

Dorea considered it for a moment but choked on her words several times while attempting to answer.

The same happened with each question I asked, all a dead end. What was she cataloguing? Where did she work? What had her daily routine looked like? The bargain was exhaustive in its coverage.

"I don't understand," I finally said. "I sympathise with you, but if she is bound by a bargain, surely there is no information that can be shared?" Had this all been a wasted trip? What was the point of sending me all this way for something that could've been covered in a letter with little risk?

Cassandra took a deep breath, turning to her daughter. "Show her your arm," she ordered, and Dorea nodded meekly, rolling up the sleeve of her unique dress.

I schooled my features, masking my shock. It was a challenge, but I owed her that, at least.

Black tendrils snaked up Dorea's arm as far as her elbow, burrowing beneath the surface. The skin they touched had lost all colour, withering, as if the life had been drained from it.

"She was found like this. Her escort dumped her on the outskirts of the Blossom Sea when they realised she'd been compromised. One of the villagers recognised her, thank the gods, and brought her to me. It took days before she could speak and that's when we encountered the bargain." She squeezed Dorea's other hand. "The veins grow larger every day. When she first arrived home, they were at her wrist. The healer has never seen anything like it. No matter how many treatments they've tried, the infection persists. If they reach her heart…"

She didn't need to continue.

"And you can't tell me how it happened?" I'd known horrific injuries through my line of work, but this one was unique in its viciousness.

Dorea shook her head. "It burns," she said, her voice so quiet my ears strained to hear it. "Sometimes the pain is so intense I black out."

Had Reuben known what I'd find here? Was he hoping I could identify the disease and report back to him?

Dorea looked so broken that I couldn't help but feel sorry for her. She seemed like a sweet girl. Blinding rage soon replaced my sympathy. Someone had exploited their family and allowed Dorea to be hurt this badly. Someone unconcerned with the devastation it had wrought. They'd simply discarded her when she'd ceased being useful to them.

If I ever found them, they wouldn't be walking away from the encounter.

I tried a different approach. "Can you remember anything distinctive?" Dorea's mouth opened, but I interrupted her before she could choke on her answer. "Not about the research, but before that. When you were travelling?"

She considered her response slowly, chewing on her lip. "Actually, there was something. It's fuzzy in my mind, but maybe it can help."

I sat up straight in my seat, listening intently. Her mother encouraged her to continue.

"The ground was cracked into two, a deep gouge in the earth. I remember wondering how we were going to cross, when I could barely see the other side. But somehow we did."

Her description was unfamiliar, but specific enough to help. I opened my map, scanning the southern region. At first, nothing jumped out. But then, there, cutting across the land, was the Threstian Gap, separating the two halves of Threstia. Of course.

"Do you think you can find it?" Cassandra asked.

"I believe so."

Dorea winced, clutching her arm.

"She's all I have. Please help her," she urged, too quiet for Dorea to hear. "If this worsens, I don't know what to do."

"I'll do what I can." I said, the vague response all I could offer.

"Thank you." Her hopeful smile nearly broke me.

Cassandra retreated to the back of the shop, returning with a glass lantern. She thrust it into my hand, a gentle glow contained within.

"Here, take this if you're venturing out in the dark. You'll have more need of it than us."

I exited the bookshop with a cloud over my head. My mission was complete, the obligation met by the information Dorea had shared.

All that was left to do was report back to the Night Ravens and await my next orders. But it felt unfinished, a tug in my stomach at the thought of returning to the Old Keep with the barest of details.

Without helping Dorea.

No one deserved the pain she suffered. And despite my distrust of others, I had a soft spot for the weak and the defenceless.

I paused at the edge of the village, eyeing the intersecting paths at the base of the hill. The best course of action was to take the information back to Reuben and wait for the Threstian Gap to be investigated by a more experienced team.

But what if that was too late? What if by the time they travelled there, all traces of the researchers had disappeared?

Dorea's face, full of pain and fear, wouldn't release its hold on my mind. For a moment, I was no longer in Valtarra, but looking into another innocent's terrified eyes as her grip on my arm slipped, and I lost her to the sea forever. A single tear trailed down my cheek.

How long would it be before the inky black veins consumed Dorea completely?

I was tired of this world destroying the kindness in everyone. I would not stand by and let it happen again.

Reuben would have to understand.

It took several minutes of hammering on the bookshop's door before Cassandra answered, her eyes red as if she'd been crying.

"I need a favour. Do you have ink and parchment to hand?"

I scrawled a brief update to Reuben, the letter phrased in a manner that would be meaningless to anyone who hadn't learnt his codes.

Cassandra took it when I was finished, assuring me she'd get it to him undetected.

Then, I strode decisively onto the path leading south, leaving Valtarra behind, and with it, everything I'd known.

Chapter 8

A gentle breeze kissed my fingertips as it danced through the fields of flowers, their vibrant colours muted by the veil of night that had fallen over the Blossom Sea.

Travelling alone in the darkness was best avoided, but time wasn't on my side. Judging by my map, barely visible with the light of Cassandra's lantern, it would take just over a week to reach the Threstian Gap.

Could Dorea hold out for that long?

The reality of my brash decision was dawning on me. My supplies were dwindling and with no knowledge of the path ahead, hunting might not be an option. I didn't know if there would be somewhere suitable to camp, or dangerous areas to avoid. Asking around could help, but it was too risky.

I'd rather struggle by myself than be sold out or exploited again.

The more I considered it, the more certain I became about deviating from my orders. Dorea's suffering aside, if I could bring a breakthrough of this calibre back to Reuben, the Night Ravens would have to take me seriously.

An unsettling feeling in my gut was the first sign something was amiss. I observed my surroundings, checking for anything out of place. It was eerily quiet, the flowers my only company.

Nothing.

I stayed alert, readying my bow, just in case. My instincts rarely led me astray, and I'd be wise to heed them. My heart pounded in my chest as I waited, vigilant of any potential threat.

There was another possibility. Was Silas still out here? My words had wounded him, that had been obvious, but he'd proven me wrong with his resilience before.

"I told you to leave me alone," I said to the emptiness, on the slim chance it was him. Only silence greeted me, the disappointment in its wake unexpected. We'd hardly become close during our previous encounters, but his presence would have softened the unease I was feeling, enough for me to consider what to do next.

"We haven't had the pleasure," a gruff voice said, a man climbing out of a nearby meadow. A scraggly white beard covered most of his face, but amber eyes assessed me coolly. His clothing was torn and poorly cared for, his pointed hat faded, but the daggers strapped to his hip shone like starlight.

I stepped backwards, preparing to attack, but rough hands grabbed me from behind. The lantern slipped from my fingers, shattering into tiny pieces. I struggled, crying out as I tried in vain to free myself, my bow becoming dislodged in the process and falling onto the broken glass.

"We've got ourselves a lively one here, Finn," his accomplice said in my ear, holding me tighter as I writhed in his arms. It was a futile effort, but I wouldn't stop fighting. Fae like this preyed on the weak. The more difficult I made it for them, the more chance I could escape unscathed.

Yet another thing I'd learned the hard way.

"Easy darling. We'll take your coin purse, then we'll be on our way," the one named Finn said as he closed in. Thieves, in the Blossom Sea of all places. It was as Cassandra had said. Cursing myself for not recognising the warning in her off-hand remark, I twisted, attempting to grab my bow, but it rested just out of reach.

"You're wasting your time," I said, as Finn grasped for the purse hanging from my waist, wrestling it free. I hoped that was all he would take an interest in. "There's nothing in there except a few coppers." I neglected to mention the silvers stashed in my new boots for exactly this reason.

He tipped the contents out into his hand, frowning at the pitiful pile of coins their efforts had brought them. "Search her for anything else of value."

My legs lifted in the air as I fought to extricate myself from the roaming hands, groaning with the effort. Escape was my only chance at continuing the mission. If I sustained an injury here, it would all be for nothing.

When Finn reached for my bow where it lay on the path, a cry escaped my lips. It was my lifeline; I couldn't lose that. I had overcome too much to get to this point. To be left at square one, either crawling back to the Night Ravens for healing, or forced to continue with nothing, no money, no means of hunting. Vulnerable.

It wasn't fair.

My hand curled into a fist. *No more.*

I stomped hard on my captor's foot, freeing myself from his grasp. He hopped on one leg, cursing me. Without stopping as I ran, I scooped up my bow. I didn't get far before Finn caught me by my collar.

"You little shit. We tried playing nice, but you've left us with no choice," he growled.

He slapped me so hard it stung, the shock of it sending tears streaming down my face. I wiped them away angrily with the back of my hand. My skin throbbed where he'd struck me, and I had little doubt it would leave a mark, but there wasn't time to wallow in the pain. I needed to make another attempt to flee before they could disarm me again.

"That was a bad idea," a familiar voice said. My traitorous heart leapt like it was the sweetest sound I'd ever heard.

Silas. He'd come back.

He stood at the top of the flowery slope, bathed in unrelenting rage. Flames danced along every inch of his body, so bright against the dark night that it hurt to look at him.

This wasn't the Silas I knew, with his easy smiles and mischievous nature. This was a god of vengeance. Judging by the curses of my captors, they thought the same.

The sleeve on the hand Finn used to slap me ignited. He flapped his arm in a panic, screaming as he tried to tear off the garment. I took advantage of the distraction to shoot an arrow into his shin. Crumpling to the ground, he clutched his leg, rolling in an attempt to extinguish the flame.

His companion, just as dishevelled as Finn had been, but with his hair shaved close to his head, took one look at Silas and bolted, not even glancing back to check if Finn was following.

"I suggest you do the same unless you have a death wish," I said, aiming my bow at Finn's chest. He grimaced, scrambling backwards on the dirty path, before clambering to his feet and limping away.

"Bitch," he cursed under his breath.

Silas' arm twitched, punishing the insult by setting Finn's hat on fire. He flung it into the fields with a yelp, exposing a newly bald patch on his head, before deciding that a quieter retreat was in his best interests.

In his haste to leave, he'd dropped my coin purse, the coppers strewn on the path. I gathered them up, tucking it into my pack.

Silas laughed heartily, picking up the singed hat and twirling it around his finger. "Shame they couldn't stay. I was rather enjoying myself."

I glared at him, unable to stop my lip from twitching. Amusement danced in his eyes, Silas captivating in his delight.

I couldn't believe he'd come back for me after what I'd said.

My smile faded. If Silas hadn't saved me, I would have lost everything. How was I supposed to help Dorea if I couldn't fend off a couple of thieves?

It was becoming apparent that I was out of my depth. This wasn't like my usual missions, where I had ample time to prepare myself, but giving up wasn't an option. There was too much riding on this.

As much as I didn't want to admit it, the only way I could continue was with outside assistance. Silas had rescued me without hesitation, despite the harsh words I'd flung at him. Could I trust him to help me find the researchers? Would he entertain the notion?

I opened my mouth, intending to investigate further, but he was already several paces ahead. I jogged to catch up, Silas turning to me in surprise. There was no trace of the fire that had raged so powerfully moments ago. Even his doublet was untouched.

"Why did you help me? I told you to go away, in no uncertain terms," I said. There was no hostility in the words, only curiosity. Why had he come back?

"You did. Luckily for you, I always did find a damsel in distress hard to resist." He was teasing me again. It was comforting to return to familiar territory, though I couldn't shake the image of him on the hill, unrecognisable.

"What's the real reason?" I pressed.

He raised an eyebrow, knowing, as well as I did, that I was in no position to make demands. His curious gaze assessed me, and I prepared to be brushed off.

"I have my reasons. Why reveal them now when it's far more entertaining to watch you stew over it?"

I scowled and he grinned in response.

"Just like that. Since I'm enjoying myself, I'll tell you one thing. I had nowhere important to be, and you were obviously hiding something. Why else would you be so keen to get rid of me? So, I followed you."

I stiffened, not only at the admission, but at the fact I hadn't caught him tailing me. I'd been more distracted than I'd realised.

Silas continued when he noticed my rapt attention. "Since there's only one entrance, I paid a child to tell me when you left the village. I came as soon as he fetched me, and, well, you know the rest."

"I would've had the situation under control, eventually." Perhaps if I was lucky, though I was loath to admit it. "But thank you."

He beamed. "You're welcome. Well, if that's all, then I'll be on my way."

What? He'd made all that effort to find me, just to leave again? It frustrated me to do so, but I chased after him. "Wait."

He paused, crossing his arms across his chest, trying and failing to keep the smug grin from his face. "Well?"

I hesitated, fidgeting with my sleeve. Trusting him was a risk, even though he'd given me no reason to doubt him so far. But if I stood any chance of helping Dorea, it was my only option. I had to take a leap of faith.

"I have a favour to ask of you."

"You're coming to a spoiled noble for help? You must be desperate." Satisfaction rolled off him in waves. I supposed I deserved that.

"There's something I need to do. It's important, but I can't tell you what it is. After today, I don't think I can do it alone. Will you accompany me?" It was a poor offer, hinging entirely on his goodwill, and that was in short supply in Idrix. I hoped my instincts were right about him.

"You expect me to drop everything and come with you without knowing what I'm agreeing to?"

It was a good point. He had nothing to gain.

He was quiet for a moment. "What will you offer me in return?"

My mouth hung open. I'd expected an immediate rejection. I had nothing of value, but if he was entertaining my laughable proposition, then he needed something. I thought back to the forest, how he'd eyed the raglaw hungrily and how quickly he'd devoured it. The relief when he'd seen me again, suffering from his lack of preparation.

He needed me as much as I needed him.

I weighed my words. "We'll travel together. If you help me complete my task, I'll stay with you afterwards for as long as you need me for, within reason." I'd have to take a sanctioned break from the Night Ravens, but it wasn't outside the realm of possibility.

"You're not an assassin, are you?" Silas took a step away from me, his eyes narrowed.

What sort of question was that? I quirked an eyebrow at him, but he was deadly serious. "No."

"And you won't make me cause harm against my will?" he said.

That's what he was worried about? "No. It's nothing like that."

"And afterwards you'll stay as long as I need?" He was enjoying this now, going beyond due diligence and drawing it out just to annoy me. I rolled my eyes at him.

"Then I'll do it, on one condition."

"What is it?" I asked, a little too quickly.

Silas grinned savagely, retrieving the aurabloom he'd tucked into his doublet. It was nearly identical to when he'd first picked it, but the change in one petal had dread pooling in my stomach.

"I had a fascinating conversation with some young men when you unceremoniously abandoned me. They saw me examining this flower and were curious about why I had it. Then they told me something rather intriguing."

The colour leeched from my face. "Really?"

"Indeed. It turns out it's an aurabloom. They reveal your true feelings, including those you want hidden."

"Silas, I…" What was once a blush pink petal had withered into the murky grey of suspicion. My chest tightened.

"Take it. I showed you mine. Now show me yours."

My breath caught, but I knew there was no use arguing, not with the grim expression on his face.

If this was the cost of earning his trust, it was a toll I had to pay.

My fingers brushed against the flower and I steeled myself for what it would expose. I wanted nothing more than to look away and not bear witness to my shame. But I had no choice but to watch and see what Silas would learn about me.

I felt naked. Exposed. Broken.

The aurabloom showed him my greatest hopes and my deepest fears, the pain that infected my heart and the armour that protected it. It bared my soul to him, leaving nothing sacred.

I held my breath, waiting for him to speak. It had been no small ask, making myself so vulnerable in front of an untrusted acquaintance. The tension that hung between us as he stared at the colours was agony.

His voice was quiet, eyes trained on the blue petal that matched his. "Who did you lose?"

I couldn't look at him. "Everyone."

He was deep in thought. I was conscious of every second that passed before he broke the silence. "Fine. You have yourself a deal. But trick me again and I won't stick around, bargain be damned."

Under no illusions that he meant it, I nodded.

"And no more brushing me off. If we're partners, then I want to get to know you. You can keep your secrets, but I won't suffer poor conversation for weeks. I'd lose my mind."

It had worked?

My relief was immediate at having a partner to help me through the challenges ahead. I hoped I wouldn't come to regret it, a thought compounded by Silas insisting on sealing the deal with a complex handshake. Beads of white light looped around our arms before fading, binding us to the terms. The bargain was struck. There was no backing out.

I continued along the path, but he made no move to follow, looking behind us.

"What's wrong?" I asked.

"I thought I saw…" He shook his head. "Never mind. It doesn't matter. Since we're allies now, do you have any snacks to share? Using my Blessing has a toll. I'm ravenous."

My meagre supplies would not last at this rate. Despite that, I handed over some leftover raglaw. It was a small price to pay for my rescue.

As Silas ate happily as we strolled through the meadows, I only hoped I'd made the right decision.

Chapter 9

It took less than a day for me to regret asking for Silas' help.

"Are you sure it's this way?" I asked, glancing between the map and dozens of winding paths. With no easy means of figuring out where they led, we'd lingered on the outskirts of the Blossom Sea for a while, frozen by indecision. The pressure of choosing the right route had only brought on a headache.

Silas was attempting to lead me down one which veered off just ahead of us, towards an arch of twisted branches, crooked and gnarly, my least favourite suggestion. Even its entrance, bereft of the vividness of the meadows, gave me an uneasy feeling. But with our alliance newly forged, I thought better of shooting him down without hearing him out first.

"Do you have a better idea?" he said.

"No," I admitted. "But we should think this through carefully."

"I'm taking this one," he said, ignoring me and striding ahead with such confidence that I felt compelled to follow.

I sighed, reminding myself that I had a purpose for bringing him along. That his powerful magic would be useful to weather the challenges ahead.

"What happened back there with your Blessing?" I asked instead, Silas' body shading me from the sunlight as I trailed behind him towards the arch. "It was like you were someone else."

"You weren't complaining at the time."

"And I'm not complaining now, either. But I've never heard of a Blessing taking over someone's entire body like that. I thought it was contained to your hands?" The power he'd displayed was staggering. I wouldn't have believed it if I hadn't seen it with my own eyes.

"No. As long as my hands are free to conjure the first flame, there are no limits, but it's easy to lose control when using so much power. It's like the magic has a mind of its own. If you don't master it, you can lose all sense of reality." He faced me, his boldness melting away, leaving behind an unexpected vulnerability.

"Then why did you?" I asked, surprised he'd risked so much.

"You helped me when I needed you. Returning the favour was the right thing to do. My Blessing tapped into that thought and channelled more power than I knew what to do with. The safest solution was to burn some of it away." He smirked. "And who can resist a dramatic entrance?"

The archway led to a crop of trees, but where the Yewdew Forest was teeming with wildlife, this forest was its opposite. There was no fear of straying from the path, because it simply wasn't possible, every inch of space taken up by thorny brambles and dead branches. A distinct chill clung to it, like it had never known the comforting caress of the sun.

Our steps crunched on a carpet of twigs that littered the ground, the only sound to be heard in the otherwise silent woodland. I kept my arms close to my sides to prevent my cloak from catching on the undergrowth. Bare trees twisted around each other, shielding the forest from any sunlight and shrouding us in near darkness until Silas summoned a flame. The fire masked the musty, stagnant odour lingering in the air with a pleasant, smoky aroma. It relaxed me, if only slightly.

I didn't have much experience with the places touched by the curse, but I knew deep in my heart this was one of them. The very essence of the forest felt hollow, like something crucial was missing.

I was familiar enough with the stories. During the Malus era, over a thousand years ago, Idrix was ravaged by war. The enemy, a warrior race, sought to conquer Idrix and its rich resources for themselves. They hadn't expected us to fight back. Years passed of death, destruction and despair, until one day, when the tide was finally turning in our favour, the enemy released a devastating curse. It ate away at everything that sustained Idrix, from its connection to the gods, to the divine magic they'd used to forge it.

If they couldn't have Idrix, no one could.

Over the years, many had tried to break the curse, only succeeding at slowing down its destruction. Pockets of decay littered the realm, where every drop of magic had been consumed, leaving only bleak emptiness behind. One day, there would be nothing left, and Idrix would cease to exist. Just a forgotten memory.

I shivered at the prospect of the rest of the realm becoming as lifeless as the forest, the crowded streets of the capital eerily empty, the Blossom Sea sapped of colour, the flowers withered and dry; carriages stopped on the High Road with no one to ride in them.

Now I realised why so many opted to take the High Road to Gladhaven, despite being hounded by merchants and opportunists. Being in this place felt wrong, an unsettling sensation that made my skin crawl.

"Silas," I grumbled, berating myself for following him without a fight.

"I had a good feeling about it. I suppose I may have been mistaken."

That was an understatement.

Attempting to salvage things before they became worse, I consulted my map, using the light of his fire to read it. My finger trailed across the parchment as I searched for where we'd ended up. "Let's retrace our steps."

Silas flopped to the ground with his legs stretched out in front of him, undeterred by the horrified look on my face. "Can't we stop for a bit? We've been walking for ages."

He had yet to build up the stamina that journeying took. It reminded me of my early missions and how long they'd taken me, needing to rest every few hours to recover my strength. Now, with decades of experience under my belt, firm muscle had built in my calves, and I only tired after days of travel.

"We should press on. There's something off about this place," I said.

"You didn't let us stop last time, either. At this rate, you'll need to carry me the rest of the way."

Our debate was interrupted by the arrival of another.

A young lady approached us. She was fresh-faced with round, rosy cheeks and kind eyes. The cloak she was wearing was too big for her, swamping her body, a basket with a lid peeking out from underneath it.

"Excuse me. I couldn't help but overhear. I know a comfortable inn nearby if you're looking for somewhere to rest for a while," she said.

Her presence in this dangerous place bothered me, but before I could decline her offer and send her away, Silas enthusiastically jumped to his feet.

He pestered her with questions about the amenities of the inn. How many rooms did it have? Was the food delicious? Was the bar well-stocked? I groaned, knowing this wasn't a battle I would win.

The young woman answered all of his questions with a good-natured spirit, but I didn't let my guard down. Appearances could be deceiving.

Over the course of the previous day, I'd imparted my wisdom, distilling years of my experience as best as I could. It had evidently gone into one ear and out of the other. The first thing I'd told Silas was to be wary of strangers, especially those who seemed too good to be true.

I let them lead the way, laughing and trading stories as they walked. Something twisted in my gut as I watched them, at the natural warmth they shared with each other, the huge grin on Silas' face and the answering smile that the stranger gave him. It was none of my business who he chose to interact with, so long as it didn't derail my mission. Yet my bad mood persisted.

Everything happened too quickly.

Silas yelped as the earth gave way beneath him, a groan of pain reaching my ears as he fell into a deep pit. Its existence had been hidden on the path by a thick covering of twigs, tricking my eyes too. The woman had gracefully leapt to the side, leaving him as the sole victim.

"Silas!" I shouted, skidding to a halt just shy of the hole in the ground. He'd landed on his rear with no visible injuries, though he was covered in twigs and dead leaves. He shook his head, dispersing the debris. It wasn't shallow enough for him to climb out, trapping him there for now.

"I'm fine," he said. "The only thing that's bruised is my ego."

I faced the lady, unsurprised at the sickly-sweet smile on her face. She opened her mouth to speak, likely to continue the charade, but I interrupted her before she could.

"What do you want?" I said, my tone curt. I had no interest in playing her games.

"I have something that's available, for a price," she said, opening the lid of her basket to show me the coil of rope inside. Of course she did. "I'll sell it to you for five silver coins."

Five silvers? The rope wasn't even worth one. The swindle was as old as time and, like a fool, I'd fallen for it, too distracted to notice what was happening around us.

I pointed an arrow at her heart. "How about a different offer? I won't shoot you if you give me the rope."

She laughed, barely flinching. "You think it's the first time someone has threatened me? I'm Fire-Blessed. If you move another inch, I'll burn it and he can rot in there."

Silas might be an idiot, but he didn't deserve that fate. However, without assistance, there was no way for him to escape. The smooth walls provided no foothold, she'd made sure of that, and it was too deep for me to reach over and help him out.

"Rot? That would be an awful waste of this face," Silas said.

Five silvers would empty my coin purse, and I'd have no hope of finding the Threstian Gap without it.

"Don't do it," Silas said to me, the gallant fool.

Despite the words, his voice wobbled. He would be far from fine. Leaving him trapped in a forest plagued by the curse, armed only with a basic knowledge of how to survive was as good as killing him myself.

I swore, knowing I had no choice. There was no other option, and I needed him by my side. Reluctantly, I handed over the silver coins, receiving the basket in return.

"It's a pleasure doing business with you." She nodded, making a quick getaway before I could say another word. It was probably for the best. If there was someone who deserved to have an arrow fired at them, it was her.

My hand clenched the handle tightly, seething with rage that she'd taken advantage of us and there was nothing I could do about it. I only had myself to blame for the oversight.

I opened the basket, aiming to help Silas and get us out of the cursed forest as quickly as possible.

It was empty.

A sick feeling grew in my stomach. "Shit."

"What's wrong?" Silas asked.

"She tricked me. The rope was a glamour." I kicked myself. She'd never directly offered the rope, only showing me the contents of the basket. And I'd yet again allowed myself to be fooled.

If I'd given myself a few minutes to think, had examined the basket more carefully, I would have seen the signs. Would have spotted the telltale flicker even from afar. But I'd thought the deception to be simpler, merely a case of overcharging for the rope. And now I had nothing to show for my expensive purchase, just a useless basket.

I sank to the ground. It was hopeless. No wonder Reuben had only trusted me with simple scouting missions until this point. The moment I didn't have a plan laid out for me, I became sloppy, reckless, an embarrassment to the Night Ravens.

As if things couldn't get worse, rain lashed from the skies, heavy enough to permeate the canopy of branches, soaking me through and leaving my skin cold and clammy.

"Hey." Silas' voice was soft. "Don't worry about it. We'll figure something out."

"Like what?" I snapped, my teeth chattering. "I should never have listened to you. First, we get lost, then tricked. What's next?"

"I'll happily be your punching bag once you help me out of here and into a warm inn," he said.

I wanted to bite back, but he was right. Taking out my frustration on him wouldn't fix the problem. I focused on my breathing, giving myself room to think.

Scouts use nature's resources to their advantage. Use the terrain, conditions, shadows, anything you can think of to help you navigate a challenging situation. Anything can become an asset if viewed from the right perspective. Reuben's words rose to the forefront of my mind, recalling my extensive training. I gazed up at my surroundings, shielding my face from the rain. Perhaps I could find a vine?

"I'll be right back," I said to Silas.

"I'll just entertain myself, I suppose. Who knows, when you come back maybe I will have floated to the top? Or drowned. Only one way to find out."

I trudged through the mud, hoping my boots would fare better than the last time. The vegetation remained similar no matter how far I walked, nothing visible that could bear Silas' weight. With the rain affecting my eyesight, I soon became disoriented, relying on the sturdy tree trunks to navigate myself back to the pit, my fingers numb with the cold.

"Thank you for not abandoning me," Silas called out.

What else could I use?

His Blessing was no use here, neither was my bow without something to fix it to. The trees were unsuited to climbing, lacking footholds and with no low branches to grip, and the only possessions inside the pit with him were the clothes on his back and the small pack he carried.

Unless...

An idea sparked.

"Silas, do you see that tree? The one that looks fairly straight?"

"The one on your left?" he asked in confusion.

"Yes. Can you use your fire to cut it down without setting it alight?" I hoped it would be possible, if his power wasn't limited to his flames, as he'd led me to believe.

"It would take a tremendous amount of skill and talent, but you are talking to me. Where are you going with this?"

"Just trust me." I moved a safe distance away. "Please."

"I hope you're watching." Silas stood in the centre of the pit, arms outstretched. Rain hammered down, soaking him in icy water, but he persevered. With a quick flick of his wrists, a red-hot line cut through the tree trunk, felling it in a single motion. It landed on the path with a crash; the sound echoing through the silent forest. Where it had been sliced, the wood was blackened and singed, smoke rising where the rainwater met the heated surface. It remained otherwise undamaged.

"What's next?" Silas asked.

"Now, you wait patiently and quietly. I know that's a challenge for you."

"I'll just stay here enjoying this fine weather while you do all the work. Don't mind me."

"I won't," I muttered. My wet clothing rubbed against me uncomfortably as I dragged the tree along the path, inch by excruciating inch, using muscles I did not know existed. I would've been sweating if not for the rain drenching me.

By the time I'd finished, the cut tree resting at the pit's edge, my palms were raw and my clothes clung to my skin, smeared with dirt.

"Stand back. Press yourself against the wall as much as you can." I said, waiting for Silas to move.

When I was satisfied with his position, I began the difficult job of heaving the log down into the hole. My movements were slow, taking great care to keep it under my control.

Silas watched me curiously. Once I was sure it wouldn't hit him, I nudged it, letting one end fall next to him. He flinched at the impact.

"Now take off your doublet," I instructed.

"I beg your pardon?" Silas said, eyeing me dubiously from below. "If you want to see me naked, you just have to ask. This hardly feels like the time, though."

"Your clothing. It's expensive, isn't it?" I'd noticed it the moment I'd met him. *Anything can become an asset if viewed from the right perspective.* "It's well made. You can use your doublet to grip the tree and pull yourself up. The material should be strong enough to support your weight."

I had no idea if it would work, but what other choice was there?

He smiled, pushing his rain-soaked hair from his face and peeling off the wet garment. "You're rather brilliant. I hope you know that."

The compliment caught me off guard, but he didn't give me a chance to recover. My breath faltered when he unlaced his undershirt slowly, making a show of pulling it over his shoulders.

"What are you doing? I said your doublet, not your shirt." He wasn't going to remove all of his clothes, was he? With Silas, I never knew what was coming next.

"It's too stiff. Here, take it." He threw the garment at my feet, splashing my boots. "My shirt will work better."

I tried not to watch the rain run down his toned chest, or the way his arms flexed as he wrapped his shirt around the fallen tree. To my embarrassment, I realised he'd noticed me staring, a smile tugging at his lips.

Silas' face screwed up in a grimace as he pulled himself up the trunk, slow and steady. At first he struggled to find a rhythm, slipping down the log as much as he climbed, but then he found a technique that worked for him. When he neared the top, I grabbed onto his arms and lifted him the remaining distance, our bodies colliding in a tangled heap.

Exhausted, we laid on the wet ground, gasping for breath. When my heart had stopped thudding in my chest and some of my energy had returned, I sat up.

"Next time," I said between breaths, "you should heed my warnings."

"I guess we're even. I saved you, now you've saved me. Let's hope that's the end of the heroics." Silas pulled on his wet shirt, not bothering to fasten the laces, allowing me to glimpse his chest. I quirked an eyebrow at him.

"You seemed to enjoy the view before. It would be unfair of me to deprive you, especially when you've been so generous with your help," he said with an infuriating smirk. I rolled my eyes, rising to my feet and throwing his doublet at his head.

"We made a pretty good team," Silas said.

"You mean me doing all the work?" I flexed my fingers where they throbbed.

"I mean us playing to our strengths. You figuring out how to solve our little situation, leaving me to provide the entertainment." He adjusted his shirt, exposing more of his damp skin. I averted my gaze.

Mud caked me from head to toe, my hair plastered to my face by rain. Silas didn't look any better. We couldn't continue our journey like this.

"Let's find this inn to clean up, and quickly. I don't want to linger here," I said.

"I couldn't agree with you more. But no more taking directions from strangers. We'll look for it ourselves. I've learned my lesson in that regard," Silas said, tucking his doublet under his arm, unable to get back into the soaked garment even if he wanted to. As we marched on, he brushed the ground with his boot, checking for more traps. "Now, what other lessons do you have in store for me?"

Chapter 10

The Traveller's Rest was filled to the rafters.

The swindler's claims hadn't been unfounded. It was a charming inn, its stone walls dressed in ivy and wisteria, far beyond what could grow without the aid of a Blessing. A small pond skirted the entrance, teeming with colourful fish that rippled the surface of the water as we passed.

It boasted a spacious common room, fully stocked with a selection of beverages from across Idrix. There was even a keg of amber ale despite its distance from the capital. The kitchen was doing a roaring trade, its swinging doors in constant motion as food was ferried to grateful tables.

Fae nestled in every corner and nook, resting on their journey home from Gladhaven's monthly market, if the packages crowding the floor were any indication. The patrons compared their extravagant purchases with each other, bragging about the bargains they'd claimed. There were vials of perfumes, painstakingly wrapped garments, and, most strangely of all, an exotic bird that squawked from its gilded cage.

I nursed my drink, my cheeks flushed with the heat of the nearby fireplace, the clammy cold of the rain now a distant memory. We'd hovered near a small table in a quieter corner and pounced when it freed up, deciding we deserved the extra comfort.

The lively chatter of the inn filled my ears as I sank deeper into the cushioned luxury of my armchair, savouring the warmth while it lasted. Silas had insisted on repaying the coins I'd lost, despite my objections. Yet even with the money replenished, I couldn't justify the cost of a room overnight, not when sleeping outside on my bedroll was free.

My limited funds had at least secured temporary shelter, a brief respite from the harsh wilderness whilst I enjoyed my goblet of moon wine. Made from berries that grew only in moonlight, it had a silky, light flavour that went down far too easily. Silas had looked at me strangely when I'd insisted on an unopened bottle, but with the help of his best smile, the serving girl had fulfilled the request. The awkwardness was worth the reassurance that it was safe to drink, free from tampering, or worse.

A bath wouldn't have gone amiss. Once we were out of the wet weather, sheltering in the porch of the inn, Silas had used his magic to dry us off, but the caked-on mud stubbornly remained, earning us judgemental looks from the other patrons. It didn't matter. We were past caring about what we looked like, desperate for a scrap of comfort.

The wine had gone straight to my head. Moon wine was heady stuff, part of why I liked it so much. And with the warmth of the inn's common room settling in my bones, I felt woozy. Content. Relaxed. I never dared to overindulge, needing to keep my wits about me in case of an unforeseen threat. An inn of unfamiliar fae, while innocuous enough, could soon take a turn for the worst.

Silas looked more at ease than he had in days, watching the inn's patrons with interest. His brown hair was streaked with dirt and sticking up at odd angles. A chuckle escaped me at the sight, drawing his attention.

"Care to share?" he asked, amused.

"You may wish to consult a mirror before we leave."

"You're one to talk. If I wasn't familiar with your appearance, I wouldn't know you had silver hair." I looked down, noticing with dismay that he was right, the ends darkened with dirt.

The corner of my mouth twitched. He shook with the effort of holding back his laughter, finally breaking me. I chuckled, Silas joining me, our laughs loud enough to cause startled glances in our direction.

It felt good to let go of the heaviness of the past few days and enjoy a lighter moment. It had been a long time since I'd been able to laugh so freely.

"You're not so bad for a noble," I said, surprising myself with the truth. He was the last fae I should trust, not only a stranger to me, but one of *them*.

I knew little of my travelling companion. Although his actions had cast no shadow of greed or deception, there was no guarantee he wouldn't stab me in the back at the first opportunity.

But as time wore on, I was finding fewer excuses to distrust him. A part of me would always be waiting for the betrayal to hit, but was he capable of that?

"For what it's worth, I'm sorry about what I said to you before." I swirled the wine in my goblet, too much of a coward to face him directly. "I haven't had the best experience with nobility, and I took that out on you."

"No, you were right," Silas said. "I am naïve. Do you know what the saddest part is? I don't have a true friend in the world. If it weren't for my cousin Valeria, I'd have no one in my corner, but she has her own concerns. It's unfair to burden her with mine too."

It all made sense now. His insistence on joining me at the campfire, his exaggerated charm, the way he'd waited for me in Valtarra.

Silas was lonely.

He'd sought companionship, and I'd treated him terribly, suspicious of his motives when they were apparently genuine.

"We have something in common." I'd been so young when I'd come to the mainland, losing everything I'd ever known. Scouting hadn't improved things. I had built a network of allies within the Night Ravens, those I trusted beyond anyone else. But none of them resembled a friend. Our bond was forged by a shared dream of what the world could look like, not true friendship.

The easy camaraderie that was blossoming between me and Silas was different. New territory.

"Well, perhaps we can help each other." He offered his goblet, filled to the brim with moon wine. "Friends?"

Could I trust him?

After a moment's hesitation, I clinked it with my own. "Sure. Friends."

We both took a sip in silence. I was unlikely to see him again after this. I would complete my mission and return for my next assignment, while he would continue his adventures, but a friend could be pleasant while it lasted.

"So, friend. Tell me about yourself. Where are you from?"

"It's a long story," I said, attempting to avoid the topic.

"We have time." Silas drank his wine, watching me expectantly. I recognised his look of stubborn determination as he lounged in his armchair, refusing to speak until I answered him. He meant what he'd said when saving me from the thieves. Dodging his attempts at conversation wouldn't be possible.

I fidgeted with my hands, clenching my fingers so tightly they turned white. I always dreaded this topic. "The Tigal Isles."

Confusion clouded his face. "I've never heard of them."

"I'm not surprised. The curse was quite thorough when it obliterated them." I prepared myself for the pity the admission usually elicited.

Silas gripped his goblet too tightly, wine sloshing over the rim and spilling onto the table. "I'm so sorry. I never would have asked if I'd known."

"It was a long time ago." Though the void it left behind would never disappear.

"What was it like? Before, I mean."

I let out a breath of relief that he hadn't wanted to know how it had happened; that was too painful to relive, even now, decades later. He rested a tentative hand on my forearm in a reassuring gesture. I didn't brush him off, to my surprise.

"It was everything. We would wake gently with the sunrise and spend the morning working. Everyone pitched in. I hunted, my mother crafted things, my father cooked and fished, and my little sister tended to the livestock. My family had a rule of whatever we were doing, we would always eat together. That family time was precious." I smiled sadly. "In the evenings, when everyone's work was done, the whole village would gather around a campfire, and we'd sing and dance until we'd lost our voices and our feet ached. Then we'd lay under the stars, lulled to sleep by the sound of the waves. The mainland was so distant, a different world. I didn't know Blessings existed until I came here. None of us were Blessed and the only contact we had from outside the islands was a merchant boat from Gladhaven once a month, bartering our produce for items we couldn't make on the island."

"It sounds wonderful. I wish I could've seen it." While he had good intentions, it was the wrong thing to say. I tugged my arm away from his touch.

"Yes, well, that won't be happening. There's nothing left there now from what I've been told," I said.

"You've never gone back?" Silas said, watching me curiously.

"Why would I? Would you return if your home was destroyed?"

It was more than that. Seeing it for myself would confirm that it was real. This way, I could pretend my village was still there, just a boat ride away. Somewhere I could go back to one day.

"No, I suppose I wouldn't." Silas sat in quiet contemplation, absentmindedly rubbing his fingers against the embossed surface of his goblet.

I'd revealed far more to him than I was comfortable with, coaxed into it by the buzz of the moon wine and the comfort of the common room. I cleared my throat. "How about you? Where is this fancy house of yours?"

"An awful place. You aren't missing out on much." He sounded nonchalant about it, but his shoulders tensed up, his jaw set in a firm line. I perked up. That was an interesting reaction.

"Silas," I grumbled. I wouldn't let him off that easily.

"If I must." He sighed, his voice becoming little more than a whisper. "I'm from Eirel."

I'd suspected he could be that day in the Blossom Sea, but the confirmation still made my eyes widen. I understood his hesitation. The mission I'd undertaken there had given me enough of a glimpse to know it was a harsh place, ill-suited for his good nature.

Eirelean fae were reclusive, hostile to outsiders, and prized power above all else. With Silas receiving his Blessing so late, I couldn't imagine it was easy for him.

"Fancy house was an understatement in that case. You must be from the Isle of Mist."

Eirel's lake divided the nobility, who lived within the shrouded island's vast castle, and the commoners, whose settlements encircled it. There was no doubt where he resided.

"How did you know that?" His shock was satisfying, but I had no intention of revealing the details of my visit.

"A great manner of things come to light when a ruler dies," I said, matter of fact.

Silas swallowed thickly, and it struck me that he must have known the lord personally. The rulers of Idrix were so far removed from day-to-day life that it was easy to forget they were fae too. Easy to forget they had lives, and fae who cared about them beyond their official role.

"I'm sorry for your loss."

"It's a big castle, more of a town really, with hundreds of noble residences within the walls. Truthfully, I rarely saw the late lord. He was always busy with his High Council." He watched me carefully. "Since you're so well-informed, what's your opinion of his successor?"

I sifted through the gossip I'd overheard, trying to recall what had been said of him. "I've heard he's particularly reclusive, even for an Eirelean. What do you make of him?"

Silas considered his words for a long moment. "He's new to the role and still finding his feet. He has an impressive legacy to live up to. The late lord had a knack for building alliances and shutting down dissent. Anyone would find that a challenge to follow."

"Time will tell, I suppose." I shifted in my seat to face him. "It makes sense now, why you were so keen to head out on an adventure."

"Does it?" His eyes flashed with interest.

"When a city closes its gates, everyone is quick to assume it's to shut out outsiders and protect the fae within. No one considers the other possibility. When trapped like that, I imagine the prospect of freedom is alluring."

"Oh, it became irresistible." He cocked his head to one side. "I never knew you were so perceptive beneath those claws of yours."

"There's more to me than you know," I said, holding his gaze.

"I look forward to discovering it." Silas' mouth curved upwards in a smile.

The air was charged, heavier, as I watched the glow from the fireplace sweep across his face. I sat back in my chair, draining my goblet.

"I'm ravenous. Shall we order some food?" he asked, breaking the spell. His body lifted from the armchair as he peered around the inn in search of a serving girl. One was pouring drinks on the other side of the room, several tables vying for her attention. He summoned her over with a polite wave.

I'd seen the large platters the kitchen served. Generous portions like that wouldn't be cheap, and I needed to save my coin for the journey ahead. The tantalising scent of fresh bread and hearty stew that swarmed the common room did nothing to help my rumbling stomach.

"I have food," I said, patting my sack. It wasn't a lie, but the berries left in there paled in comparison to the inn's offering.

He surveyed me with a curious gaze, like I was a puzzle he was trying to solve. "I'm feeling rather indecisive today. I'll choose a few things, and you can do me a favour by helping me eat it all. My treat."

I protested, but the serving girl had already noticed him. She wove through the throngs of fae that were summoning her to take our order. Silas read out a selection large enough to feed five. My gratitude burned in my throat.

He handed her a pile of coppers, far more than the cost of the meal. When she tried to return some, he closed her hand around it, urging her to keep it. She nodded gratefully.

It wasn't a sensible move to spend so generously, not when the path ahead was unpredictable, and there was no telling who was watching us in the inn. But just this once, I would ignore the consequences. For once, I would let myself enjoy some home comforts.

I'd misjudged Silas. There was an undeniable goodness to him, one that couldn't be faked. Perhaps good existed in the world, and I'd been unfortunate to not experience it until now.

I took my first step towards making amends the only way I knew how. "Willow. My name is Willow."

His answering smile stole my breath.

"Willow," he repeated, as if testing the way it felt on his tongue. "It suits you."

"My mother named me. She told me willow trees are strong and can prosper in any conditions, just like I could." My lip trembled at the thought of her. We were robbed of enough time together, the wound still excruciating.

"She chose well." He rested his hand on top of mine and I felt every tiny movement, my focus glued to where our hands met.

The serving girl arrived with the feast Silas had ordered, bringing over a few plates at a time. He withdrew his hand to make room for the food, and I mourned the warmth of him.

"Help yourself." He grabbed a meaty rib from a still-steaming platter and tore into it, abandoning all decorum. I laughed. "What?" he said, his mouth full.

"I'm curious if you learnt those manners on the Isle of Mist."

"I'd never be invited to a formal gathering again if the nobility could see me now." He licked his lips clean. I realised I was staring at the same time he did. Dimples broke out from his grin. "Come on. It'll get cold if you're not quick."

I didn't need to be told twice. I wasn't polite, tearing into the meal with the same ferocity he'd displayed. We ate in comfortable silence, polishing off as much of the food as we could manage.

I couldn't remember the last time the weight had been lifted from my chest. For once, I wasn't living and breathing my mission, planning my next steps and tracking my target. I just existed.

I'd never considered what I'd missed out on due to my lifestyle. There had always been a purpose to my life. Growing up, that was hunting, biding my time before I was selected to lead the island's hunters. Then, after everything happened, it was survival, before the Night Ravens gave me a new purpose. There hadn't been a chance to dream of anything else.

But here, with Silas, in a warm, comfortable inn, my stomach so full I'd had to loosen my trousers, and the haze of the moon wine still caressing my mind, I dared to dream of more.

"I need some fresh air." I didn't wait for his reply before rushing out into the cool evening air, barging past a dawdling group of fae at the inn's entrance. The breeze sharpened my senses, bringing everything back into focus.

I was alone outside, my only company the gathering fireflies, leaving enchanting trails of light behind them.

Leaning against the wall, I sucked in a deep breath. This was dangerous, more dangerous than any situation I'd faced as a scout. I had an important job to do, one few others were capable of. The Night Ravens relied on me, on my information, to protect our existence. Yet here I was, enticed to want more by a decent meal and a friendly conversation. A fantasy I couldn't afford to indulge. There was too much at stake.

I thought of Reuben, Sal, my fellow scouts. What they would say. My face burned in shame. Even a novice knew to keep your focus on the mission at all costs.

I marched back into the inn, intending to bid Silas goodnight, ready for a fresh start in the morning. But when I returned to our table, he was gone. In his place was a hastily written note and an old, worn key. Attached to it was a wooden disc engraved with a room number.

I picked up the note in disbelief, reading the elegant handwriting.

Thank you for a magical evening.
Even the strong need a break sometimes.
Rest well,
Silas.

The gesture was far too generous. I couldn't accept it, especially with nothing to offer in return. But he was nowhere to be found. I swallowed the lump in my throat, clenching the key tightly in my hand as I walked up the stairs to the rooms above the common room.

Silas knew. He'd watched me decline the food, then devour it like a starved wolf. If a meal was out of my budget, he'd realised I'd be forced to huddle under my bedroll in the bitter cold, struggling to light my fire yet again. He'd known that if he'd offered me this directly, I would have declined, spun up some story to save face in front of him.

So he'd waited for the opportune moment to gift me the room, with no expectation of reciprocity.

The only bed I knew aside from my bedroll was my cramped bunk back in the Old Keep, where privacy came from a makeshift curtain. The dormitories were freezing and I could only fall asleep by burying myself under a pile of blankets.

My key led me to a room in desperate need of renovation. The wooden furniture within was chipped with frequent use, the thin curtains did a poor job at covering the window, and green paint peeled from the walls, exposing the plaster beneath. Evidently, the inn's priority was providing a comfortable resting place for patrons looking for a warm meal, the same effort not extended for overnight guests.

I nearly sobbed at the sight of the bed. The lumpy straw mattress would undoubtedly itch my skin through the cheap linens, and it had seen better days, but it was a proper bed, large enough to sleep two. There was no greater luxury after a week of sleeping on the cold, hard ground. And I had the entire place to myself, no snoring to keep me awake, no being disrupted by a creaky door opening all night. Just me.

It was the greatest gift I'd ever been given.

I took full advantage of the prepared tub despite the lukewarm temperature of the water, submerging myself without hesitation.

The day's events had been unexpected, to say the least. Silas' links to Eirel raised some questions about my new friend. The Eirelean commoners I'd eavesdropped on during my mission had little love for the nobility. I'd seen my fair share of villagers beaten by the city guard for a less than complementary remark.

But he didn't possess their cold, detached cruelty. He wore his heart on his sleeve, his emotions easy to read. Then there had been his unwavering generosity in the face of my hostility.

Nothing added up.

I scrubbed my dirty skin until it was red, the water turning a murky brown once I'd washed off all the mud. Afterwards, I sank into the bed, my hair still wet, unable to recall the last time I'd felt so content. I drifted off as soon as my head hit the pillow, sleeping more soundly than I had in years.

Silas didn't know what he'd done for me. I would never forget it.

Chapter 11

"**P**ull the string taut so it touches your nose and lips...Good. Now, keep your arm straight. Can you feel the breeze? You'll need to factor that in and aim slightly left of your target...No, don't drop your hand."

Silas flinched at my touch as I adjusted the position of his arm, but maintained his concentration. This close, his scent filled my nose. The inn's cheap soap, mixed with his natural, earthy smell and its hint of vanilla.

Something had shifted between us after our night in the inn and the common ground it had uncovered. I had grown accustomed to his presence, no longer finding him a hindrance.

We were partners now. *Friends.*

Our friendship was destined to be a short one. Once my mission was over, and the terms of our bargain satisfied, we'd part ways. The scout lifestyle, with its sparse comforts and stability, was no place for someone like him, a noble accustomed to the opulent surroundings of the Isle of Mist.

We'd avoided the topic of his generous gift. I'd broken my fast alone that morning, unable to stop my gaze from drifting around the common room in search of him, unexpectedly disappointed when he'd failed to appear.

Later, when I'd packed up my belongings and readied myself for another day of travel, he'd been waiting for me outside the Traveller's Rest, greeting me with a dazzling smile.

Overnight, Silas had traded his elegant doublet and tailored trousers for a set of simple travelling clothes in dark colours, blending in with the other patrons leaving the inn. He wore them well, but there was no masking his confident stature, even with his black cloak trailing behind him.

To my surprise, when we'd stopped for a short rest, he'd asked if I'd teach him to use a bow. With flames at his fingertips, he had no need for weapons. But Silas had insisted, and after he'd paid for my room, it felt good to do something for him in return.

It was a shame he was a terrible student.

The arrow missed its mark by a wide berth, joining his previous attempts as it wedged itself into the ground uselessly. The tree he was targeting remained undamaged. I gathered the fallen arrows, returning them to the quiver for the fifth time.

"Oh, come on!" he groaned, resting the bow against his thigh. "This is impossible. You made it look so easy." It was refreshing to see him outside of his comfort zone. He seemed to breeze through life effortlessly, taking everything in his stride and never struggling.

"That's what happens when you can't rely on a Blessing. If I failed to hit my mark, I didn't eat."

I omitted the full truth. I was better with a bow the first time I'd picked one up than islanders who'd trained their whole lives to hunt. There was no explanation for my luck. As soon as the bow was in my hand, everything else ceased to exist. It was just me and the target. My natural talent didn't make me popular with the hunters, although that was forgotten when I provided a bountiful feast for the village.

"You're rushing into it. Take your time and observe your surroundings before you release," I said.

Silas looked like he wanted to talk back. I smiled, relishing his struggle. He wisely decided against provoking me, and instead, raised a hand in the air, studying the feel of the breeze against it.

"That's it. Now close your eyes and adjust your aim to the wind."

This time, when he wielded the bow, he aimed left of the target, looking at me for confirmation before he released the string.

I rewarded him with a small grin. The arrow sailed through the air, embedding itself into the tree with ease.

It was a beautiful shot, especially for a beginner.

"Did you see that? I did it." Silas collided with me, engulfing me in a tight hug. He laughed merrily, spinning us in delight. I could only hold on for dear life, hoping he wouldn't drop me or send me flying into the trees.

"Thank you," he said, when my feet were on the ground.

Dazed, I could only nod. I was consciously aware of his hands on my lower back, Silas pressed up against me so closely I could feel his heart thudding in his chest.

He cleared his throat, stepping away. I shook off the feeling, distancing myself once again.

"Let's see you hit the target a few times," I said, acting like nothing had happened.

He obliged, adjusting his stance and firing arrows into the tree. Soon, it was littered with small holes, Silas managing consecutive hits.

"Looks like I may have to swing by Gladhaven. I'll need an impressive bow to show off my newfound talent for archery," he said, plucking arrows from the tree.

I groaned. He shot me a lazy grin as he reached past me to return them.

"I can just picture it; all style and no substance."

He clutched his chest, feigning a stagger backwards. "I'm wounded that you hold me in such little regard. Besides, what's wrong with coveting beautiful things?"

I kicked mud in his direction, splattering his pristine new boots. His eyes sparkled in challenge.

"I bet the ladies swoon at your feet with lines like that," I said.

"Is it working? Should I prepare myself to catch you?" He stretched out his arms towards me, mockingly, barely able to contain his laughter.

"I don't swoon and the only thing you should prepare yourself for is my hands shoving you forward if we don't get moving. We're wasting time lingering here longer than necessary."

"You'll be needing this, in that case." He passed my bow back to me and I slung it over my shoulder. "Lead the way."

Our route south had an eerie feel to it. It lacked the unsettling emptiness of the dark forest and the curse that plagued it, yet the open grasslands, bereft of any fae, buildings, or other signs of life, put me on edge.

Anyone venturing in this direction would take the High Road unless they had something to hide.

The black rock of the Threstian mountains had become visible when we stopped for the day, their dark shapes cresting over the horizon, the light fading so quickly we could hardly see the ground we were walking on.

"Why don't you set up camp and leave the fire to me this time?" Silas said.

He busied himself gathering firewood while I positioned our bedrolls on a flat patch of grass, sheltered by bushes. It gave a good vantage point over the path, providing ample warning of any intruders when combined with the protective wards I wove around our camp. A comfortable silence settled over us as we worked, and it reminded me of carrying out my duties on the Tigal Isles in quiet focus.

I felt the heat of the fire before I saw it, my back to him as I unpacked my supplies.

"Here. Courtesy of the inn." He produced a bottle of moon wine from his pack, waving it in the air. My face lit up. He'd remembered it was my favourite. "Don't worry, it's sealed. Thought the journey would go smoother if I sweetened you up."

"You think me so easily swayed?" I reached for it, but he snatched it back before I could take it. Bastard.

"I'm here, aren't I?" he teased, holding the wine out of my reach.

I pounced at him, colliding with his chest, catching him off guard and swiping the bottle from his grasp before he could find his balance. The cork popped audibly as I opened it. "Against my better judgement."

"Don't forget, you were the one who proposed our bargain. I'm helping purely out of the goodness of my heart."

"If you say so." I took a swig, handing it back to him. Silas' neck worked as he drank the liquid, drawing my gaze. The campfire cast a red hue over his face, like he was made of flame, and for a moment, I was stunned.

"What are you thinking about?" His voice was softer than usual, more relaxed. He passed me the moon wine, settling on the edge of his bedroll and watching me curiously. My skin prickled at his scrutiny.

I avoided the question, replacing it with one of my own. "How does it feel when you use your Blessing?"

He thought about it, staring at his hands.

"My fingertips burn long after I've used the magic, like the fire is reluctant to part with me. It passes after a while. If I push myself too hard, it drains me and I want to sleep for a week. I have a healthy level of stamina though. There's nothing to worry about in that department." He grinned wolfishly. "Are you jealous? Of my Blessing, I mean."

"No." My answer was instant. "Magic isn't the only power, and I've got this far without it. I don't consider myself lesser because my strengths lie elsewhere."

"Good. Because there's nothing lesser about you. You're one of the most impressive fae I've ever met."

I drank deeply from the bottle. "You might be growing on me too. Sometimes."

"Coming from you, that's a hell of a compliment." He leaned closer, the moment between us charged. "Careful now, you'll get my hopes up."

It was too hot, the air in the clearing stifling. Was it his Blessing? I willed my racing heart to slow down, to give me one moment of coherent thought.

"What's your story, anyway?" I asked, desperate for a change of subject. "Why the adventure? Were you just so eager to escape Eirel's closed gates, or is there more to it?"

"I don't want to talk about it." The colour drained from his face. That was unexpected. The question had been innocent enough. I thought the nudge would inspire him to share tales of his glamorous life on the Isle of Mist, how he tired of lavish balls and scandalous gossip. But he didn't.

My eyes narrowed. "Yet you want me to spill all my secrets. Seems fair."

"You're right. I won't pry, not anymore," Silas said. He was weirdly quiet, just like when I'd questioned him in the inn. It unnerved me. All I'd needed to do to shut down his curiosity was to ask him personal questions. But now I wanted the opposite.

"How about a trade?" I said.

"Sounds dangerous, but go on." He sat up straighter, giving me his full attention. Some colour had returned to him.

"One truth for another." I didn't want to share my truths, not really, but his extreme reaction was unsettling, and my curiosity demanded to be satisfied.

"Deal." He didn't even take the time to think it over, agreeing instantly.

"You first." I said, racking my brain for something I could give him that wouldn't compromise my mission.

"Fine. You resent me for being part of the nobility, but the truth is, I hate it. I haven't been free to make a single decision in my life until now. This is the first thing I've done for myself. And I think it's going pretty well, don't you?"

He watched me expectantly. The more I learned about Silas, the less suited he seemed for the treachery of Eirel. He'd made mistakes on our journey, many, many mistakes, but he'd adapted far quicker than any scout I'd known, certainly one from such a privileged background.

It was my turn. I took a deep breath, steeling myself to open up to him.

"Since losing the Tigal Isles, I've felt adrift. Travelling takes a toll, but it's the only thing that makes sense to me. On my travels, I'm in control of my life. But one day, I hope I can find where I belong."

"I know exactly how you feel."

Everything was silent, aside from the crackling of the campfire, but it was an easy silence.

"I do have some fond memories of Eirel," he said, after a while. "When I was young and foolish, I decided I wanted to be normal, just for one night. So I snuck out of the castle, borrowed some clothes to blend in, and had myself an evening on the town. I didn't realise the swill in the local tavern was many times more potent than the wine I was used to, and I made a fool of myself."

"I imagine you were quite the spectacle."

"You know me. I'm not shy. Supposedly I forced the whole tavern to give their finest rendition of a bawdy tune, danced on a table which then collapsed beneath me, performed a striptease for the furious landlady and ordered a round of drinks for everyone before realising I'd lost all my money. It sounded like a riot; if only I could remember it."

He leant back, resting his weight on his elbows. "My brother discovered me in the early hours being thrown out of the tavern by the landlady. Apparently, he'd never seen such an inventive use for a broom. He smoothed things over with her, sobered me up, then made sure I was presentable before we met our father for breakfast.

He never breathed a word of it. He was like that, always had my back without question when I needed him."

"He sounds like a great brother."

"He was." Silas smiled sadly. "He passed away when I was still in my early years of adulthood. I lost my father recently too. Now it's just Valeria and me."

"I'm so sorry." I knew what it was like to lose everyone you loved. The loneliness that always haunted you, even on the lighter days. The ghost of the beautiful memories and the ache they left behind.

"I noticed grief was on your aurabloom too. Was that from the curse?"

I nodded. He didn't pry further, understanding my hesitation. "They live on in us, even when you don't notice their presence."

"I carry them with me always." It was my burden to bear. As the sole survivor from the Tigal Isles, it was my duty to do whatever I could to stop the curse. I couldn't let their deaths be in vain. I owed it to their memory.

"Me too."

He smiled, easing back into his story. But the warmth of the moment lingered, as comforting as the wine we drank. "No one realised who I was. It wasn't like we ventured into town often. Stories spread though of the legendary drunk and their entertaining antics who was never seen again. I'm wiser now, and have a much higher tolerance for alcohol, you'll be pleased to know."

"So, no more performing a striptease to get yourself out of trouble?" I teased.

"Only if you ask nicely," he said with a wink.

"You'll be waiting a while."

"It's a good thing I'm extremely patient." Silas looked at me like he was seeing me for the first time. "It seems like we have more in common than we thought."

"I guess so," I said.

He fumbled with his belongings. "I have something for you."

"More wine?" My voice was tinged with hope. The bottle hadn't lasted long with the two of us drinking it.

"No, you've finished my supplies. This is something else."

He retrieved an amulet from his pocket, but there was no jewel hanging from the chain. Instead, the stone was dull, resembling an ordinary rock if not for the lines carved into its face. He fastened it around my neck, his breath ghosting on my skin and sending shivers cascading down my spine.

Magic thrummed through it, unlike anything I'd experienced before. I'd seen enchanted artefacts, but nothing close to this level of power. It was what I'd hoped to find from my mission in the capital, though I would've been pleased with a fraction of the power the necklace possessed.

"You're giving me an artefact?"

"I'm *lending* you an artefact," Silas clarified.

"This is too much. I can't accept it." The stone should be stored in a vault somewhere, guarded under lock and key.

"I want you to have it. While we journey together, at least."

"What does it do?" I asked, examining it. It was cold to the touch.

"It's a seeking stone. I have its twin". He pulled down his collar, a matching amulet hung around his neck. The hairs of his chiselled chest peeked through the neckline of his shirt. "They're connected. The wearers can always find one another."

"You want to track me?" I asked nervously. Allowing him to do that could put the entirety of the Night Ravens at risk. Our new trust was still fragile, and this risked fracturing it completely.

"No, it doesn't work that way, I promise. It's a relic of protection, passed down through my family for generations. But the magic is complex. You must wish to be found just as much as I'd want to find you, otherwise the connection will fail." He paused, uncertainty casting a shadow over his features. "I can take it back if you don't want it."

"Having someone looking out for me wouldn't be the worst thing in the world." I tucked it under my shirt, unable to find the words to thank him. The amulet was priceless, and he'd chosen to lend it to me. Because he'd wanted to.

He didn't let me get away with that response. "I think the words you're looking for are 'thank you'."

"Don't push your luck," I said. But later, when he was in a deep slumber, I spoke again.

"Thank you. For everything."

I fell asleep to Silas' soft breathing and the reassuring weight of the seeking stone on my chest.

Chapter 12

"Poisonous," I declared at the clutch of berries in Silas' grasp. He pulled a face, dropping them in protest, one of the fruits breaking away from the bunch and bouncing off my foot. It left a green smear behind, but with how dirty my boots were it wasn't noticeable.

The wind whipped my hair against my head as we crossed the endless grasslands that made up the majority of southern Idrix, our journey taking us ever closer to Threstia and whatever answers we'd find there.

Silas' third attempt at foraging hadn't yielded any improvement. It was tempting to give in and do it for him, particularly with the urgent ache in my stomach, but he would never pick up the survival skills he so desperately needed unless I gave him the opportunity to learn from his mistakes.

"You barely glanced at them. How can you tell?" His voice bordered on indignant.

"The colour, for one. I told you to avoid the green, yellow and white ones. They have a far higher chance of being dangerous to consume," I said, as patiently as possible, though it didn't come naturally to me. Had I been this difficult to teach? If so, I owed Reuben a thousand apologies.

"Have you looked around? That's all there is." In his defence, since leaving the inn, there were slim pickings for foraging, the grassy plains bare of anything except, well, tall grass. But each cluster of bushes we encountered appeared promising until Silas returned with yet more poisonous berries.

"Look higher, in the difficult to reach places. The ones you can gather with minimal effort will be just as easily found by wild animals. You must be smarter than them if you want to eat."

"Did you insinuate that I'm less intelligent than an animal? And I thought we were friends."

"I've yet to see any evidence to the contrary."

His eyes flashed. "Are you baiting me?"

"Is it working?" I hoped so. At this point, I would try anything to ease my hunger. "Prove me wrong then."

He huffed, hurrying to the bushes ahead and disappearing into the greenery.

I sighed. My patience was wearing increasingly thin the further we travelled. It was no fault of Silas', though he certainly didn't help things.

I hadn't returned to the south since I'd joined the Night Ravens. There had been an opportunity to, with Reuben frequently sending scouts to monitor Gladhaven's criminal undercity, but he'd always assigned those missions elsewhere, likely concerned about the memories it would dredge up for me.

I wondered what he'd think of me heading back with only a clueless noble for company.

Though I supposed that wasn't the case anymore. Silas had proved himself capable on more than one occasion, taking to our quest with an earnest enthusiasm. He no longer grumbled about what a terrible night's sleep he'd had, and his navigation abilities had come a long way since the Blossom Sea. Several times, I'd let him read the map and tell me which direction we needed to walk in, and he was becoming more and more adept as time went on.

We'd fallen into a surprisingly natural routine, covering as much ground as we could in the morning while he told me more about his Blessing and the entertaining mishaps it had landed him in. After a long rest for lunch and target practice, we carried on, finishing our travel for the day when we found a good spot to camp.

With a loud cheer signalling his victory, he emerged triumphant with a handful of purple berries. His hands were stained with sticky juice where he'd accidentally squashed some of them, but it didn't appear to bother him. Small cuts littered his forearm, the cost of battling the brambles for the edible fruit.

"Ready to judge my efforts?" Silas asked, depositing the berries into my palm.

"Let's hope they're worth the wait." I ate a few, savouring their tart flavour. "Not bad."

He didn't respond, staring at my lips. I frowned at him, unnerved by the attention.

"You have a little something..." He trailed off. "Here, let me."

Silas' thumb brushed the corner of my mouth, surprisingly delicate as he wiped away the juice that remained there, his gaze fixed on me. I froze. The touch was functional, but the sensations it stirred were anything but. My breath hitched at the contact, the warm stroke of his thumb making me feel fuzzy, like I was drinking moon wine. When he pulled back, the skin he'd touched tingled.

"All done," he said, oblivious to my thoughts. I intended to keep it that way. It was just my body's reaction to an unfamiliar touch, nothing more than that.

I brought my hand to my face, to where he'd touched it, dazed.

"Well?" he said, watching me expectantly. I realised he'd been talking to me.

"What?"

"I asked if you wanted more," he repeated.

"No, I'm finished." I wiped my mouth with the back of my hand, ensuring the juice was gone. He cleaned his hands with a rag until only a tinge of purple remained.

The High Road loomed ahead of us, a paved path cutting across the grasslands, wide enough for two carriages to pass by each other with room to spare. Dread settled in my stomach at the sight. Facing it was inevitable. I'd always known that. But it didn't make the thought of it any easier.

Unaware of my discomfort, Silas pointed ahead with a smile. "Look it's the High Road. We've met up with it again."

I forced my legs forward, each step as difficult as walking through mud. The sooner I faced my fears, the sooner the road would be behind us.

"Where are you going? I thought we were avoiding it?" he said.

"We must cross it to get to Threstia. It's the only way."

"If the road was here all this time, why didn't we use it in the first place?" He waved his arms dramatically. "We could've saved ourselves days."

"Spoken like someone who has never travelled along it. It's only worth it with a carriage. Walking is unsafe. Thieves would be the least of our concerns," I said darkly.

"You're acting strange. What's wrong?" Silas, too perceptive for his own good, sidled up to me, separating me from the road ahead. "You can tell me."

"What do you mean?"

"Don't act coy. You're frowning so hard it's going to leave a permanent wrinkle on your forehead. Friends are meant to confide in each other, you know."

"Friends also know when to mind their own business."

He drew himself up to his full height. "Whatever it is, you have nothing to worry about with me by your side."

I laughed bitterly. "Have you not learnt your lesson by now about storming into situations unprepared? Magic can't solve everything."

"It certainly helps though," Silas said, undeterred.

I let out an exasperated sigh. "You have no idea what you're dealing with. Do you think you're the only noble cavorting around the realm?"

"I wouldn't exactly call sleeping outside and eating scraps cavorting." His eyes narrowed as my words sunk in. "Why, who else is here?"

"You can't be surprised. Do you know what happens when arrogant nobles are given too much power and little responsibility? They become restless. In their boredom, they seek increasingly extreme forms of entertainment. The rest of us suffer the consequences." It was always the same.

Silas looked shaken. "Like what?"

"This isn't the time." I didn't want to think about it, not with the High Road so close.

"Fine, I'll drop it." His voice softened. "But rest assured that I'll protect you from whatever harm comes our way. The seeking stone is proof of that."

"I don't doubt it." I said, my fingers finding the amulet and clasping its cool surface. "But don't let your guard down."

"I know, I know, and situations can quickly take a turn for the worst. I do listen to your lectures. Well, sometimes."

The long grass became thicker and more difficult to traverse as we climbed the slope at the edge of the road. So many things had changed in the years since I was here last, but it looked the same as ever, like it was frozen in time. A shrine to one of the worst moments of my life.

I listened out for signs of a carriage approaching. Crossing at the wrong time was deadly, a collision dangerous to everyone involved. For a moment, there was nothing but the grass swaying in the breeze. Then the wind shifted direction, bringing with it the sound of voices. Voices I'd hoped never to hear again.

No. This couldn't be happening.

I couldn't move, my limbs locking together in terror, every breath a struggle. Darkness danced at the edge of my vision, and I feared I would pass out.

"Willow." Silas noticed the change in me, at my side in an instant. "Are you feeling ill?"

"Yes. Get me out of here," I croaked out. It took all my strength to back away, kept on my feet solely by his firm grip on my shoulders.

"Aren't we crossing here?"

"We'll do it further down." I didn't care where.

But it was too late. At the approaching footsteps, my hand found Silas', clenching it so tightly it must have hurt him. He made no complaint, but his other hand was outstretched, ready for the threat.

Three finely dressed fae approached, one female, the others male, clad in burgundy cloaks with gold embellishments. The woman's blonde hair fell to her waist, twisted in perfect curls, her eyes so dark they looked black. The men couldn't look more different from each other. One was tall, with bronze skin and black hair slicked back in a neat bun, the other short in stature, his messy brown hair covering his hazel eyes. Three faces I could never forget, their names branded in my mind forever.

"Hightower nobles," Silas whispered under his breath. He was correct, the trio originally from Hightower, but frequent travellers to the mainland.

"I didn't realise we had company. We're not used to it this far along the High Road, but we always relish the opportunity to meet new friends," the woman, Lilith, said. Hearing her voice was like tasting ash in my throat.

"If I'm not mistaken, we know this one. Ithan, it's your little archer, back for more," Ares, the shorter of the men said, his features lighting up in delight. Silas tensed beside me.

The world was closing in on itself, and all I could do was force myself to keep breathing.

"There's no fucking way." Ithan laughed, nudging Ares. "I thought she was long dead."

"She was a stubborn one, if you recall. It's unsurprising that she survived."

"And this time she brought a friend," said Lilith, her eyes raking over Silas in interest. He said nothing, squeezing my hand reassuringly.

I waited for them to question him, to ridicule him for lowering himself by travelling with an Unblessed. But with his plain clothing, they hadn't realised his status. They saw exactly what they expected to see, and Silas made no move to correct them.

"We're just crossing. Let us pass and we can all carry on with our day," he said brightly.

"And why would we want to do that pretty boy, when the fun is just beginning?" Lilith replied. My stomach churned, and I prayed to the gods I wouldn't humiliate myself in front of them.

Silas made a point of taking in the roadside, their carriages parked neatly in a row and the makeshift camp beside them. "Looks rather lacklustre to me."

His subtle confidence in the face of being outnumbered cut through my fear. That's right, I wasn't alone.

Lilith scowled, a gale whipping up and buffeted us as she harnessed her Air Blessing. She was quick to lose her temper. Nothing had changed in that regard. I planted my feet into the ground as best as I could as the wind howled in my ears. It was just a taste of what she was capable of. Her favourite game was to test how long someone could stay conscious once she stole their breath. If her victim didn't wake up, they were merely a broken toy, soon forgotten.

"Shut up and stand in the middle of the road. Or I can drag you there myself, if you'd prefer?" To prove her point, a gust lifted us off our feet momentarily.

I gave Silas a look, urging him to go along with it. He winked in return. With every passing moment, his presence stoked my courage. I wasn't alone.

"Doesn't this feel familiar? How many years has it been now?" Ares said.

"Nearly a century," Ithan answered.

"And yet it feels like yesterday." Ares' hazel eyes narrowed at me. "Do you remember your lesson, or do we need to give you a reminder? Ithan, why don't you do the honours?"

Ithan's steps echoed on the stone as he approached us. If Lilith was carelessly cruel and Ares a slave to his bloodlust, then Ithan was the most terrifying of all. Because he had played the part too well when he'd won my heart. After years of suffering on my own, I'd thought he was my salvation. How wrong I'd been.

"Get down on your knees and beg for your lives," Ithan ordered, summoning a vine from his fingertips, thorns protruding from the stem. My body shook viscerally at the memory of it whipping me the last time I'd ignored the instruction.

Silas went rigid next to me. If I didn't intervene soon, the entire road would become engulfed in flame.

Over the years, I'd thought about this moment. What I would do if I ran into them again. The bullies who had left me for dead, discarding me when they had no use for me anymore. If it wasn't for Reuben, I might have been another casualty. In my nightmares, I would awaken, still trapped within their torment.

But I wasn't the same naive girl who they'd deceived before. I'd reined in my sentimental heart. I was stronger. I was a survivor. And I would never let them hurt anyone else again.

After all, I wasn't alone.

A slow, wicked smile spread across my face. It was dangerous, lethal. Unhinged. Silas gave me a subtle nod. This was my moment, and he would only step in if I needed him.

"I always hoped this day would come. The day you get what you deserve."

"How dare you talk back to us?" Ithan snarled. The vine lashed towards me, and I released a shaky breath. Silas burned it to cinders with a casual flick of his wrist, the magic posing no challenge for his power.

"Don't interrupt when she's talking to you. It's rude," Silas bit out, fury burning in his eyes.

Ares' mouth hung open, the smug expression wiped from his face.

"He's Fire-Blessed," Lilith said. "Do something."

"I'll deal with it," Ares said, sending a torrent of water directly at Silas. My heart caught in my throat. But Silas merely waved a hand, his flames colliding with the water and burning it away into steam. Ares winced as his hands were scalded, forcing him to drop them.

It wasn't possible. Each Blessing had its weakness. A Fire-Blessed fae could never hope to win against a Water Blessing. Yet Silas had done it, dealing with the torrent like it was a minor inconvenience.

"He's a bloodline heir. He must be, to counter you like that," Lilith said to Ares, her face white. Her shock was mirrored by my own expression. The bloodline heirs were among the most powerful families in Idrix, with lineage that could be tracked back to the first fae. Only the five rulers and the Circle of the Enlightened were stronger. I glanced at Silas for confirmation, but he was occupied with staring down the noble trio, making no effort to hide his disdain.

"Who the fuck are you?" Ithan asked, caught off-guard.

"I'd claim to be your worst nightmare, but I think she has that covered."

On the face of it, I would disagree. It was his vast power that had rendered them speechless. It would be easy to ask Silas to take them out. But death was quick, and I wanted them to suffer for what they'd done to me.

I'd had many years to plan my revenge, should the opportunity rise. And Silas had set the stage for me.

Vanity was the nobility's ultimate weakness. Their reputation meant everything to them, and I'd done my research. It was fortunate that Reuben had sent me away to Hightower for a year, more than a coincidence, I suspected, and while my mission had been my focus, there had been plenty of time for personal research.

When the usual rules don't apply to you, it makes for interesting reading.

"I've changed a lot since the last time we met. I've travelled the realm, and it's incredible what you can find out from talking to the right fae." I took a deep breath. This was it. "I wonder, Lilith, would your friends treat you so well if they knew you were illegitimate?"

Lilith turned an impressive purple colour. "How did you..."

"Your mother may have taken care of your birth record, but she didn't realise that Hightower's scholars take meticulous copies in case of disaster. They were all too willing to lend me theirs. Your father advocated for their funding to be cut and, well, they hold grudges," I said, unable to keep the satisfaction from my voice. Silas gazed at me with such awe it made my heartbeat falter.

"We'll fix it," Ares said. "Once we make sure she dies for real this time."

I addressed him next. "Did you think I'd stop there? It must have been so difficult for you when your family lost its fortune. Gambling is a disease that's terribly cruel to those it claims. How did your friends react to your ruin?"

Ares snarled, raising his hands as if to attack. Silas moved in front of me, shielding me with his body. "Lay a finger on her and it will be the last thing you do."

"And what secrets of mine have you uncovered, little archer?" Ithan asked, smiling with amusement. This was still just a game to him, but the stakes were higher than ever. I met his gaze, the one who had offered me a helping hand after I was picked apart for anything of value. The one I'd let my guard down around. The one who had whispered sweet promises of a future together before he betrayed me.

"You are very good at cleaning up after yourself, I'll admit," I said. It had taken me the better part of six months to find any dirt on him. "But your brother isn't. I hear treason is punishable by death." The smile fell from Ithan's face. I had him.

Silas was shaking with the effort of holding back his laughter.

"I'll offer you the same terms you gave me. Beg for your lives and I'll spare you from ruin. And what else was it?" I pressed a finger to my mouth in contemplation. "Ah yes, sell it to me. Make me believe it."

"You can't be serious," Lilith said, outraged.

"Oh, I'm deadly serious," I said, a thrill going through me. It was intoxicating to hold such influence over those who had wronged me.

"I'd rather die than beg," Ares muttered.

"That can be arranged," Silas said, fire blazing in his hands.

"Just shut up and do as she says," Ithan said. "If these rumours spread, we're finished. We'll be banished from Hightower."

Lilith was the first to break. "Please," she said, her eyes shining with tears.

"You're not on your knees," Silas said. "Weren't those the terms?"

Her jaw clenched, but she listened, climbing to the ground awkwardly. The others followed, motivated by a lick of heat Silas sent in their direction.

"You don't have to do this," Ithan said, his voice soft, vulnerable. I knew better than to fall for his act again.

"Why did you do it?" I asked. "What possible reason did you have to hurt me?"

"We were bored. And you were nothing. Nobody. Expendable. It's not our fault you took it so seriously," Ares said.

"You're not even worth the ground she walks on. Having a Blessing is meaningless if this is how you choose to squander it. I hope the gods are watching and decide to revoke yours, because you are an embarrassment to every Blessed fae. Grow up."

"We will," Lilith said. "Please, give us a chance."

I stepped forward, towering over them where they knelt on the hard stone. "I won't write to Hightower with my findings since you begged so nicely for me. But if you come after us, now or in the future, I'll release everything I have on you, and my friend will make sure you know why you should never threaten a bloodline heir. Do you understand?"

They nodded.

I looked up at the sun, still at the highest point in the sky. "Make a bargain with me. You won't move from this position until darkness falls this evening. I'll make an exception if your life is threatened by a carriage or otherwise, because unlike you, I have a soul. Only when day has turned to night may you continue on with your journey."

"Absolutely not," Ares scoffed.

"Swear it, or the deal is off the table."

Ithan looked at his friends and sighed. "We swear it." They held out their hands to mine and the magical thread of a bargain wound around them, binding us together.

I masked my relief with a savage smile. We'd be able to put a great distance between us and them before they moved, and with the leverage we had, it was unlikely they'd try anything ever again. I'd done it. *We'd* done it.

I crossed to the other side of the road, towards Threstia, not sparing a glance at the nobles I left in my wake.

Silas' steps bounced as he caught up with me. "Vengeance suits you," he murmured in my ear. "You should wear it more often."

Chapter 13

As soon as the High Road was out of sight, several hours after we'd left it behind, I fell to the ground. My breath came out in wheezes, each one feeling like being punched in the gut. I may have faced the ghosts of my past and emerged victorious, but it had taken a toll.

The anguish I'd buried during our confrontation rose to the surface in an overwhelming surge. A wave of dizziness hit, and I struggled to get enough air into my lungs. I'd been foolish to believe that facing my tormentors wouldn't leave its mark, but at least I'd waited until they were gone before falling apart.

"Look at me," Silas' voice called to me through the panic. My eyes, unfocused, found his with difficulty, their striking green colour a comfort to my frayed nerves. "I'm here and you're safe. You just need to breathe."

If only it was that simple. Each breath I attempted was agony, like hands were wrapped around my throat.

Silas persevered, an unquestionable authority to his tone that I hadn't heard from him before. "Listen to my voice. Breathe in, now out. In and out. You can do better than that. I know you can."

It was no use. I desperately gulped in as much air as I could with each shallow breath, but it wasn't enough. I was lost to the terrifying sensation, the world spinning.

Silas loomed over me, brushing his hair back, and I realised that he'd joined me on the ground. His scent flooded my nose, and for a moment, I felt like I was back in the forest, the comforting blend of pine and vanilla soothing me. "Try this instead." He held his fist in front of my face, opening and closing it in time with his instructions. "See if you can match the motion."

I can't, I wanted to scream at him. Couldn't he see that this was out of my control? And at first, it was. But Silas, stubborn as he was, refused to give up. If my breakdown fazed him in any way he didn't show it, his body language relaxed as if this was an everyday occurrence. His words became my mantra. *In. Out. In. Out.*

Eventually, the heavy feeling in my chest began to lift, each breath becoming easier. My breathing returned to its usual rhythm, and the panic released its grip on me.

"Where did you learn that?" I asked once I could speak again, my throat rough and scratchy.

Silas was sprawled out, absentmindedly brushing off the dirt that clung to his clothes. He considered me quietly. "My mind can be an overwhelming place sometimes. I've picked up a few techniques over the years."

"Thank you," I said, swallowing hard. I don't know what I would've done without him.

He shook his head, his hair falling into his face again. "There's nothing to thank me for. You were incredibly brave back there. Your body just needed time to process everything." He dusted himself off as he stood, helping me to my feet. "Maybe we should stay for a while and let you recover."

"No. I need to get away from here." The panic may have passed, but I wouldn't feel like myself again until we were a great distance from the High Road.

He nodded, following the brisk pace I set even as I pushed us harder than usual. It felt good to move, to have the purpose of my mission to distract me from my tumultuous emotions, and it became my driving force. Everything would work out as long as I kept moving.

The ground beneath our feet transformed, the grass becoming patchy until all that remained was black, rocky soil. For a while, neither of us spoke, the quiet punctuated by the crunching of our boots on the stones.

"I understand now why it took you so long to trust me," Silas said, eventually breaking the silence. The sun bowed behind imposing mountains that seemed like they were built from shadow, casting a red glow over the horizon. It bathed him in a pink hue as we sat down on two of the large rocks that protruded from the ground. It was the time of day when we usually set up camp, but we made no move to do so. "I hadn't realised how the nobility treated others. It's a disgrace."

"I feared you would side with them. You're one of them, after all." But he hadn't. He'd had my back the entire time, resolute in his support when I'd needed him the most.

"I never want to be associated with scum like them," Silas spat out.

"They called you a bloodline heir. Is it true?" My voice quietened to a whisper. I'd known he was noble, that was true, but a bloodline heir? He was part of the elite, possessing power that most fae could only dream of. It hung in the air between us, threatening to taint the relationship we'd so painstakingly built.

He sighed. "I suppose there's no point holding back now. I'm from one of the most influential families in Idrix."

My eyes fluttered shut. I had my own secrets from Silas. I could hardly begrudge him his. But it had been difficult enough to trust him as a noble. This revelation made everything more complicated.

"Willow." I opened my eyes, meeting his gaze. His brow was furrowed in concern, his jaw clenched tightly. "You know me well enough by now. Do you truly think I'm like them? Cold, conniving, only looking out for my own self-interest?"

"I don't know what to think anymore," I said. The flash of hurt that crossed his face made my chest tighten, but it was the truth. Seeing Ithan again had been a stark reminder of the cost of letting my guard down. I didn't know whether my intuition could be trusted.

His fingers drummed against the rock. "I should've been honest with you from the start. I thought that if you knew my background, there would always be a rift between us, and you would never fully trust me. If this has been your experience with the nobility, I couldn't blame you for it."

"And once you knew me better?" I said. "Why not come clean?"

"I didn't want to lose my only friend." His voice cracked.

I wavered. If I wasn't limited by my bargain to the Night Ravens, would I have risked the same? I knew myself how difficult it was to make a true friend in Idrix. "You've never given me a reason to doubt you. Even when I looked for one."

The dimples in his cheek appeared as a small smile graced his face. "I would never betray you. Please know that."

I wished I could believe him as much as he believed himself. "I can't handle another betrayal. I don't know if I will ever fully trust you."

"Then trust me for today," Silas said.

"What do you mean?" I asked in confusion, twisting on the rock to face him directly.

"Ever feels a little daunting, don't you think? All I ask is that you trust me, just for today. I promise I won't betray that trust." He took my hand in his, threading our fingers together into a steady hold. The warmth of his skin invaded mine, promising protection.

"And tomorrow?"

"Tomorrow I will ask the same. And the following day. I will ask the same question every day, and my promise to you won't change. But I will ask, for as long as you need me to."

In that moment, I realised several things. The first was that I'd never met anyone like Silas and was unlikely to ever again. I realised that I may have found the one who was most worthy of my trust, someone who would treasure it and never take it for granted.

And most staggering of all, as heat rose in my cheeks at the feel of his hand in mine, I realised that what I was beginning to feel for him had surpassed the bond of friendship.

My feelings had crept up on me. I'd believed my heart was too shattered for love to ever be a possibility. But Silas, with his enduring optimism and fierce loyalty, had stitched the broken pieces back together, helping me see the good in the world again.

"Very well. Today, it is," I said, not wanting to acknowledge those feelings. This close to Threstia, they were an inconvenient distraction. And besides, he had given no indication that he was feeling the same. What would a bloodline heir see in someone like me? I gazed down at where our hands met. "There's something I still don't understand. All this time, you've had power and influence at your fingertips. Why did you need me?"

He chewed on his lip thoughtfully. "Heading out on this adventure was an impulsive decision. I had no plan. I'd never left Eirel until now and I didn't know what I'd face. And you were so… competent in the forest. I thought if I stuck with you, I'd stand half a chance of surviving."

"It wasn't your wisest move. With me, you've fended off thieves, fell into a trap, and faced three nobles." And all on the same mission. It was a run of bad luck I prayed never to repeat.

"What's life without a little adventure?" Silas smirked, and I felt my blush deepen. I hoped the pink light of the fading sun was enough to mask it.

"Speaking of, how about we continue ours for longer today? I won't sleep easily until I know we've put some distance between us and those nobles," I said.

"Of course."

We set off quickly, keen to cover as much ground as possible. As darkness fell, Silas sent a flaming sphere ahead of us, lighting our way as we closed in on the outskirts of Threstia. I was no longer worried about what we'd face there, not with Silas by my side. For everything he'd done for me, I'd given him so little in return. It felt out of balance, and I wanted to change that.

"I should explain what happened back there. Who they were to me," I said, my steps slowing.

"You don't have to talk about it if it makes you uncomfortable."

"I want to. That is, if you're willing to listen. Perhaps then I can finally leave everything in the past where it belongs."

"In that case, go ahead," Silas said, shadows dancing over his face where it was lit by his magic.

I took a deep breath, watching the glow from the sphere flicker as it illuminated my way forward. Our surroundings were difficult to make out in the darkness, a flat expanse of rock all that was visible. It felt like we were the only two fae left in the world.

With Silas' gentle attention on me, I began. "When the curse destroyed my island, and I lost everything, I was vulnerable. Alone. I wasn't prepared for what I'd find here on the mainland. I thought if I asked for help, I would easily receive it."

"And you found the opposite."

I nodded. "For fifteen years, I wandered Idrix seeking aid. When I was lucky, the fae I encountered ignored me, focusing on their own survival. Others tricked me out of my remaining possessions or trapped me in predatory bargains." Losing my faith, when that had been one of the few things keeping me going, had felt like hope itself had died. I was nothing but an empty shell.

"You tried to warn me when we met." Silas' hand flexed by his side.

"I didn't want anyone else to suffer the same fate." Even someone I didn't trust. "Ithan was the first to show me kindness. When I met him, I didn't have a copper to my name. He was alone by a campfire when I skulked past, and he stopped me and offered to share his meal."

"That sounds remarkably similar to how we met."

"Exactly. I thought history was repeating itself. We travelled together for months, but it wasn't like this, like me and you. Equals. I was blind to it at the time, but there was a condescending undertone to our interactions. I was more of a pet than a companion. He never respected me, but I overlooked it because I was safe, and protected, and things were looking up."

"And you fell for him." It was a statement, not a question.

"Against my better judgement. I never truly loved him for who he was. I fell for the dream he sold me, one where I didn't have to worry about where my next meal would come from or fight for my life. It was a fairytale, and he was the prince saving me from the evil of the world. A pretty story, but nothing more." And I'd believed it all.

"What happened?"

"We met up with his delightful companions on the High Road and the truth came out. You see, it was all a big game. A bet between friends. Whoever made an Unblessed fall in love with them first was the victor. My humiliation for the grand prize of two gold coins."

"Those bastards." His eyes darkened, reminding me of the Silas that had rescued me from the thieves, none of his usual softness remaining.

"There's one positive. I didn't give them the dramatic reaction they craved. There were no tearful outbursts, no accusations. I'd suffered so much by that point, was so broken, that I felt nothing at all. I could only stare at them in silence, unable to process Ithan's betrayal. But that wouldn't do at all, not when he'd invested weeks of his precious time to win my heart."

I hesitated over whether to continue. Silas was shaking with barely suppressed rage beside me. But I had come this far, and I wanted him to understand my initial hostility towards him. Why I'd had no choice.

"They decided to do whatever it took to break me. When I wouldn't beg for their mercy, they used their Blessings to force me to my knees. When I wouldn't admit that I was unworthy of their presence, they filled my mouth with water until I nearly drowned. When I still didn't yield, they decided to beat me the Unblessed way so I'd understand. My eyes were so swollen they couldn't open and I was incapable of standing afterwards. If it weren't for an approaching carriage, they wouldn't have stopped until I was dead. At the time, I wished I was. But instead, I made a promise to myself to fight. So that one day I could be strong enough to face them and stop them from hurting anyone else."

Silas stiffened, the sphere's shape distorting as he struggled to retain control of his emotions. His voice was dangerously low as he spoke, sending a shiver down my spine. "I need you to keep talking to me, because if you give me even the briefest window of opportunity, I'm going to go back there and kill them all. First, I'll make them experience everything you went through. Perhaps more, depending on how unforgiving I feel."

I extended an arm, stopping him from moving forward. "I appreciate the offer, truly, but I have a better idea. They were lax in their negotiation. I promised not to reveal their secrets so long as they cooperated, but I never said anything about you."

A wide grin spread across Silas' face. "How may I be of assistance?"

I released him. "I have useful contacts in Hightower, but none within the nobility. Can I leverage that bloodline heir influence of yours to get the information into the right hands?"

"It may be a challenge. Tensions between Eirel and Hightower are strained. But that doesn't mean they wouldn't pay attention to a bloodline heir's concerns. When we return to civilisation, I will send some scandalous letters. Without means or titles, they'll be in for a rude awakening when they're cast out. That's the least they deserve," he said.

"What will happen to them?"

"They only have two options realistically. They can join the sacred guard of the White Temple, sworn to protect the Circle of the Enlightened in the Amber City. But that demands lifelong dedication. Members forsake all personal relationships and aspirations, letting all ties to their past life burn in the pure flames of the temple's hearth. Alternatively, they could roam Idrix penniless and unwelcome in any ruling seat. They'd have no choice but to stay in the countryside, fighting for survival."

Panic coursed through me. "If they decide to fight, won't they come after us?"

"They won't take that path," Silas said confidently.

"How do you know?"

"There's honour in serving the White Temple, influence and power too, though that's all in service to the gods. Navigating a complex hierarchy is what they've known their whole lives. They'll have to give up their autonomy, but that's an easier sacrifice for them than living a life of obscurity, with no guidance to follow."

"Would you make the same choice?" I asked, curious.

"No. Power never had its claws in me in that way. I'm sure I could carve out a satisfactory existence without Idrix's cities. I mean, look at me." He gestured to his travelling clothes and my gaze followed the movement, drifting down the firm lines of his body before I realised I was doing it. "I haven't shied away from getting my hands dirty."

"You've adapted well, all things considered." It was almost easy to forget his position until the strength of his Blessing removed any doubt.

"I'm enjoying myself. I always wanted to see the realm and check if the reality matched what I was taught, and the company is a vast improvement from what I'm used to," Silas said.

"I'll take that as a compliment," I said nonchalantly, like the words didn't affect me.

"You should, although you have little in the way of competition. There's a reason you're my first friend."

"Is it really that bad, even as a bloodline heir?" Surely fae begged for his favour in his enviable position?

"On the Isle of Mist, the fae can be just as cruel as your tormentors. It's just... not so blatant. It's all backstabbing and double-crossing, and honourable, at least on the surface. What happened to you sickens me."

"Then change it." There was no reason for the cruelty that infected Idrix, except for a thirst for power and dominance left unchecked. Silas, by his own admission, didn't play those games. He had a duty to do something about it.

"It's not that simple," he said with a frown.

"It sounds simple enough to me." I stopped dead, facing him, the pleasant buzz that lingered from his compliment vanishing.

"You sound just like Valeria." I looked at him blankly. "My cousin," he clarified.

"She must be wise."

Silas quirked an eyebrow at me. "She is. Tough too. You'd like her a lot. And she'd love you."

"I don't understand. You have the power to make a better world, one that protects the weak and innocent. How is it more complicated than that?" I gave him a pleading expression. His next words could change everything between us.

"Do you really want to know? Because I can go into excruciating detail?" Silas asked.

"Yes. I want to understand your way of life. It's all a mystery to me." I'd rather be bored than uninformed, and the sneaky treachery of the nobility was hidden to outsiders. It could be valuable information for the Night Ravens.

Silas gazed out at the surrounding darkness with a resigned expression. "Fine. I'll tell you everything once we've rustled up something to eat."

"Do you promise?" I asked, stopping at a spot with fewer stones. It was well-sheltered by a wall of black rock, only leaving one side open to the elements.

"I do," Silas said. He deposited his pack on the ground, unrolling his bedroll. "And like every promise I make to you, I'll stop at nothing to keep it."

Chapter 14

Silas let out a string of curses that would've made Sal blush, as unflappable as she was, as he scoured the area for viable firewood. It was usually a straightforward procedure. He'd come a long way since his debacle with the damp wood, developing a knack for finding good kindling that would keep our fire lit through the night. Stones scattered as he kicked at the ground, crouching down to examine it.

"What's wrong?" I asked, pausing my task of setting up our bedrolls. Were they always positioned so close together, Silas sleeping within arm's reach? I adjusted them several times over, second-guessing myself. What if he questioned it on his return, dragging them further apart? I repositioned them a final time before deciding it would suffice.

"It's the wood here," he said in a frustrated tone. "The twigs are crumbling in my hands and the trees aren't much better. They're brittle and will make terrible firewood. I'm afraid if we want to keep a fire going, we'll need to take shifts to tend to it."

From the limited scenery that the flaming sphere exposed, I could see he was right. Vegetation was sparse, and what little there was looked stunted and wrong. I'd be surprised to find anything to hunt here. We'd been lucky to discover a lone raglaw soaring over the hills as we left the grasslands, Silas securing his first kill, and our dinner, but it wouldn't last us long.

"Can't we make do with your ball of fire instead?" Enough heat was emanating from it to take the bite out of the cold night air, even with him several paces away.

"While I'm awake, sure. But it requires concentration to maintain its form. As soon as I fall asleep, it will disappear, and we'll be left with no campfire."

That wasn't wise, not when we were both unfamiliar with our surroundings and what could be out there. The rocky landscape could be hiding all manner of threats, the unassuming quiet no guarantee that we were alone.

"Fine, I'll take first watch." It would be difficult to sleep after the events of the day. I may as well use that time productively. "Build what you can, but we'll save the wood until we settle down to sleep." I retrieved the raglaw from my burlap sack, plucking its feathers. "If I spear an arrow through it, can you cook it without burning my fingers?"

Footsteps echoing on the rocky ground signalled his return to our camp, the sphere floating in front of him. "You should know by now that the answer is usually yes when it comes to my Blessing."

His confidence wasn't unfounded, the magic searing the skewered bird without so much as brushing my hand. I handed Silas his portion, taking care not to burn myself in the process.

I tore into a raglaw leg, the salty meat coating my lips with grease as I ate, growing concerned about our future meals. Our packs were stuffed with berries from the grasslands, but I didn't hold out hope that Threstia would offer us anything else. It wouldn't be the first time I had to ignore the ache of hunger on a mission. There had been several occasions where I'd had to ask for second helpings of dinner on my return to the Old Keep. But I would need my mind to be as sharp as possible to uncover the researchers, and the distraction of an empty stomach wouldn't help in that regard.

I picked the bone clean, savouring every bite, noticing Silas doing the same.

"You still owe me an explanation of the inner workings of the Isle of Mist," I said between mouthfuls.

"I haven't finished my dinner yet. You're so demanding sometimes." I cocked my head at him, Silas staring me down before eventually relenting. "You're familiar with the lords and ladies of Idrix?"

"The five ruling seats." Drei and Hightower across the Sapphire Sea, Tirrim and Eirel to the north and Gladhaven to the south, with neutral territory in between.

"Exactly. But their power isn't absolute. Everything is a careful negotiation, requiring a delicate balancing act to govern the realm. There's their High Council who advises them on their decisions, the other members of the nobility, particularly the bloodline heirs, who they maintain alliances with, and then, of course, the common fae, those without title who reside within their lands. Each group must be satisfied if the ruler wants to keep their seat. The High Council is a valuable resource when they're on your side or can be your worst adversary, blocking your every decision if you lose their favour. The nobility's allegiance is key. Without it, a ruler can be challenged or usurped by a rival. And the common fae are often underestimated, but they have more power than it appears. When they lose faith in their leader, everything grinds to a halt. Before you know it, the pitchforks will be at your door."

"So, to change things, you must convince all three," I summarised.

"Indeed. That's where the complexity lies. Agreements are meticulously negotiated over decades, sometimes centuries. And the established nobility, especially the council, despise change. They like everything as it is, within their control. The advisors, so they can keep their lucrative positions and the influence it affords them, and the nobility so they can plan their moves and feed their selfish ambition."

"Is the Circle of the Enlightened involved too?" The mysterious vessels of the gods never left the White Temple.

"Their authority is unquestioned. The rulers will always defer to the gods if they make their judgement known. But it's never happened. The Enlightened don't interfere outside the Amber City, and in return, the rulers treat the capital with the reverence it commands, an independent district."

"And where do you fall within this?"

"I want reform as much as you do. I've long believed the system holds us back from our true potential. What I've witnessed on this journey has only confirmed that. But despite my position, I lack the support to drive through any meaningful change."

That caught me by surprise. "But you're...you know." I trailed off.

Silas trapped me with his gaze. "I'm what? Please elaborate."

He was going to make me say it. "You're charming and eloquent. I don't understand how you can lack support. Surely the lord listens to you?"

"Reputations are shaped over years. My brother was always the serious one. I had a penchant for mischief and fun and took it too far as a foolish youth. It's likely the nobility will never take me seriously." He blinked several times. "Sorry, this must be terribly boring."

"Not at all. It's refreshing to see this side of you. And for the record, anyone who doesn't support you needs their head checked. If more fae like you were in positions of power, maybe no one else would have to go through what I did."

He didn't respond, sitting quietly in deep thought.

"Silas?" I said.

A muscle ticked in his jaw. "I'm going to light the campfire and then retire for the evening. Wake me when you need me to take over."

"I..." His abrupt change of mood left me stunned. I studied him as he moved to his bedroll, draping his blanket around himself. He looked drained, like the day had caught up with him too. I supposed that was understandable. "Of course."

He fell asleep quickly, his back towards me. I watched him for a while, wondering if I'd pushed him too far. At some point, he rolled onto his side, his brow furrowed as he rested his head on one arm. Only when my eyes grew too heavy to ignore did I wake him, Silas unusually subdued at the interruption to his rest, conjuring a new flame in silence.

I managed to steal a few hours of sleep, helped by the comforting warmth radiating from the sphere. When I stirred, gently woken by the morning sun, he hadn't moved, watching the flames dance with that same frown on his face.

His sullen mood persisted while we packed up our camp. That wouldn't do. It didn't feel right to travel without his cheery optimism.

"I believe it's time," I said as formally as I could muster.

"Time for what exactly?" Silas asked. He feigned disinterest, adjusting his cloak around his shoulders, but his tone betrayed his curiosity.

"For you to officially become the navigator of our quest." I hoisted my pack onto my shoulders.

"Really?" He raised an eyebrow. "Why?"

"You've proven yourself more than capable, and it would free up my attention to monitor our surroundings." It wasn't my key motivation, but I was happy to let him think that. I handed him the map, his fingers gently closing around the fragile parchment.

"I don't know where I'm taking us," he said.

"That's easily resolved. Deeper into Threstia. We need to find a way to cross the Threstian Gap."

He studied the frayed parchment, tilting it in his arms to find a good angle. "Cross the gap? But nothing's marked on here."

"Exactly. Threstia is rarely visited. Any maps are likely to be inaccurate. But that doesn't mean you can't use logic to determine the most likely place for a bridge." Deduction was an essential skill for a scout. Information could be hidden away anywhere, requiring careful thought to uncover.

He rolled his eyes. "Wonderful, just when I'm in the mood for a lecture."

"Silas," I warned.

"Fine, I'll try." I tried not to laugh as he held the map right up to his eye, examining it intensely. "It's just rock. All of it."

"Go on," I prompted.

He went back and forth between the map and the view ahead of us, his face screwed up in concentration. "No one would come here unless they had a specific purpose, and convenience wouldn't be necessary without an established settlement. So it would make sense to build bridges where you could monitor them." He rolled up the parchment, tucking it into his pocket. "They'd be positioned to the north or south, sheltered by the mountains."

"Couldn't have put it better myself," I said. Silas caught my eye, smiling proudly, and I held his gaze longer than I'd intended.

I cleared my throat. "So, which way should we go from here?"

"South. I've had my fill of the north."

Whilst his reasoning had been flawless, it hadn't factored in our string of bad luck. Our progress was soon halted by a wall of stone blocking the path. Fragments of dark rock, some as large as a carriage, had broken away from the hillside, piling on the ground. The resulting obstruction was an unstable peak, impossible to pass.

"Damn it. Rockslide. We'll have to find another way." I kicked a stone in frustration, watching it skitter across the hard surface. We were so close.

Silas, to my frustration, decided it was time for his sunny demeanour to reemerge. "You know, when I experience a setback, I tell myself I need to dust myself off and try again. Let's take a deep breath and stay positive," he said, grinning from ear to ear. He picked up a small rock from the pile, tossing it in the air and catching it one-handed. "Why are you looking at me like that?"

I made no effort to hide my glare. "I'm debating what would shut you up the quickest, strangling you or lodging an arrow in your heart."

"I love it when you flirt with me." He winked.

"You and I have different definitions of flirting. If one of us is, it's you."

"You think I've been flirting with you?" Silas' face crinkled in genuine confusion. He hadn't been. My face burned. I wished the ground would swallow me like the pit in the dark forest to spare me from the humiliation.

I was under no illusion that it was harmless fun, born out of enjoyment, not intent, but with the surprise on Silas' face I'd been mistaken in that too. After years of distrusting strangers, I was out of practice, and evidently, out of my depth.

He stalked towards me and his voice dropped low. "If I was flirting with you, you'd know about it."

He moved closer, until there was only a hair's breadth between us, lowering his head towards mine.

I froze. Was he... was he going to kiss me?

I was no stranger to kissing, but since Ithan I'd avoided it, afraid to make myself vulnerable again. Sex was like scratching an itch, something that didn't require putting my heart on the line. There had been the odd encounter on my missions, stolen moments of pleasure in taverns and city lodgings, though none where I'd stayed until the morning.

But kissing was different, more intimate somehow. My gaze fell to Silas' soft, full lips, my chin tilted upwards in anticipation. What would it feel like to kiss him?

Would he tease me first, trailing sensual kisses along my neck, coaxing sighs from my lips before confidently capturing my mouth with his? Or would his enthusiasm be infectious, devouring me with an intensity that stole my breath? Or maybe it would be neither and his eyes would darken, his fingers knotting in my hair as his kiss claimed me, fierce and demanding.

Suddenly, I felt hot all over.

However, Silas didn't satisfy my curiosity. His breath brushed the soft skin of my ear, tickling me as he spoke. "If I was trying to seduce you, I'd say something like when I earn one of your rare smiles, it makes me feel like I can take on the world. Or how when you made those nobles kneel at your feet, resplendent in your vengeance, I was struck with the urge to do the same. Or perhaps that when I catch a glimpse of the real you, the one that's hiding beneath those thick walls of yours, I want to grab hold of that moment and make it last forever." His mouth curved into a slow, deliberate smirk, as if he knew the power his words held over me. "Something like that."

I forgot how to breathe. Silas wasn't playing fair. Those weren't shallow compliments, easily spouted without thought. No, he'd seen me, seen right into the core of my being, and hadn't flinched. He backed away, never taking his eyes off me.

"That would be adequate, I suppose," I said, when I was capable of speaking.

"Are you blushing?" Silas asked, holding back a smug laugh.

"What do you think?" I raised a hand to my cheek, mortified to find the skin warm.

"That my words affect you more than you let on." The full force of his charm ambushed me. His eyes twinkled in mischief, made more devastating by the dimples that played at the corner of his mouth, and his hair fell across his face in a way that made me itch to run my fingers through it.

I narrowed my eyes at him. I wasn't going to let him tie me in knots like a love-struck fool. Our growing trust didn't mean I'd lost all sense. "You have a high opinion of yourself."

"It's earned, I assure you." He strutted away, checking I was watching him.

"Where are you going?" I shouted after him.

"Finding a way around the rockslide. Come on, keep up."

Sensing I would regret making him our navigator, I trailed after him.

Chapter 15

"Over here," Silas called, gesturing to a small gap between the rockslide and the surrounding hills. "Let's crawl through."

I examined it, peering into the narrow space that would require us to be on our hands and knees. Squeezing through wouldn't be pleasant, with sharp rocks sticking out at odd angles. It would take us slightly off course, requiring us to climb the rocky hills and later descend to the Threstian Gap, bypassing the path blocked off by the rockslide.

With no viable alternatives, I led the way, my back scraping against the rock as I inched along. Shaking off the tiny stones I dislodged while manoeuvring through the gap, I took great care not to damage my bow in the process. I was grateful when the passage finally opened up, pushing myself out of it. It had deposited me partially up a hillside, peppered with jagged rocks.

Silas followed closely behind me, his body brushing against mine, leaving a trail of warmth in its wake.

"After you," he said, assessing the slope.

My legs scrambled for purchase as I ascended, offering my hand to Silas to help him reach me. After a few slips and plenty of curses, we reached the top. I dusted off my hands, dislodging the dirt that covered them.

The peak granted us generous views, the Threstian Gap visible below. I could see why Dorea had remembered it so vividly. The scale of it was astounding, the two sides of Threstia separated by a chasm as wide as it was deep, a thin blue line the only evidence of the river at its base. Crossing it would require nerves of steel and steady footing.

"I knew we were due some good luck for a change," Silas said. I nearly agreed before realising that he wasn't staring out at the horizon, but further along the hillside. I followed his gaze, noticing what had caught his attention.

A small waterfall from the mountains looming above us trickled into a wide pool, brimming with clear water. It was an oasis in the otherwise bland scenery of dark rock, its inviting beauty beckoning me in.

He leapt towards it in excitement, discarding his cloak along the way.

"What are you doing?" I prayed to the gods that it wasn't what I suspected.

"What does it look like?" He said, loosening his collar.

"Like you're about to dive into that pool when you have no idea what's inside it."

He pulled his shirt over his head, tossing it to one side. I took in his toned chest, unable to look away. "Loosen up," he said. "I haven't washed in days and the water is beautifully clear."

"I once heard about a fish that bites unsuspecting swimmers, devouring their flesh. I hope you're not too attached to certain body parts." I'd overheard it from a merchant in Hightower, fresh from his travels to distant lands, but they could be in Idrix too.

"Why? Do you spend a lot of time thinking about me naked? Can't you swim? I'm sure the water's not that deep."

"Of course I can swim. I grew up on an island," I shot back.

"If you're scared, you're welcome to sit this one out, but I'm not passing up an opportunity to freshen up."

Silas untied the fastenings of his trousers as if I wasn't standing next to him. I turned away abruptly, slamming my eyes shut, ignoring his delighted laugh. I heard a splash as he jumped in, droplets raining on my back, making me question why, of everyone, I had to fall for him.

My eyes snapped open at the sound of a scream. I rushed to his side to assess the threat, my bow in my hand. But when I reached the pool's edge, he dissolved into another fit of laughter. "I'm fine. The water's freezing though."

I opened my mouth to give him an earful but was hit with the sudden realisation that he hadn't been exaggerating. The water was completely clear. I could see everything, *everything*, in perfect clarity.

"What are you doing? Cover yourself!" I flung my arm over my eyes, but it was too late, the image of his naked body seared into my mind, refusing to relinquish its hold on me. It was for the best that the pool was free of carnivorous fish, because depriving the world of *that* would be a terrible shame.

No wonder he was always so cocky.

"You're the one looking where you shouldn't," Silas said, utterly unfazed. "It's perfectly safe. Are you sure you don't want to get in? I'll give you room." He headed deeper, his arms raised in surrender.

I wavered. It would be refreshing, and a chance to wash outdoors was a rare luxury. Was it worth the awkwardness of bathing together? As long as he kept his distance, I was sure I could master my discomfort. "Fine. But turn around. If you peek, I'll abandon you here to fend for yourself, whatever the consequences of breaking our bargain."

"I won't look. You can trust me." He ducked his head under the waterfall with his back to me, leaving me to it.

I stripped off quickly, depositing my clothes in a neat pile next to where his were strewn chaotically on the ground. The rock was warm beneath my feet as my footsteps padded over to the pool. Was I really doing this? I only hesitated for a moment before stepping in, nearly releasing a scream myself at the icy water biting at my skin. Silas was true to his word, staying firmly on the other side, granting me as much privacy as he could.

I wasn't shy about my body. It was lean from years of rations and constant walking, my arms and legs toned where I relied on their strength. But that didn't mean I wanted to flaunt it in front of Silas, especially with my growing feelings towards him.

Being in the water together, knowing that he too was naked under the surface, was overwhelming. I shivered, the sensation nothing to do with the coldness of the pool. Needing a distraction, I focused on methodically cleaning myself, scrubbing my dirty skin with my hands.

I began to relax, my body adjusting to the temperature of the water, and enjoying the relief of washing off the grime and sweat

I'd accumulated since the inn. I felt renewed, ready to take on the challenge of Threstia.

I forgot Silas was there until he spoke. "Can you help me? I can't reach my back."

He wanted me to do what? I glared at him. "You must be joking. Do it yourself."

"I can't get it. Please." He swam closer, keeping his eyes firmly on mine, making no attempt to glance at my exposed body beneath the surface. His hair was slicked back against his head, dripping rivulets of water onto his broad shoulders. Beads of moisture ran down his chest, trailing down the firm lines of his stomach, and I tracked the droplets with my eyes until they disappeared past his navel. He turned, baring his back to me.

I didn't know if I could trust myself to touch him. It would be an exquisite kind of torture, the thought alone making my body tremble. But Silas had never balked when I needed his help. If this was how I could return the favour, how could I refuse?

"If I must."

I could do this. My hands skirted over his wet skin, warm as it always was, rubbing in a circular motion. His back was corded with lean muscle, more than I would've expected considering his position in the nobility. Yet another surprise to him. The more layers I peeled back, the more I found to like, each discovery solidifying my fascination with him. I couldn't resist exploring further, tracing my fingers along his upper back, enraptured by the way he flexed in response. I splayed my hands across his shoulders, letting them glide down his body slowly.

Silas groaned, and I stiffened.

"Sorry," he said sheepishly. "It feels good. I've never carried a pack before, and my back has ached for weeks."

Before I could question it, I dug my thumbs in, massaging the knots that had formed in his shoulders. He melted, pushing back against me as I relieved the tightness. He'd probably never carried anything heavy in his life. As a bloodline heir, he would've had fae at his beck and call, never lifting a finger himself. Well, until I'd put him through his paces.

"If you ever breathe a word of this to anyone, I will kill you in your sleep."

"You're feeling very murderous today," he said, his voice breathy.

My hands shook slightly as I continued my ministrations. "You're in decent shape, for a noble," I said.

"Thank you for noticing. Better late than never."

I flicked water at him, catching him by surprise. "They work you hard on the Isle of Mist?"

"Something like that. The nobility are expected to represent the very best of the fae, both in appearance and power, proving ourselves worthy of our proximity to the gods. Every year, we're pitted against each other in a tournament, our performance defining our place in the social hierarchy, regardless of our official position. I make a point of training tirelessly for it with every spare moment I have. Anything to ensure I don't besmirch my family's reputation more than I already have."

He seemed to grow smaller before me, like he had before when recounting his past. I distracted him by raking my nails down his spine. Silas shuddered in response, letting out a strangled noise. I kneaded him with deeper pressure in a bid to release the muscle tension built up over weeks of travel.

He made noises of appreciation as I touched him, sweet moans that made my wicked mind conjure up all kinds of erotic images. I found myself wishing he wasn't so expressive, as a bolt of desire shot through me, not helped by my nipple accidentally brushing against his skin.

I bit down a moan of my own. I didn't recognise myself. If it weren't for the freezing water tempering my need, I feared I would lose control, rubbing against him without restraint, seeking any form of stimulation.

It was a sobering thought. I jumped away from him.

"That was incredible. Thank you," Silas said, wearing a satisfied grin.

My desire coiled tighter around me, threatening to trap me in its grip and make me do something ill-advised. I released a breath, needing to get a hold of myself. "We've wasted enough time. I'm going to dry off, you should too."

Panic flitted across his face before he could hide it. "Actually…I need a moment."

I nearly questioned why before realisation washed over me. *Oh.* I hadn't been the only one affected by our impromptu bath.

"Find me when you're finished," I said, giving him a knowing look. He sank into the water, and I chuckled, climbing out of the pool, not bothering to cover myself. I had nothing to be ashamed of, after all. My skin prickled with the awareness of being watched.

I dried myself as best as I could with my blanket before dressing, tying the material to my pack to let it dry. I had no intention of letting my mind wander to what Silas was doing in the pool, so instead I busied myself looking for the easiest place for us to climb down the hill. He met me a little while later, his hair still wet and clinging to his forehead, the neckline of his shirt damp.

We gazed out at Threstia as the sun set, seeing it from an angle I doubted many had. Great-winged beasts had once roamed its skies, back when it was saturated with magic. Now it was desolate, a barren wasteland devoid of any signs of life within its rocky domain.

Silas was mesmerised by the unique landscape. "I can't believe a place like this exists," he said. "What happened here?"

I wasn't surprised he didn't know. It had been forgotten by most, frozen in time and left to waste away.

"I've only heard stories." Stories born from evidence the Night Ravens had unearthed, but stories all the same. "Threstia was always wilder than anywhere else in Idrix. Its inhabitants were wanderers, preferring to travel with the seasons rather than making a permanent home. The forest was its heart and soul, its magic granting life to the surrounding land. When war hit, it became a major battleground. The forest was destroyed in the crossfire, and without its protection, there was nothing to stop the curse from turning it barren."

We clambered down the hill, clumsy and inelegant, the chasm within walking distance once we were on steady ground.

"What a waste." Silas said, staring at the endless rock surrounding us as we walked. I hummed my agreement.

"It's only a matter of time before the rest of Idrix looks like this." The curse would destroy every last kernel of magic, the source of life in Idrix itself, and eventually this would be all that was left. Not unless it was broken.

I wouldn't rest until we'd figured out the key to breaking it.

"Are there other places so badly affected?" Silas asked. "My education focused on the history and military tactics of the war, less so on the damage caused by the enemy's curse."

"A few. Some are dangerous to go near, like Adrak." The frosty island was forbidden to visit, not that anyone wanted to travel there. "There are pockets of decay all over the mainland, just like the dark forest we passed through. Perhaps even further afield." I tilted my head towards him. "Aren't you worried? You may possess a Blessing but that doesn't make you immune to the curse's effects. The nobility will lose their magic one day too."

"It's monitored very closely. At the current rate of deterioration, the bloodlines won't be significantly affected for several generations."

"And that's acceptable?"

"The brightest minds Eirel has to offer are sent to the academy in the Amber City, the same with the other districts. Their studies are devoted to finding new ways of breaking the curse, or at least slowing its destruction. Our future rests in their capable hands. Do you think it can be broken?" Silas asked, picking up a fallen branch and watching it crumble to dust in his hand.

"I don't know." It was our only hope. None of us stood a chance the moment it claimed the last of Idrix's essence. Perhaps we'd still be alive to witness it. It was a startling thought. I shivered, wrapping my cloak around me.

"I never realised how bad it had become," he admitted.

"What did they teach you?"

"That before the curse, magic was abundant. All fae received Blessings from the gods, and it wasn't limited to the elements. Magic was strong and flexible, and it flowed through Idrix as plentiful as the air we breathe. That's how artefacts were created." He reached under his shirt, clutching his amulet. "It's weird to think that the seeking stones were crafted by a Blessing. Can you imagine what it was like back then?"

"It sounds like we could've done anything." Though based on what I'd seen Blessed fae do, I couldn't imagine it was all good news.

"There's still so much we don't understand. I've always wanted to visit the academy. Every year, they uncover more about what life was like before. Mythical creatures of untold power, diseases that have long disappeared, ancient civilisations that vanished without a trace…"

I flinched and a look of horror appeared on his face. "I'm so sorry. I completely forgot. I'm used to the curse being a historical thing, a list of facts to study."

"I wish more than anything that it was," I said.

"What happened to your home, if you don't mind me asking?"

I'd bathed naked with Silas, yet talking about that day felt more exposing. "There was a great wave. Not like you're picturing, choppy waters crashing against the shore. This one swallowed the Tigal Isles whole. It all happened so fast. By the time we saw it coming, there was nothing we could do. We didn't stand a chance."

His brow furrowed. "When did you say this happened again?"

That wasn't what I expected him to say. "A little over a century ago."

"But how long? Exactly?"

I chewed my bottom lip as I thought about it. "It must be one hundred and five years."

"It can't be." He crouched to the ground, holding his head in his arms.

"Silas?"

His eyes met mine, and I was struck by the raw emotion in them.

"I told you I lost my brother, but I never explained how. Exactly one hundred and five years ago, his ship was caught in a storm, one that raged over the Sapphire Sea in a way that hadn't been seen before. The wreckage washed up on the coast of Tirrim, but him and his crew were lost to the sea forever."

"That's…" I was rendered speechless. It was the same year. How could it be?

He nodded sadly. "It can't be a coincidence."

Tirrim was located far from the Tigal Isles, at the opposite end of Idrix, but the Sapphire Sea connected them. For there to be two disasters at the same time was inconceivable. "All this time, I thought we were the only ones affected."

Silas looked shaken, his legs wobbling beneath him. "I won't ever forget that day. They were sailing to Hightower, a small party. It was meant to be the start of a new Eirel, one where we forged relationships with the other rulers. That was the last I saw of him. And do you know what the worst part is? What haunts me to this day? He asked me to see him off at the jetty before he left. And I turned him down. It was such a stupid reason. I'd pushed my tutor's boundaries too far, and he'd told me I would never measure up to my brother. I was too busy licking my wounds to say goodbye. And now I never can."

"How could you have known?"

"It doesn't matter. I should have cherished every moment while I could." His legs gave out, and he fell to the ground, distraught. "I thought it was just a bad storm. How can you bear it? Knowing that the thing responsible for taking away everyone you love is still out there."

I rested a hand on his shoulder. "All I can do. Fight. There must be a way to break it. That's the only thing that keeps me going."

"I want to fight too." His features hardened into fierce determination.

"We can talk about it later. But one step at a time. Let's cross the Threstian Gap first."

Chapter 16

The next day, we had our opportunity. The Threstian Gap was even more breath-taking up close. The other half of Threstia loomed an intimidating distance away, the chasm appearing much wider from a closer perspective. It had an air of finality to it, like we were standing at the edge of the world.

The last remaining settlers had vacated it many years ago, unable to reliably transport supplies across the unforgiving cliffs, leaving a handful of rope bridges in varying conditions. Some had collapsed entirely, others looked reassuringly stable.

Tucked behind the shadowy mountains, we'd discovered a surviving bridge. Most of its planks remained, though there were several gaps along its length. It swayed gently in the wind, and I felt every movement in the pit of my stomach.

Silas rubbed the fraying rope between his fingers, frowning. "Is this safe?"

I peered down, suppressing a shudder at the crevice's depth, the cerulean water of the stream below only just visible. It was a long way down and there would be little chance of survival if we slipped. "I guess we'll find out. Unless you've changed your mind about accompanying me?"

"Nice try."

I didn't let my relief show. His presence was a constant reassurance, even if it was distracting.

Silas paled as the bridge wobbled with a particularly strong gust of wind. "Let me go first. If I watch you cross, I'll lose my nerve."

"Be my guest."

He took a tentative step onto the wooden plank, wincing as it shuddered beneath him, amplifying the shakiness of his legs. "If you ask me, this bridge is in dire need of repair."

He wasn't wrong. No one had maintained them since the settlers left, and there was no telling if they remained strong enough to support our weight. But we had come too far to give up now and the end of the mission felt tantalisingly close.

"Are you going to spend all day criticising the quality of the bridge, or are you going to cross?" I said. There was no bite behind the words, but with every moment I waited, I found my own resolve faltering.

Silas moved, albeit slowly, his legs trembling beneath him with each step he took. "I suppose this is a bad time to mention I'm scared of heights."

"That would have been useful to know beforehand," I replied. When he was several paces ahead, I joined him. With the extra pressure of my weight, the bridge swung from side to side, and I clenched the rope support so hard my knuckles turned white. Silas wailed, nearly slowing to a stop in front of me.

I tried to ignore the glimpses of the stream below visible through gaps in the wooden planks, but several of them were loose, unstable as I stepped onto them. I couldn't afford to look away. Putting one foot out of place would mean certain death. "Come on, let's get this over with."

He didn't speed up, but he kept moving forward at least.

"Since these may be my final moments, can I tell you something?" he said, his voice wavering.

"What is it?" I asked.

But I never found out. One moment he was shuffling gingerly across the bridge, the next he trod on a loose plank, the wood plummeting into the valley below. My heart caught in my throat as his legs plunged through the gap, dangling over the chasm sickeningly. His desperate hold on the rope was the only thing keeping him safe, but even as I watched, his grip started to slip.

"Willow!" he shouted, but I was already launching myself across as quickly as I dared, not wanting to do anything to jeopardise his balance. I sank to my knees, wrapping my arm around his waist, gripping him tightly. The planks beneath us creaked, threatening to fall as the other had.

"Don't let go," I said, distributing my weight carefully. I'd have to act swiftly but cautiously, otherwise we'd both end up in the ravine. But panic had me in its clutches, and it was difficult to think past the all-consuming fear with Silas' life hanging in the balance.

"I wasn't planning to," he panted, his face set in a grimace.

I couldn't lose him, even if it put my own life at risk.

The bridge groaned loudly again, and I knew it was now or never. I threw myself backwards, using the momentum to pull Silas up.

His body lifted out of the gap excruciatingly slowly. It was a painful endeavour, my bow stabbing into my back as I heaved him upward to safety, my arm burning from supporting his weight. A muscle twinged in my shoulder, and I bit down a cry.

By the time he was free, both of us were shaking and drenched in sweat.

"Thank you," he breathed, his whole body trembling. I laid my hand on his shoulder, squeezing it in what I hoped was a reassuring way.

"You can do this." I needed to get him back on stable ground urgently. Every quiver of his body was sending vibrations through the fragile bridge. "We're nearly on the other side. I'll go ahead of you, and you can hold on to me. Would that help?"

He nodded gratefully, accepting my hand to help him to his feet. I stepped carefully, testing the structural integrity of every plank as I went and holding the rope even tighter. I didn't dare relax until our feet were on the other side, my body swaying like I was still on the bridge.

Silas fell to his knees, panting for breath. I clapped him on the shoulder. "Well done. It's over now." At least until the journey back to civilisation.

"Thank the gods for that," he said, getting to his feet. He looked rattled from the ordeal.

"What was it you wanted to say to me?"

He shook his head. "It doesn't matter."

I studied him for a moment, but Silas remained tight-lipped.

"Do you know where we're going?" he asked.

"Not exactly". Dorea hadn't narrowed down a specific area, but I'd completed enough scouting missions by now to know what to look for. Tracks left uncovered, remnants of campfires, disturbed vegetation. Few fae took precautions to mask their presence, and with the isolation here, I doubted it would be different. "I'll know it when we see it."

There was nothing but cracked earth and withered trees littering the horizon. If the dark forest was dying, Threstia was already dead, the smell of rot cloying, sticking in my throat. Every instinct in my body screamed at me to leave this place and never look back.

We trudged on, a tense silence hanging over us at the sight of what the curse had done. The scenery remained unchanged as far as the eye could see. Every fissure in the rocky ground was a reminder of what was lost.

"There's nothing left here. What are you hoping to find?" More questions. The breadcrumbs of information I'd been feeding him evidently weren't enough.

I considered my options. The bargain I'd made when joining the Night Ravens forbid me from sharing any details about my orders. But those had ended back in Valtarra when I'd taken matters into my own hands. There was nothing preventing me from telling Silas about the researchers, provided I trusted him enough.

I gazed at my companion, the one who'd conquered his fear and risked his life to get this far. He deserved to know why, at least.

"I'm helping someone. She was working here when she was injured by something that's causing her a great deal of pain."

I told him of the inky black veins that snaked up Dorea's arm and the suffering she'd endured, omitting the details of how I'd become involved.

"How did it happen?" he asked, his face shining with concern. The compassion he showed for someone he'd never met caused a pang in my heart. It was lucky that I'd found Silas when I had. This cruel world would have ruined him, making him just as jaded as I'd become.

"That's what I'm here to find out. She was hired by a team of researchers, but that's all she could tell me. A bargain prevented her from telling me more."

"Researchers?" His eyebrows rose in surprise. "What could they be looking for here? It's just dead trees and some boulders left."

"I'm not so sure." There was something more to it, a heaviness that lingered in the air.

"Do you think they could be researching the curse?" he asked, his face lighting up with interest.

"It crossed my mind," I said. "I won't know for certain until we find their camp."

We continued on, pausing occasionally while I examined the terrain for signs of disturbances, and Silas adjusted our direction. It wasn't until several hours later, our legs tiring as darkness fell, that we saw it.

"It's not possible," I whispered as I struggled to process what I saw.

"What is that?" he said, his jaw hanging open.

Tents were set up on the rocky plains, but this was no mere camp. It was a city, a bustling hive of activity, large enough to house the Old Keep several times over. Hundreds of fae scurried between them, protected within the confines of a heavily guarded settlement. This had to be the researchers Dorea had mentioned, but it was far beyond the scale I'd imagined.

"Nothing good." The tiny part of me that hoped they had pure aims despite the way they'd treated Dorea shrivelled into nothingness. The resources needed alone to sustain an operation of this size were enough to know that. Guards paced the perimeter of the site, the sharp blades of their swords glinting in the sunlight. They wouldn't go to such lengths to protect the research unless they had something to hide.

I'd known that investigating Dorea's illness wouldn't be easy, but I hadn't expected anything like this.

"I don't suppose I can convince you to stay here?" I asked, already knowing the answer.

"Not a chance," he said. It was a relief, but something still twisted in my gut. If something happened to him, it would be my fault.

We'd need to sneak into the site, find out what they were researching, and escape without being caught. I hadn't attempted anything on that level before, and Silas certainly hadn't. We would need an airtight plan to succeed, and that would require time and careful thought.

"This way," I said, dragging him towards a cluster of rocks perched on higher ground. It provided a crucial vantage point where we could monitor the activity within the camp without revealing our presence, and, more importantly, carved into one of the boulders was a secluded nook offering us shelter for the night.

I set about my usual task of organising our sleeping arrangements while Silas watched our target. We didn't dare risk a fire in case the smoke gave us away, relieving him of his camp duties. The element of surprise was all we had and if we lost it, this would all have been for nothing.

After a pitiful meal of leftover berries, the portion too small to satisfy our hunger, we settled down for the evening.

It would be a long night of suffering. I could feel every lump of the hard ground beneath me, digging into my back uncomfortably. Shivering, I curled up as tightly as I could under my threadbare blanket. It did nothing to stop me from shaking as the cold clung to my skin like a wet cloak.

"Get over here." A voice cut through the quiet. Silas.

"Excuse me?" I was sure I'd misheard him.

"I can hear your teeth chattering from over here. My blood runs hot. I can keep both of us warm if you don't mind the company."

He wanted us to cuddle up? My heart betrayed me as it raced at the thought.

"Absolutely not." That was a bad, bad idea. It was hard enough to keep my head clear in his presence, let alone in such an intimate position. Opening up to him had been dangerous. Sharing a bedroll would be playing with fire.

"Willow," he said, like he was chastising me.

"Silas," I replied, matching his tone.

"Must you be so stubborn?" His voice softened. "You won't get a wink of sleep shivering like that. Let me help you, please."

I tossed and turned on my bedroll, but I knew he was right. And with so much ahead of us, a good night of rest was essential.

I sighed. "If I even suspect you of having wandering hands, it will be the last thing you do. Understand?"

"Whatever you say," Silas said. There was a rustling noise as he picked up his bedroll and brought it over to mine. He slid in next to me, under my blankets, the delicious heat from his body providing immediate relief from the bitter cold. His scent was intoxicating, the heady mix of earth and vanilla filling my nose, easing the tension that plagued me. He wrapped me in a gentle embrace, keeping his touch purely functional. It didn't matter. The feel of his skin on mine had already caused enough damage, my every nerve lit up in awareness at his proximity.

I shifted, attempting to find a position where it was easier to forget he was pressed up against me.

"Stop wiggling," Silas said, his arm snaking around me to hold me still. With him so close, it took all my determination to resist nuzzling against him. It was an effort to keep my breathing even. To not show how much he affected me. But there was no time for complications. I needed to stay strong, if not for myself, then for all who relied on me.

I lifted his arm off my chest, letting it fall back against his side, before shuffling into a better position. "I'm trying to get comfortable."

"And I'm not trying to prevent that," he said, "but you're rubbing against me and it's a little distracting."

"I just need a moment." I was so close to finding the perfect spot where his warmth enveloped me, but I could still think clearly.

"I'm serious. Every time you squirm like that, you're grinding against my cock. Don't get me wrong, I'm not complaining, but it's not very conducive for a night of rest." His voice was like silk in my ear, the admission sending chills rippling across my skin and making heat pool between my thighs. My body ached, every place where he was touching me burning, not only with the warmth of his Blessing, but flames of desire. We were treading towards dangerous territory and there would be no turning back.

My skin was flushed, need thrumming through me, and Silas' strong arm locked around my waist. It was so tempting to throw caution to the wind and writhe against him, teasing him mercilessly until he snapped, losing control and igniting this temptation between us.

But this was all just a harmless flirtation for him, a fun diversion that lacked deeper meaning. As much as I would enjoy crossing that line, I knew my heart would get too involved. It would only end in hurt for me.

After everything I'd shared with Silas, I couldn't bear that.

I settled for a more subtle gesture, shifting slightly so the curve of my rear dug into his groin.

In a flash, he pounced, wrapping me in a tight grip and pinning my arms to my sides. I couldn't move, a thought that thrilled me and annoyed me in equal measure.

"There, that's better," he said, ignoring my growls of frustration. "Sweet dreams, Willow."

When I woke with the sunrise, I discovered we'd moved during the night, locked in an intimate embrace. I was snuggled up against Silas, my legs entwined with his. My hand rested on his chest, and I could feel the steady rhythm of his heartbeat beneath my fingertips.

His arm had slid around me, resting on my lower back, holding me against him, and there was a hard shape pressing into my stomach. The realisation of what that was brought a furious blush to my face. He was still asleep, thankfully, and I got to work extracting myself from him.

"Just five more minutes," Silas said, his voice thick with sleep.

I persisted in freeing myself, disturbing him in the process.

He scowled at me as his eyes snapped open. His hair was a mess, forcing him to push it back from his forehead. "Spoilsport."

I ignored him, packing away our belongings instead, trying to forget how safe his embrace had felt. How right I'd felt in his arms. This was a dangerous game and it would only end in heartbreak if I carried on. I knew better than this.

"How'd you sleep?" he asked, rubbing his eyes, still half-asleep.

"Terribly." I wanted to answer, but the words stuck in my throat, preventing the lie. "Thank you for the help, but it will never happen again."

Silas wore a lopsided grin that made my heart skip a beat. "If you say so."

I ignored him, retrieving a few scrolls of blank parchment from my pack and beginning the arduous task of plotting our next move.

Chapter 17

I sipped the last dregs of water from my canteen as Silas returned to our makeshift shelter, clutching a crudely drawn map of the site. He'd volunteered to take a closer look to help us determine ways to use the terrain to our advantage. What he lacked in artistic talent, he made up for with his attention to detail, his drawing accurately plotting the layout of the camp.

"The sides are just as guarded as the main entrance, I'm afraid," he said, wiping the sweat from his brow. I'd hoped he'd return with better news, but fate was working against us. "Looks like that's still our best bet."

"Then we'll move at nightfall." I scrunched up my sheet of parchment and tossed it into my pack, its contents now irrelevant. We needed to sneak past the guards to infiltrate the camp, but with so many researchers milling around, it would be difficult to avoid detection.

"What about a glamour?" Silas asked. "Disguise ourselves as researchers or guards?"

"It might work," I admitted. "But there may be powerful wards in place, if their level of security is any indication. The last thing we'd need is to reveal ourselves by accident." We'd be sitting ducks. As sure as my aim was, against that many enemies, it would be a struggle to fight our way out.

We sat in quiet contemplation, suggesting ideas to each other and assessing them for weaknesses. It was surprisingly natural to work together. In the handful of missions I had undertaken with a partner, there was always a sense of distance, a hesitation to let down our guard which prevented us from true partnership. But with Silas, it was like we shared a stream of consciousness, one shouldering the mental burden whenever the other needed a moment to recharge.

"We need a distraction," I mused. "It's a shame we can't torch the place."

"Remind me to never get on your bad side." He sat up straighter. "Wait, that gives me an idea."

"Fire and stealth don't go well together," I said, not following his line of thought.

"They don't. But how about the opposite?" A slow smile spread across his face.

His confidence sparked the first rays of hope within me. "Go on."

"What's going to happen at nightfall? This isn't the type of place that winds down. And if you're working into the night, what do you need?" A flame flickered in his hand. "Light." He closed his fist, smothering the fire.

I leapt to my feet. "And if they experienced a sudden blackout, that would both provide a distraction and grant us the cover of darkness." It was exactly what we needed. "That's brilliant. Can you really do that?"

He laughed as if the question was ridiculous. "Don't you dare underestimate me. Of course I can."

It could work. For the first time, I dared to have faith. Maybe we could pull this off.

With a distraction decided, the rest of the plan soon came together. It was far from perfect, but it was enough. At least I hoped so. The sky darkened around us as we ran through it so many times that I had each movement memorised. Only fate could betray us now.

It was time to move.

Silas counted down from five, and I steadied my breathing, waiting for my window of opportunity. My heart thudded in my chest, the only sign of my nerves. I'd learned to ignore the sensation. It was a distraction I didn't need. Only the adrenaline served me at this stage. There was a lingering unease in my gut at the thought of what was at stake today.

We raced forward as darkness swallowed the research site, crouching in the shadows just beyond the entrance. Its potency was unnerving, like night had smothered all the light in the world. The magnitude of Silas' power was hard to believe, even as I experienced it. But this was our shot, and I couldn't falter. Not now.

The guards shouted orders to each other, racing to relight the torches with urgency. Silas was next to me, his eyes closed in concentration as he thwarted their every attempt to restart their fires. Not a spark made it through his control.

The research camp was in disarray, fae scurrying from tent to tent, clutching candles, torches, and anything else they could think of. A complaining crowd surrounded a stressed looking researcher as he tried in vain to light anything with his Blessing. The flames igniting in his palms were immediately smothered, the mob growing increasingly irate.

No one so much as spared a look in our direction, rendering us invisible amongst the chaos. The plan was working exactly as we'd intended.

"This way," I said, dragging Silas with me. His hand was warm in mine, a reassuring presence that steadied my erratic heartbeat.

We weaved between small, plain tents that were practically on top of each other, venturing deeper into the site. Occasionally, we would duck behind a tent, hidden in the shadows, as panicked fae rushed past.

The camp was squalid, the stench of it making me gag. I'd had more pleasant nights sleeping on the ground than the conditions we glimpsed. They'd packed as many as they could within the space, but for what end?

The tents became more lavish and spaced out the deeper we walked. The material they were crafted from was thicker and more vibrant, the living quarters comprising several rooms. Here, the foul odour was less pronounced, though it still lingered faintly in the air. This was evidently where those in charge resided, afforded slightly more comfort than the masses.

It was as Silas had observed during his reconnaissance. The outer edges were of little significance, each layer further inside becoming more important to the camp's operations.

What we needed was at its heart.

Past the edge of the tents, we found what we were looking for. There was a substantial tent, larger than any other, situated precisely in the centre, surrounded by a vast expanse of uneven pits where the ground had been disturbed. They dominated the land within the camp's perimeter, likely the reason for the cramped living conditions. Small groups of robed researchers gathered around each pit, taking shovelfuls of earth, bagging them, and carrying them to large boxes. Others took those boxes when full, stacking them into carts.

Out in the open, we were vulnerable and exposed. We needed cover, and fast. A cart, filled to the brim with supplies, offered us the perfect hiding place. I nudged Silas towards it, dropping to the ground and wiggling in the dirt underneath until we were fully sheltered.

A tall man in dark robes paced between the groups, projecting his voice, laced with authority, across the area. His hair was as silver as mine, but fell to his hips, billowing out behind him as he walked. "We're experiencing a blackout, but do not let this affect your labelling standards. It's imperative that we're able to match the analysis with the sample location. If I catch one slip up, you're out."

"Gods, he's even worse than usual," a member of the group nearest us whispered, a young man with broad shoulders. I leant in closer, straining my ears. Complaining fae were a useful source of information. I poked Silas, gesturing to them wordlessly. He nodded.

"He's probably on edge, like the rest of them. What's going on with the torches? They can't expect us to work in these conditions. I can't see my hand in front of my face," another said, his hair dusted with grey specks.

"It's all pointless. How do we know this is even the right zone?" added a blonde woman, dirt smudged on her nose.

"Didn't you hear Ridrick? They narrowed it down to a few areas, and this one's the most likely. Apparently, it used to be a forest."

The woman laughed. "He said that in the last location, and the place before that. Haven't you learned by now? They have no idea what they're doing."

"Be quiet. Do you want him to hear us?"

"I'm hearing too much talking and not enough digging," Ridrick said from a distance away.

"What's so special about these portal remains we're looking for, anyway? Not that I'm complaining. They're basically throwing money at us to dig in the dirt all day."

My gaze locked with Silas'. Portals? They were little more than a myth from before the war, their ancient magic providing shortcuts between territories, and, if the stories were true, gateways to other realms. The curse had rendered them useless, leaving no evidence they'd even existed. Yet, apparently, not everyone believed that.

"Whoever unearths a viable sample first gets a hundred gold coins. I'm not turning that down. I could retire and still have money to spare."

"If you don't quieten down, you'll be lucky to receive your wages." I flinched. Ridrick had appeared out of nowhere to scold the group. "Now, where are the blasted torches? Podner, I need light over here." His voice faded as he marched away.

I puzzled over the information, something not sitting right with me. So many resources, all this effort, just to find evidence of a portal that may not even exist?

One thing was for sure. Dorea had been processing these samples when she'd been inflicted with her condition. They were searching for traces of ancient magic. Could that have been what caused her harm?

Silas' nose scrunched up, concentrating desperately on holding it together. I inhaled sharply. He was going to sneeze and give us away.

I clamped my hand over his face, glaring at him. His breath was hot, tickling my skin.

We were paralysed, our eyes wide in matching panic. But then he took a deep breath, the tension leaving his body as the sensation passed. I sighed in relief, letting him go. The group had fallen silent after their scolding. We watched them for a while, but they revealed nothing further.

"Let's go," I whispered to Silas, sliding out from underneath the cart. I eyed the main tent. If I wanted answers, there was no avoiding it. And with Ridrick occupied with shouting at someone, we had a window.

"Hold still," I said, tapping my fingers on Silas' ear. He shivered as the glamour trickled over his skin, coating him. I did the same to myself, unable to suppress a shudder. Wearing one felt uncomfortable, like trying to wear clothes that didn't properly fit. To all unassuming eyes, we now appeared in the brown robes of the researchers, my bow disappearing from sight.

Silas stared at me in confusion. "I thought glamours are too risky?"

"They are," I replied. "But we don't know what's inside, and I'd rather we blended in, for as long as it lasts."

Two guards stood either side of the tent's entrance, with a further two patrolling around it. They hadn't been visible when we'd crafted our plan, assuming the guards would be focused on the perimeter. To stand any chance of getting inside, we'd need another diversion.

"Any ideas?" I asked Silas, tracking the guard's movements as we ducked behind a cart.

"Only one, and it's risky. Are you ready?"

I nodded. A bead of sweat ran down Silas' forehead, but otherwise nothing happened.

"What are you doing?"

"Be patient." His breathing grew quick, and for a fleeting moment, light returned to the camp with the extra strain on his power.

"Silas…"

"Now." Everything went dark again. Suddenly, a crate exploded behind us, soil and shrapnel raining down. The researchers screamed, diving for cover, and chaos erupted once more. Three of the guards surged forward towards the fire, their swords raised as they assessed the threat, the one remaining guard dividing his attention between the tent and surrounding area.

We took advantage of the few seconds his head was turned to slip inside, the tent's heavy flap shifting no more than it would in a breeze. Mercifully, it was unoccupied, but that could change in an instant.

"Can you give me some light? A dim one. I don't want to attract any unnecessary attention."

Silas summoned a tiny ball of flame, far smaller than his flaming sphere had been, letting it hover in the air next to me, providing just enough light to examine my surroundings.

The first thing I saw, which was unsurprising given its huge size, was a grand table, most of the surface taken by a map of Threstia divided into quadrants. A wire square sat on top of it, marking our current position, but it was littered with indents. Beside it, parchment was stacked neatly. I picked up the nearest sheet, a report summarising their results from the previous camp. This was it. There was more than enough evidence here to bring back to Reuben.

Returning the document to the top of the pile, I rifled through the stack, selecting random sheets as I went.

"What are you doing?" Silas asked, not shielding his curiosity.

"This is evidence I need, but I need to be cautious. This way, they shouldn't discover that something is missing until we're far away.

And if they do, they'll be more likely to blame incompetence over foul play."

"Clever."

I rolled up the parchment, carefully tucking it inside my robes. "I'm known for it occasionally."

The sound of approaching voices signalled that we wouldn't be alone for long. I swore, looking around for somewhere to hide. There was nothing. Silas quickly extinguished his flame.

The tent flap opened, and I did the only thing I could think of. I pushed Silas, hard. He stumbled, falling back against the table, perched on its edge once he'd steadied himself. I stepped into his space, leaning over and bracing my arms on either side of him.

And then I kissed him.

We had an audience, and our survival depended on selling the illusion. Luckily, Silas caught on and followed my lead without missing a beat.

The kiss was all-consuming, everything around us melting away. Silas met my intensity and returned it with an eagerness that left me dizzy. The simmering tension between us reached its breaking point, igniting in one surge, his mouth hungry and desperate, stoking a passion that quickly blazed out of control. A low moan rumbled in his throat as I deepened it, needing more of him. It would never be enough.

His hand slipped inside my glamoured robes, reaching my bare back, his fingernails lightly raking down the sensitive skin. I gasped. He took advantage, his tongue skilfully exploring my mouth until my hand fisted in his hair.

I'd never been kissed like this before.

I forgot everything. Who I was, where we were. The only thing that mattered was that he didn't stop. I craved more, the urgency of my desire robbing my senses.

Someone cleared their throat. We broke apart, facing our audience. Ridrick had entered the tent, joined by a woman with grey hair and stern eyes, wearing the same robes as him. They were flanked by two of the guards, their swords pointed at us.

Ridrick had turned a concerning scarlet colour. "What exactly is going on in here? It may be dark, but we're not blind."

My hand shook. It was all over.

"You'd better have a good explanation for cavorting in a restricted area, otherwise you'll both be cast out at first light," Ridrick finished.

I released a shaky breath as Silas' hand slid into mine.

"I've resisted kissing her all week. Can you blame me for taking advantage of the blackout?" The tips of my ears tingled at the admission, and I was certain they'd turned pink. Was it true? Had he wanted to kiss me once we'd become friends?

I couldn't respond, only able to catch my breath.

"They're just young, lovesick fools, Ridrick. They're not the first to be caught in a compromising position," the woman next to him said. "I seem to recall you were once involved in a similar incident."

"That was different. I would never show such disrespect for my supervisor's office. How did they get in here?" Ridrick spluttered, his eyes narrowed suspiciously at us.

"There was no one guarding the door. We thought it would finally give us a chance for privacy." I skirted the fine line between truth and lie, the words catching in my mouth, difficult to speak.

"Is this true? Did you leave your posts?" The woman shot an accusatory look at the guards.

"For a brief moment. There was an explosion. We thought the camp was under attack."

"I'll be having strong words with your commander. You should be attached to your post at all times. I don't care if the whole camp is on fire." She looked at Ridrick. "What was it?"

"A box of soil overheated." He looked sheepish. "It's not the first time it's happened. Hazard of the job."

I squeezed Silas' hand in silent thanks at his quick thinking, him returning the gesture.

"I'm surrounded by imbeciles," she muttered under her breath. She fixed her steely gaze on us. "Are you hiding anything from us? Anything you wish to confess?"

The parchment burned a hole in my pocket, and for a moment, I swore she could see it.

"We've answered your questions truthfully," Silas said, and I had to admire the way he'd answered an entirely different question naturally enough to evade notice.

"Ridrick, search the tent. Check if anything is amiss."

He nodded, prowling around the room and leaving no corner untouched. As he reached for the stack of parchment, my heartbeat faltered. But he merely examined the top sheet, moving swiftly on.

"Judging by your silence, I take it everything is in order."

"It is," he confirmed bitterly.

She sighed. "I'm not paid enough for this." She addressed us directly with a stern look. "Do you promise not to do it again?"

"Yes," we said in unison.

"Very well." She pointed at Silas. "You, come with me. I have a cart that needs loading, and you appear to have some free time."

Her gaze moved to me. "You go back to your patch. We'll need to work overtime to make up for the delay."

Ridrick opened his mouth to protest, but she shook her head. He thought better of it, promptly closing it.

Doing anything to raise the woman's suspicion would be asking for trouble.

"Yes, of course," I said.

My gaze met Silas' in silent apology. He knew, just as I did, that my priority would be smuggling the parchment out of the camp. But it hurt to leave him here without a plan for his escape.

He had surprised me at every turn. If anyone could do this, it would be him. It was new to have a partner I trusted so implicitly, who always had my back. I liked it.

I strode out of the tent like I belonged, moving through the site without being questioned, everyone remaining distracted by the blackout. I retraced my steps, blending into the shadows to mask my presence when I reached the overcrowded living quarters.

I crept forward, barely able to breathe. The guards had lit one flame, and had crowded around, attempting to light other torches from it, a sign that Silas' influence over the camp was weakening. I sneaked past, then ran towards our earlier shelter, finding a vantage point where I could look out for him.

"Come on, Silas," I prayed. "Come on."

He had to escape. I couldn't do this without him.

And after the way his lips had felt on mine, there was no chance I would.

Chapter 18

I couldn't relax, could hardly breathe as I watched the research camp's entrance without blinking, searching for any sign of Silas. A group of guards crowded around the remains of a fire on the perimeter, cheering as they successfully relit it. The shadows receded to only the darkest corners, and my stomach dropped.

Where was he?

With every passing moment, I regretted leaving him behind more. What if something had happened to him because of me? What if they'd caught him tampering with the fires?

I'd spent so long worrying he would betray me. I hadn't considered the possibility that I would be the one betraying him.

The light from the fire intensified, a sign that Silas' ability to smother it was fading fast. The window of his escape was closing. I hovered, stuck between the urge to go back for him and the need to protect the parchment, now securely tucked into my pack. If they captured me in the process of saving him, this would all have been for nothing.

A warning bell rang out, every clang a harbinger of doom. I froze, my heart in my throat. Nothing happened at first. It was as if the camp was suspended in time. Then the campfires flared wildly, dancing in the wind.

The flames swelled, blazing into an unrelenting torrent of fire that escaped the bounds of their containers. The guards cursed, one rushing to fetch a nearby Water-Blessed fae, who splashed the containers in a feeble attempt to control the blaze. It barely stifled it.

In the commotion, Silas appeared, running towards me in a dead sprint, pursued by a dozen guards. A cry nearly broke free from me at the confirmation of him alive and well.

My relief was short-lived. Arrows rained down around him as I watched on in horror. Silas incinerated most with a flick of his arm, but with the strength of his Blessing waning, he had to dodge several that made it through. I felt each one as if they were piercing my heart.

"Run, Willow. Now!" he shouted, panting between every word.

I didn't need to be told twice. I sprinted as fast as my legs would take me, grateful for the head start.

We couldn't outrun them if they were determined to chase us, not with Silas unaccustomed to a life of adventure and me more used to stakeouts, but with the right terrain, we could stand and fight. I scanned our surroundings as we ran, searching for any advantage.

In the distance, a peak of dark rock emerged, flanked by a dozen smaller hills. It had a craggy, uneven surface that would make climbing challenging, but it towered above everything else nearby. An arrow lodged into the ground where my feet had been moments before. They were closing the gap.

"This way!" I shouted. It would have to be enough.

My legs were on fire. I'd never ran so far before, even when chasing the thief through the capital, and our escape was taking its toll. I kept my gaze locked on the peak, urging myself to make it, one step at a time. Silas was behind me, breathing heavily.

We would make it. We just had to make it to the hill.

An arrow grazed the top of my shoulder, a searing pain slicing my skin. I whimpered, clutching the wound.

"Willow."

"Don't. There's no time. Get to the hill." Any distraction would make us a target, and I didn't intend to die here. Not when we'd come so far.

With my pace slowed by the injury, Silas bridged the gap between us. His arm hooked around me, a sure and steady comfort, pulling me towards the base of the hill.

The climb was like no pain I'd experienced before. My body ached with the ascent, my shoulder throbbed where the arrow had struck, and my lungs burned as I desperately tried to catch my breath. Still, we persevered, driven by the singular thought of making it to the peak.

Silas sent a wave of fire around us, keeping the arrows away while we climbed. My shirt clung to my back with sweat, but it was a worthwhile price to pay for protection. It didn't stop one catching my ankle, another narrowly missing Silas' head. I salvaged as many arrows from the enemy as I could, knowing that could be the difference between life and death.

By the time we reached the top, tears streamed down my face. Silas sagged against me. A handful of guards had made it to the hill and were finding their footholds, relentless in their pursuit.

I tuned out everything around me, my focus on myself and my target. I released the arrow. It struck true, as I knew it would. A body fell to the ground, numbness unfurling within me at the sight. There was no chance to process the feeling, only to unleash more arrows. It wasn't the first time I'd killed for self-preservation, and it would unlikely be the last.

As I picked off the guards one arrow at a time, and Silas pushed the others back with a wall of fire despite his exhaustion, I came to a startling realisation.

It wasn't enough.

My jaw clenched at the sea of guards flooding over the horizon. There had been no Blessed within our initial pursuers. The fallout from the blackout had likely kept them occupied. But I was willing to bet every coin I had that we wouldn't be as lucky with the next contingent.

I swallowed thickly. Was this really it?

I screamed, wiping my tears before taking out another guard with my bow. Only three arrows remained in my quiver, and retrieving the rest was impossible.

Overcoming this was futile.

Silas read it on my face, clasping my hand tightly.

"I'm sorry," I said, a lump in my throat. "This is all my fault. I should never have brought you into this."

"You have nothing to be sorry for." He squeezed my hand. "I don't regret any of it."

"Really?" I asked in disbelief.

"Well, now you mention it, I would have preferred not to fall in a pit or cross a rickety bridge. And a more comfortable bed wouldn't have gone amiss. But no, I don't regret it. You've opened my eyes to what's out there."

"Me neither. It hasn't always been easy, but I couldn't imagine doing this without you."

The guards closed in, a dozen more climbing the hill. If these were truly our last moments, there was an urgent question burning in my mind. There were no excuses left, no time for hesitation.

"Did you mean it before? When you said you'd resisted kissing me?"

"Every word."

Could it be? Hope, the most dangerous thing of all, bloomed in my chest.

"But the kiss meant nothing to you. You just went along with it to save our necks."

"Did I?"

He tilted my lips towards him with a tender touch, his closeness making me forget the bleakness of our situation, if only for a moment.

"Let me make one thing clear. If I'd had any notion that you would be receptive to my advances, I wouldn't have held myself back. I would have kissed you when mud caked your face in the inn. I would have kissed you when you repeatedly lectured me on how to read a map, and I definitely would have kissed you when you stubbornly insisted my flirting wasn't affecting you."

My breath hitched.

His eyes twinkled in that way I'd grown to love. "And if we weren't in such a precarious position, I would show you just how much I want you. Unfortunately, we'll have to test my patience a little longer."

"Silas," I whispered. "It's too late. We can't hold them back forever." Even as I said it, the guards had made it halfway up the hill.

His breaths were laboured, his voice rough. "I told you before, you shouldn't underestimate me."

He sank to the ground, pressing his hands to the rocks in front of us, and gods, they *melted*.

At first, they glowed red in the darkness of night, like the dying embers of a campfire, but then pressure built as they hissed and steamed, releasing an acrid smell into the air. Silas roared with the effort, dragging his fingers along the surrounding rocks as they sizzled and bubbled into lava. Soon, the edge of the hilltop fell to the fiery onslaught, becoming a molten stream that oozed down the cliff towards our pursuers. Their screams of agony went right through me as it engulfed them, and I knew I would never forget the sound.

I scrambled up onto the highest ground I could find, balancing my weight on the tip of an uneven rock, hoping that Silas had a plan. He may have been fire resistant, but I certainly wasn't.

A sob burst from me at the terrible beauty of the scene before me. The lava spread as it consumed more of the hill in its endless hunger, speeding its descent. The stifling heat it unleashed saturated me in sweat, and I gagged at its rotten scent. Silas had turned our peak into a small volcano, and the guards that had once attacked were now fleeing in terror.

He clambered to his feet on shaky legs, staggering as he closed the distance between us. Gasping in a desperate breath, he scooped me off the ground and into his arms. He was submerged in the lava but showed no signs it was burning him. It was as if he was standing in water up to his ankles, not molten rock.

Our eyes met, his set with grim determination and a shade of fear.

"Silas..." I could only say, incapable of anything else. He had saved us, done the impossible when all hope was lost. I ran my hand down his cheek tenderly.

Considering how much magic he had used, his hold was surprisingly firm as he carried me to safety. He slid down the other side of the peak, keeping me cradled in his arms, only stopping when we'd travelled far enough that the lava became a narrow stream.

"Told you so," he said, his voice no more than a quiet whisper. His legs buckled from underneath him, both of us collapsing in a heap.

Wincing at the impact to my injured shoulder, I carefully climbed off him. He was still, too still, a single drop of blood running from his nose.

"Silas," I said uncertainly, nudging him.

Nothing.

"Wake up," I pleaded, shaking him harder. "Wake up, please."

It couldn't be.

There was no response. I slapped at his cheeks, urging him to open his eyes, but he didn't move. His skin was cold under my fingertips.

No.

The heart he'd painstakingly pieced back together shattered, and I knew it could never be mended. A strangled noise escaped me, my face dripping with tears as I sobbed, clutching him like I'd never let go.

Then I felt it. His chest rose. It was feeble, too small to see even up close, but the tiny movement sent hope pulsing through my veins.

There was still a chance.

I dragged his limp body towards a large boulder, leaning against it and resting his head in my lap. I kept my bow, with its pitiful amount of arrows, within reach, but my attention was firmly on the man lying against me. My heart. My everything.

I stroked his hair in what I hoped was a soothing motion, waiting for him to come back to me.

As the top layer of the lava cooled, a thin black crust settling over it, I waited. My teeth chattered with the bitter cold of the night air, but I ignored it. Silas was my only priority.

The sun was rising with the pink glow of morning, illuminating the drastic shifts to the terrain from his power, when he finally stirred.

His eyes fluttered open. "If I'd known overexerting myself would lead to waking up in your lap, I wouldn't have waited until now."

I swatted his head, Silas letting out an exaggerated yelp.

"Never do that to me again. I thought I'd lost you."

"I have no intention of going anywhere. You're stuck with me, whether you like it or not." He sat up, stretching. His lazy smile faded to a devastated expression that made my chest tighten.

"Are you hurt?" I asked, examining him for any signs of injury.

But Silas was looking at the volcano he'd formed, steam rising from it even in its subdued state. The jagged rock we'd navigated as we'd climbed was smooth, sculpted by the lava, the nearby hills flattened. The ground was black and shiny where it had begun to cool, leaving the landscape of Threstia unrecognisable.

"What have I done? I've damned us."

"No Silas, it's over. You saved us." I said, resting my hand on his shoulder. He'd been incredible.

"You don't understand." He stood, swaying as he did. "I've put a target on our backs. We need to leave immediately."

I climbed to my feet, joining him, leaning on the boulder for support. "But you're exhausted. And no one's crossing the lava anytime soon. Not until it solidifies. The researchers will have to find a way around and that will cost them days. And after that display, I'm not sure they'd want to."

He shook his head. "It's not them I'm worried about. There's something I need to tell you."

Chapter 19

"What's going on?" I asked, looking to Silas for reassurance, but he had none to offer me.

His face had gone white, his boots catching on the uneven ground as he paced nervously. He couldn't look at me. "I haven't been entirely truthful with you about who I am."

What was he talking about? He'd already revealed his position, back when we'd first crossed into Threstia. "You're a bloodline heir from Eirel."

He wrung his hands, taking a deep breath. "There's no easy way to say this, so I'll blurt it out. I'm not just a bloodline heir; I'm the Lord of Eirel."

He was... what?

It made no sense. Silas, one of the rulers of Idrix? Ash coated his face, his clothes torn and filthy. Anyone would've passed him without sparing him a second glance.

"No. You can't be. You've spent the past two weeks gathering firewood and sleeping outside," I said.

He leant against the boulder, never taking his eyes off me. Their emerald depths shone with an unexpected vulnerability. "I'm afraid I am. It was never meant to be me. My brother was raised to be lord, and I was the spare. Then he died and my life changed in an instant."

"But we've travelled the length of Idrix. No one recognised you." Surely, someone would have approached us?

"Why would they? I've never left Eirel's borders and the common fae don't know my face. It's long been Eirel's strategy. Reality can't measure up to someone's imagination, and you can't prepare to face an enemy if you don't know them. Intimidation tactics at their finest."

My mouth went dry in a way that had nothing to do with the ash still lingering in the air. Blood roared in my ears. "You tricked me."

The fae I'd gotten to know during our quest, the one I'd developed feelings for didn't exist. Did I even know him at all?

Silas took a step towards me, resting a hand on my arm. "It's not like that. Please let me explain."

Shrugging off his touch, I spoke, my voice quiet and laced with venom. "Was any of it real? Or was this all just an experiment for you? A pleasant break from the pressures of ruling where you could dress up in your plain clothes and sleep on your little bedroll, and see the realm."

"Of course it was real. It wasn't like that." Tears danced in his eyes, but it did nothing to soothe the bite of his betrayal.

"How? You're a *lord*. You could have done something about this rotten place this whole time. Thrown resources at the curse, sheltered the vulnerable who needed your help, protected your subjects from harm. Yet you've been playing the charming adventurer without a care in the world. I can't look at you." The realisation hit me like a rock slamming into my chest. "You're just like the rest of them."

And I'd fallen for it yet again.

"Listen to me, please. That's not what happened. I had to escape. They were going to kill me." He was desperate, pleading with me like his life depended on it. "I'll tell you everything, if you just let me."

It was too late. "You could've told me. You had the perfect opportunity to explain when I found out you were a bloodline heir. Yet you still didn't."

"You were recovering from confronting those nobles. I wasn't sure how you'd handle the truth."

"You never gave me a chance." Maybe I could've understood back then. But too much had happened since. I'd let him in, opening up to him and leaving my heart exposed.

"And do what?" Silas raised his voice. "Drag you into my mess? I couldn't do that to you. I needed some time to get my head straight and think of a plan. Unfortunately, that time has run out. There's no chance my enemies won't have witnessed this and known it was my doing."

"I wish you would have." I gazed out across the hostile landscape, watching smoke rise from the volcano in the distance and billow out into the sky, mirroring the inner turmoil I felt.

His voice softened. "I've never felt like this before. Don't let this ruin what we've built."

"Don't you see? I would have ripped out my own heart and given it to you willingly, but now I don't know if you'd treasure it or burn it to ashes. I trusted you and this whole time you've hidden everything from me."

Silas' features hardened. "How can you say that to me? You talk of trust, but when have you ever trusted me? You've told me next to nothing about why we're here. And don't try to tell me we're helping your injured friend. I saw you stealing those documents. What's the big secret? After everything we've shared, don't I deserve to know?"

I was momentarily stunned, my haze of frustration clearing. "It's complicated."

"And you have the gall to bite my head off for hiding my background. Didn't you think for one moment that if you'd confided in me, I might have been able to help? We've both held onto our secrets for too long."

My shoulders slumped. Perhaps he was right. It was like he'd thrown water over me, my anger no longer burning so much with the shock.

He was the Lord of Eirel, possessing the power and influence to make a better Idrix, one where the Blessed fae didn't hold their superiority over everyone else, one where a stranger wasn't more likely to trick you than offer help, one where the curse wasn't stealing our hope for the future. Instead, he'd deserted his subjects, trailing after me instead.

But this was Silas, not a stranger. He was kind, loyal to a fault, and supported me through everything, asking for nothing in return. He wouldn't abandon Eirel without a good reason. And hadn't he explained the difficulties he faced when I'd pressed him? I just hadn't known back then that he faced them as Eirel's lord.

It would be a long road to trusting him again, and he owed me an explanation, but there was no denying the fact I owed him one too.

"When we made our bargain, I was telling you the truth. I'm doing something important, but I can't tell you what. I'm bound by another bargain. It prevents me from telling anyone."

He was sceptical, but I could see his brain working, sifting his way through the words. "Can't you work around it?"

"No, you don't understand. This isn't a simple bargain, with one term. It's complex, the terms twisted together and difficult to decipher. A precaution in case I was ever caught." It was the price to pay for being a scout.

"Please, there must be something you can tell me." Exasperation clouded his face.

I released a deep breath, thinking. The bargain protected the Night Ravens, keeping its secrets in case we were captured, or worse. If I focused on myself, maybe I could share something.

"I find information where others cannot. Information that helps those far more intelligent than I am to uncover answers." I considered him. If only I could make him understand why I had to do this. "I told you before, I'm fighting against the curse. This is how."

I thought he'd understand; the curse had taken so much from him too. But Silas' eyes narrowed at me. "And whose secrets are you selling?"

"What?"

He staggered backwards from me. "I've been such a fool. Is this why you wanted to travel together? You knew I was noble. All this time, you've been stringing me along while you learn all my secrets?"

"What? No!" I hadn't considered how it would look, binding him to me once I'd uncovered his position, pestering him with questions about how the nobility worked. "Silas, listen to me. The only reason I wanted to travel together was because I thought you could help. I'm completely out of my depth here. I can't do this without you."

"Then tell me what's going on! Because I don't know if I can trust you anymore."

"I can't. There's only one way I can tell you. You would have to be bound by that same bargain, and you can't. It's a lifelong commitment."

"What if I walk away now?" He sounded just as defeated as I felt.

A numb feeling spread through me. It had been inevitable. From the moment we'd set out on our journey, it had been doomed to end. I just hadn't realised it would cut me so deep.

"You'll never see me again." It was the only way. A clean break, no more distractions. My work would only become more challenging, more dangerous from this point onwards. Having someone I cared about outside the Night Ravens was a weakness ripe for exploitation, especially when that someone was a ruler, his world the opposite of mine.

He sucked in a breath, a deep frown etched into his face.

Something broke in me at that, leaving behind a void that could never be filled. I'd always known I wouldn't be enough for him.

"I need space. I'm going for a walk." Silas said, swinging his pack over his shoulder.

"But you just told me we're in danger," I said.

He stared me down, his eyes burning with an intensity that made the argument die in my throat. "I don't give a fuck. Let them come for me. I could do with letting off some steam."

He didn't look back once as he walked away, hopping over the narrow stream of cooling lava. There was a finality to the moment, despite his words, and I feared that would be the last I saw of him.

And I could only blame myself.

Silas had shown me exactly who he was. He fought for me, putting his life on the line without a moment's hesitation. And what had I done? Pushed him away when he'd bared his soul to me.

Even as a tear slid down my face, I didn't stop him. I wanted to beg him to stay, urge him to give us a chance. But I bit my tongue until he'd disappeared from my line of sight.

The sting of his absence was like ice in my veins.

Ithan's betrayal had paled in comparison to the anguish I felt as Silas walked away from me. My heart had already been scarred by then, part of me still closed off.

With Silas it had healed, allowing me to dream of more.

There had only been one moment that compared to this agony. The day I'd lost everything.

It had been a sweltering day, the sand against my feet hot enough to burn, but my quick footsteps hadn't lingered. The unbearable heat of the afternoon had forced the islanders to abandon all labour and seek refuge in the shade, as they often did during the summer months, only surfacing when relieved of the sun's presence. If I had been sensible, I would have joined them. But a head start had been too irresistible to pass up.

Everyone had agreed that I deserved the honour of first hunter. I was a natural with a bow, and no one had come close to my success rate. I'd even taken down a bear that threatened a neighbouring settlement. But the position wouldn't have been mine until I'd emerged victorious from the great hunt, and there had been no rules about when the competition would start.

I had been climbing a tree in the forest, hoping to use its cover to mask my presence from the wildlife, when a voice had called out to me.

"Going somewhere?"

I'd slithered down the trunk, facing Aster with a frown. My younger sister had grinned back at me, unrepentant.

"You should be sheltering from the sun," I had said.

"So, should you. But since we're both out here, can I watch?"

Her excitement had been too adorable to turn down. "Fine. But if you scare off my prey, I'm sending you home."

We'd straddled the branches of the tree as we waited. My gaze had been fixed on the forest's undergrowth, my bow drawn and ready as I'd watched the rustling leaves of a bush intently.

"Willow," Aster had said just as I'd released an arrow, the rodent scurrying away when I'd missed it by a large margin.

"What did I tell you?"

But she'd stood, holding onto the tree trunk as she faced the water.

"The sea. It's gone."

I'd been sure I'd misheard. I'd joined her, gazing out across the horizon.

But she had been right. The tide had withdrawn from where it had been moments before, revealing the ocean floor underneath. The sea was only a small line in the distance.

"Have you seen anything like it before?"

"No." I had masked my shock, keeping my voice steady, not wanting to panic her. "I'm sure there's a reasonable explanation for this. Let's head back to the village."

But Aster had still been watching the water, her mouth hanging open. "Look!"

The sea had started to return to the shore, but it was fast. Too fast.

There wasn't time to warn anyone.

The wave had speeded towards the island, growing greater in height as it surged in our direction. I had pressed my back against the trunk, climbing to Aster's side.

"Listen to me very carefully. I need you to hold on to me tightly and not let go. No matter what you see or hear, you must not let go."

"What's happening?"

The wave had become as tall as the treetops.

"I love you. I will always love you." I had hooked my arm around the tree, pressing her body against mine. Her tiny arms had hugged me as I pressed a kiss to her head.

When it hit, the wave hadn't felt like water. It had been unforgiving, like being thrown against a rock, ripping us from the trunk effortlessly. I had clung to Aster with an iron grip. I had known then that I wouldn't make it, with my body flung around in the chaos and water seeping into my lungs, but I would do anything to make sure she did.

Something solid had collided with my back, perhaps a tree, or part of someone's home. It had been impossible to tell with my eyes tightly shut. All that mattered was that it had forced my arms open, ripping Aster away from me. I had frantically reached for her, managing to grab her hand.

I had held on with every fibre of my being. *Don't let go*, I had screamed in my head. But, as the sea had continued to batter us, and black tinged my vision, her grip had loosened and she'd been stolen from me forever. The last thing I'd seen was her wide eyes, full of fear.

I'd failed her. Aster had relied on me to protect her, and now she was gone.

I had welcomed the darkness when it had finally claimed me.

I thought I'd known loss then. But watching Silas leave me after finding out the truth, rejecting everything I was when I'd just regained my hope, that caused a wound so deep I doubted I would ever recover.

Please come back. The whisper was carried away by the wind, a distant plea never to be heard by the one it was intended for.

Chapter 20

S ilas never returned.

Part of me had known when he'd asked for space that it was a flimsy excuse, but it did nothing to ease the impact of losing him.

The sun had risen, a pink light cresting over the horizon. It illuminated the wisps of smoke that danced in the sky, making it feel like a spark of magic remained in Threstia. The agony of Silas' absence faded to a dull ache that I would never be free of.

The retreating darkness was the only sign time had passed. Aside from patching up my injured shoulder to the best of my ability, I hadn't moved for a whole day, keeping my gaze fixed on the spot where I'd watched Silas leave, like at any moment he would materialise through the smoke and scoop me into his arms, his reassuring warmth enveloping me as he kissed away my remaining doubts.

But he was gone.

The world felt too quiet without him by my side. I was left alone with my spiralling thoughts, and that was a harsh place without Silas' sunshine to brighten my spirit.

He hadn't said goodbye in his desperation to leave.

I'd known this would happen, eventually. Known that when he'd understood who I truly was, it would push him away. It had all been a foolish hope, a longshot at best. And now I'd woken from the dream. He'd deserted me and I was by myself again.

Why did it feel so much worse this time?

My body protested when I finally moved, propping myself against the boulder for support. I packed up my limited supplies as quickly as I could, mourning the loss of Silas during our morning routine. The ghost of his presence haunted me, lingering just out of reach.

Seeing no point in hanging around, I walked back to the Threstian Gap. Waiting wouldn't bring him back to me, and with the lava rapidly cooling, the guards could be right on my tail. Staying put left me vulnerable, an easy target, and I was already fragile enough.

Besides, the Night Ravens needed to know what had happened in Threstia. It was my duty to give Reuben the parchment I'd stolen from the camp, relying on his wisdom for dealing with what I'd unearthed. I'd wasted enough time on sentimental matters.

Every step echoed through my bones, but I kept up the ruthless pace, ignoring the sweat crowding my brow. My breaths became strained, and my calves burned, but I marched on.

The heat of the midday sun bore down on me, sapping my strength until I couldn't avoid stopping for a rest. I blinked. With my aggressive speed, I was able to reach the outskirts of the Threstian Gap in half the time it had taken me with Silas. I had no recollection of the journey, not with the monotony of the unremarkable scenery, everything blending together in a confusing blur. Only my turbulent thoughts had left their mark on my mind.

Water trickled down my parched throat, and I mopped the sweat from my brow with my ash-covered sleeve. Pushing through the brutal heat was an option, but it wasn't worth suffering from sunstroke and slowing my journey by days.

The only shade came from a nearby crop of rocks, the shadow it cast almost too small to shield me. I pressed myself against the largest boulder, grateful for the cool relief it provided from the afternoon sun.

At some point, I dozed off. Without the adrenaline coursing through my veins, there was nothing to stop the events of Threstia from catching up with me, my body unable to fight the resulting fatigue. Fortunately, no one discovered me, but I reprimanded myself for the rookie error.

Silas wasn't there to watch my back and cover my slip ups anymore. I had to be perfect.

The air was much cooler after waking, making it possible to continue. Soon, the chasm loomed before me, as daunting as it had been the first time. A shiver slithered down my spine at the memory of crossing with Silas, how close we'd come to plummeting into the darkness.

Bidding farewell to half of Threstia felt like closing the chapter on my mission, leaving behind everything that had transpired. Instead, my focus shifted to returning as swiftly as possible with the information I carefully guarded, no more distractions.

I should've known it wouldn't be so simple.

The first sign something was wrong was the absence of the bridge we'd used to cross. It had been fragile even then, but my brow furrowed as I examined what was left on the cliff side. The only remnants of its existence were the rusted metal posts that had once anchored it to the ground. The rope, the wooden planks, everything had gone. This was no accident, a case of the frayed rope finally giving out.

Someone had tampered with it.

An unsettling feeling gripped my stomach. Had the guards cut off the escape route? They would've had to cross the lava and overtake me while I'd slept; not impossible, but highly unlikely. Had Silas crossed before it was destroyed? I grimaced. There would be another bridge, a failsafe, but I'd have to find it myself, delaying my journey further.

I picked up a rock and flung it as hard as I could into the chasm, my scream echoing through the valley. One thing. Why couldn't one thing go my way?

Whoever had sabotaged it couldn't have gone far. They could be waiting in the shadows for me to fall into their trap. I had to be prepared for that possibility. I drew my bow, holding it ready in my hand.

Keeping the Threstian Gap to one side, I surveyed every inch of my surroundings while I searched for another bridge. My background had shocked Silas. Could he have been the one to destroy it, knowing it would slow me down until he escaped?

My heart ached at the thought. Who could blame him? I was a complicated mess, and it was dangerous to be involved with me. He would've had to forsake everything he knew.

I wasn't worth that.

A noise behind me had me aiming my bow at the intruder.

A head of silky black hair strolled towards me; the experienced scout's arms outstretched in greeting. He was the last fae I'd expected to see.

I lowered my bow. "Norwyn? I thought you were missing. You didn't return from your mission."

"There were…complications, something you appear to be familiar with." He gestured to the smoking volcano, visible in the distance, his brown eyes crinkling in amusement behind his round spectacles.

"What are you doing here?" My mind couldn't reconcile the image of him standing next to me, Norwyn acting as if we'd casually crossed paths in the Old Keep, with the depressing scenery of Threstia. He wore identical clothing to me, a plain shirt and brown trousers, but where on me it was awkward and ill-fitting, he made it seem respectable.

"Reuben sent me. He got your note and wanted you to have backup if things got ugly. Turns out he had no reason to worry. Nice work."

I'd forgotten all about the note I'd asked Cassandra to send for me, back when I'd first decided to stray from my orders. It was a relief it had reached Reuben, but sending Norwyn all the way out here, when his expertise was highly sought after? It was strange, even for him.

"Sit down. I can tell you're exhausted. When was the last time you ate anything?" He rifled through his pack as I perched on one of the many stones that peppered the ground, handing me a canteen of fresh water and a cloth stuffed with something. I unwrapped it, finding hard cheese and dried strips of meat inside.

"Eat. You'll need your strength for the journey back," he said in a way that left no room for debate.

"Is he angry?" I asked, guzzling down the liquid, letting it soothe my dry throat.

"Why would he be angry? You've shown initiative. I wish more of the scouts would. Everyone's too afraid to step out of line. But when Reuben realised where you were going, he freaked out. The day

I returned to the Old Keep, he sent me straight after you. I hitched a ride on the High Road and followed your tracks from there."

"I thought I hid those."

He smirked. "Not well enough for me."

"Wait, did you say the High Road? Did you happen to see any nobles along the way?" I asked.

"No. Why do you ask?"

"No reason." I kept my mouth shut, not wanting to share that particular story with him yet.

Norwyn didn't notice my awkwardness, unwrapping his own parcel of food. "I remember the first time I took a step up. I was terrified. Kept thinking about all the ways I could mess up. Thought maybe Reuben had misplaced his trust in me."

"What happened?" I asked. Norwyn and Calliste had always seemed infallible. I couldn't imagine him plagued by the same uncertainty as I was.

"I aced it. Just like you have, by the sounds of it."

"I had a lot of help along the way," I said. It wasn't my victory alone. It had been Silas' too, wherever he was. My hand clenched into a fist.

"A true scout uses all the resources at their disposal," Norwyn said, mimicking Reuben's deep voice. He cocked his head at me. "Why are you trying to deflect the praise? I don't give it out freely, you know."

"In that case, I appreciate the recognition." I devoured the food he'd given me, feeling the lingering grip of hunger when I'd finished. Still, it was better than the dull pain in my stomach I'd become used to.

"I must say, I didn't expect this of you. I'd heard that you were stubborn, wilful, unbearably hostile. I thought it would be years before you were ready for more responsibility. What changed?"

"I met someone. They helped me see things differently, or at least they did while it lasted." I buried my feelings deep down before they could threaten to destroy me.

"It's the way of the scout. This lifestyle isn't well-suited for anything long-term," Norwyn said.

His confirmation settled in my chest. It was as I'd always known. I folded the cloth into a neat square before handing it back to him.

"Why were you back so late, anyway?" I said.

He chuckled. "I got caught sneaking into the caves of Drei. The Chief wouldn't release me until I'd bested her strongest fighters in the pits. And then I proved my worth to her in other ways. I think she secretly likes me."

"You're not supposed to share the details of your missions with me. It's forbidden." Every scout knew that. It was drilled into us from the moment we started our training.

"Who said anything about a mission? When you've been doing this as long as I have, you figure out how to have fun too."

"But the Night Ravens..."

"Are my priority, as they will always be. Don't question my loyalty. I complete my missions to the highest standard, but what's the point in a better world if we neglect ourselves to achieve it?"

I frowned. "But that's always been the way."

"That's Reuben's way. I've known him a long time, and he's always used work to distract himself. You don't have to follow his example."

"What are you suggesting?" I climbed to my feet, finding myself restless at the implications of his words.

Norwyn stood beside me. "Nothing. You know your own mind. But you're young and there's a whole world out there. Don't lose your chance to explore it just to please a bitter man who cuddles his scrolls for company. Serve the Night Ravens well, but make it serve you too."

I didn't know what to say to that.

Norwyn took my silence as a sign our rest was over. "We should cross the chasm while we still have light. The Old Keep is a fair distance away."

"You're coming with me?" Surely, he had better things to do with his time?

His eyebrows rose. "Why? You don't want an escort?"

"It's nothing like that. It's just…" I hesitated, stumbling over my words. "For decades, I've heard tales of your heroics. Working together is an honour, and I haven't wrapped my head around it just yet."

He chuckled, the sound echoing around us. "The shine will wear off soon, I assure you. I snore, I complain when my legs get tired, and I can't start a campfire to save my life."

"Ah," I said. "About that…"

Darkness had started to fall once we'd found a second bridge. This one looked more secure, more of its wood remaining intact and the rope reassuringly thick where it was fastened to the posts. Norwyn didn't give me a chance to think about it, striding across so quickly I nearly missed it. I hurried after him, ignoring the swaying sensation beneath my feet and jumping over the planks two at a time, desperate to not appear cowardly in front of him.

I stopped dead on the other side, panic rising within me.

Scorch marks marred the earth in every direction, like an inferno had blazed through Threstia, leaving nothing but destruction behind. The rock was blackened with soot, staining my skin as I ran my hands along it, rubbing the residue between my fingertips. It was cold to the touch, the fire long burned out.

Only one fae had the power needed for something like that. Silas.

There had been a struggle. The signs of it were obvious with every glimpse of the charred ground, the burn marks scattered and interrupted. He'd thrown the last morsel of magic he had remaining at his attackers, but based on the way the streaks trailed away from the bridge, he hadn't been successful.

He hadn't left me.

The realisation thrummed through me, waking me from a deep slumber. I felt alive, revived, colour returning to the world. He'd spoken truly, going for a walk to clear his head when he'd been ambushed.

My relief was short-lived as fear took hold. Who had taken him?

Silas was in trouble, and only I could save him.

"I can't go with you," I said to Norwyn. "There's something I need to do first."

His features darkened, all traces of amusement vanishing. "I wasn't aware that I'd given you a choice."

Chapter 21

My stomach lurched like I was still on the bridge as it swung back and forth. I took a step away from Norwyn, assessing the terrain for advantages. There were the hills surrounding us, the rockslide, now half-cleared and crumbling in places, and a few loose stones on the ground. "But you just said…"

"I know exactly what I said. But Reuben will skin me alive if I return without you. He's a stubborn bastard. I wouldn't put it past him to reassign me to training duty for a few months out of spite, and I happen to appreciate my freedom."

I raised my voice, unable to contain the emotion welling up inside me. "You don't understand. My friend's in danger and he needs me."

"I'm sure he can fend for himself. You need to focus on your mission right now. After that, you can look for your friend." He moved towards me, closing the gap between us.

"No. Because of him, I succeeded. I'm not leaving him behind." I never would again. "I made a bargain, but more than that, I made a promise."

"You know that we can't save everyone," Norwyn reminded me.

Those words might have convinced me before, an echo of what I'd been told every time I'd tried to go beyond the scope of my orders. But I'd changed. I'd met Silas, his light brightening my world in a way I hadn't known I'd needed. All it took was one look at the scorched ground for my resolve to harden.

I would fight for him. I would always fight for him, now and forever.

"He isn't everyone. He's *everything*," I said, needing him to understand. "He revealed himself to his enemies to save my life, and now he's in danger. It's my fault."

Norwyn grabbed my arm, his grip painful as he wrenched me towards him.

"Let me go," I said, shaking him off with difficulty.

"And if I don't?" His voice was dangerous, testing me.

I reached for my bow.

He laughed. "You'll shoot me? That's a new one. What are you going to do? Drag my body back to Reuben?"

Would I go that far? My hand shook. "I will, if you try to stop me."

There were no bounds to what I would do to ensure Silas was safe.

"You don't have the guts," Norwyn said.

"Then you don't know me at all. The guilt I'd feel over hurting you pales in comparison to the agony losing him would inflict. There's nothing in this world that could prevent me from going after him. I would suffer an eternity of the torture that forged my worst memories to have him back by my side."

"You're a fool," he said, making to grab me again. I swerved, dodging his arm, and used the momentum to scoop a rock from rubble.

Time slowed, and I realised what I needed to do.

"I'm sorry," I whispered as I smashed the rock against of Norwyn's head, the force of the impact sending vibrations through my hand. His legs buckled from beneath him as he lost consciousness, hitting the ground with a thud.

Breathing heavily, I stared at his limp body. The hit had been clumsy, leaving an angry red bump. Checking his wrist for a pulse, I was relieved to find it beating strongly against my fingers. He'd wake up with a hell of a headache, but he would wake up, at least.

I was in for a world of trouble when I returned to the Old Keep, if they let me back in. For all I knew, I'd be branded a traitor, exiled forever. But I would gladly take any punishment once I knew Silas was out of harm's way.

Dragging Norwyn's body by his legs, I hid him behind a boulder, sheltered from view. It was better to play it safe, even though I doubted anyone would pass by this close to the Threstian Gap.

I hesitated for a moment. Norwyn had earned his reputation for excellence over the years. Was knocking him unconscious enough to prevent him from following me and dragging me back, kicking and screaming?

Likely not.

I carefully prised the spectacles from his head, tucking them into my pocket, trying not to imagine his face when he realised what I'd done. They'd hear him cursing my name from Hightower.

Burying the worry of what awaited me at the Old Keep, I set off to save my partner. My friend.

I'm coming for you, Silas.

I'd already wasted too much time; every second counted. He had been terrified at the prospect of being discovered, the thought filling me with dread, but I couldn't let that discourage me.

I hopped over the scattered remnants of the rockslide, watching my footing as I searched for clues in the dark. In Threstia it was easy, each subtle change in the scenery another piece of the puzzle. But after that?

Silas' attackers could have taken him anywhere. I was a capable scout, but there were limits to my abilities. Once I reached the High Road, it would be difficult to decipher whether they'd headed north or south, with any tracks soon eroded by the constant footfall. If someone was determined to remain hidden, I would stand little chance of finding them, and one wrong move could seal his fate.

My concern grew with every step, knowing the odds were stacked against me.

But what if someone *wanted* to be found?

My fingers found the amulet still hanging around my neck. I exhaled a relieved breath, ripping it off me and clutching it in my fist. The seeking stone.

After everything, would Silas want to see me? We'd left on frosty terms, the steely expression on his face lingering in my mind. The artefact could reject the connection, a final shard in the ruin of my soul.

It rested in my hand, feeling as warm as his skin, and hope rose up in me. I knew. His heart sung to mine, every beat sending an answering pulse of heat to the stone. It bonded us, stronger than any bargain, and I knew for certain the artefact would lead me to him.

I pressed it against my heart, thinking of Silas, recalling the way his mouth curved up in a smirk when he was about to misbehave, how his eyes burned when he summoned his fire, how he'd felt so right cuddled up against me. I poured the very essence of him into the seeking stone, willing for it to find him.

A tugging sensation made me loosen my grip. The amulet glowed with a pink light as it rose from my hand, floating in the air ahead of me and lighting my way. I moved towards it, the artefact bobbing away at equal speed. It had worked. It had actually worked!

"Thank you," I said, like it was perfectly normal to speak to a stone. It seemed to shine even brighter in response.

I set off in a sprint, following the pink light over the rocky ground. It twisted left and right, the lines carved into its face pointing me to Silas' position, correcting my course as I crossed into the grasslands.

The darkness lifted with the arrival of morning, and I realised I'd travelled through the night, but still, I didn't stop. I desperately needed to rest, even for a little while, but I pressed on regardless. Every moment mattered if I stood a chance of catching up with Silas' captors.

Even the High Road posed no challenge, besides a short pause to let a carriage pass.

It wasn't until the next afternoon, when I was close to breaking, that I saw them. The seeking stone hummed happily before dropping into my palm.

A dozen fae had set up camp in the grassy plains that separated the Travellers' Rest from Threstia in a secluded area. It was meticulously organised, three tents pitched in a row, and next to them, a campfire where most of them gathered. Silas was bound at the centre, but alive at least.

The men surrounding him wore emerald uniforms bearing a golden emblem I didn't recognise, the crest of a noble family. What did they want with the Lord of Eirel?

A thicket provided me with all the cover I needed. I crept closer, shrouding my presence with the leaves. Fighting sleep as it stubbornly tried to claim me, I laid on the ground, listening to the sounds of the camp. There were the low voices of the fae, the crackling of the fire as slabs of meat cooked above it, and the clinking of goblets as they congratulated each other on a job well done. I was alert, poised to take in anything that would help me rescue Silas.

"Imagine having everything you could ever want and throwing it all away to go to Threstia, of all places." The guard spoke as if Silas wasn't there, snorting. "Not too bright, this one, is he?"

"That's what happens when you never learn the word no. Does 'em no good. I told my wife the same thing. Coddling them only creates spoilt brats."

"Makes you despair, doesn't it? The leader of Eirel, a runaway. We're screwed."

I winced. Silas had told me himself he'd needed to escape, that his life had been at risk, but I'd been too angry to see it as more than an excuse. The enemy who had captured him, the ones he was so terrified of, were his own guard.

All this time, he'd been fleeing home. I'd given him so much grief for his grand adventure, when he'd had no choice but to follow me on my mission, with nowhere else to go. I'd been so harsh to him. Guilt tightened my stomach.

I had to save him. No one fled a privileged life without reason. His desire to leave had outweighed the risk of being caught. Silas must have been desperate.

"The council will whip him into shape. They have no choice, not when Valeria is next in line. Their claim to power hinges on having him within their possession. Without him, there will be a challenge."

That was why they'd stopped at nothing to capture him. He was valuable to them, solely for his position. I clenched my fist. No wonder he'd been so betrayed by the thought of me spying on him.

Even with my skill with a bow, I'd be foolish to take on so many guards by myself with only three arrows remaining. I was vastly outnumbered. I'd only succeed with Silas on my side, and for that I'd need to free him without them realising.

I assessed the camp from my hiding spot. It was open, vulnerable. They'd assumed with their numbers they were protected. There's no need for additional security if you intimidate any would-be ambushers. Their arrogance provided me with a golden opportunity, one I'd be foolish not to pursue.

I smiled, formulating a plan.

Silas would have his revenge on those who had wronged him. And I would be only too happy to assist.

My body was stiff with inaction, the price to pay for my rapid journey to him. I stretched my neck, earning a little relief.

The guards only grew more complacent as the night wore on. Some were already drunk, staggering around the camp and roaring with laughter as they toppled over each other. Even those abstaining weren't keeping watch, huddled over maps and discussing things in hushed tones. It was like they'd forgotten Silas was there, their job complete now they'd retrieved him. All that remained was to celebrate their victory.

It sharpened my determination. Showing such little regard for their leader was unforgiveable; they didn't deserve the honour of wearing their uniforms.

I crept closer, maintaining my usual levels of stealth. Tonight was my window. All routes leading to Eirel would be too busy for any rescue attempts, but here, secluded from the main path, I could strike without causing a scene.

I listened carefully, hoping for a morsel of information that could aid my plans. Luckily, the alcohol had loosened their lips, Silas' captors speaking so loudly it wasn't a strain to overhear them.

"Do you reckon we'll be rewarded for this? We braved Threstia and grabbed him without being incinerated."

"Are you joking? The Master of Coin is a stingy bastard."

"Then what's stopping us from ransoming him off? I'm sure someone would pay a pretty penny for him. With the lord in your possession, you can control Eirel."

The other uniformed man slapped the back of his head. "That's treason, you idiot. Keep your voice down or you'll be headed straight for the prisons. I've seen the state of them. They reek of piss and desperation. Trust me, you don't want to mess with the council."

"I was just saying!"

Silas had sat up at some point, his hands still bound behind his back, suppressing his magic. His head was tilted downwards, gaze on the grass and shoulders slumped. Defeated.

It was agony to see him like this. There was no spark left in him; his spirit broken. I shook, struggling to contain my rage. They would not get away with this. Silas would never return to Eirel against his wishes. I would make sure of that.

Notice me, please, I willed, watching from the shadows. My plan wouldn't work without his involvement. I risked more exposure, peeking out of the bushes while keeping a careful eye on the guards.

Come on, notice me.

As if he'd heard me, Silas' head snapped up. A symphony of emotions played out on his face. Surprise, relief, gratitude, and something else I couldn't place.

Then he winked.

Only Silas would consider a wink an appropriate response to the dire situation. Despite what they'd done to him, he was still in there. Any remaining doubts evaporated, leaving me with the quiet confidence I relied on during missions.

He shifted imperceptibly, clearing my shot. I waited, biding my time, the guards casting occasional glances his way. The minutes stretched by, punctuated by my steady breaths. Soon. Silas held his position, his gaze roving over the camp, marking every inch of the terrain.

Another round of ale was poured. A heated argument broke out between two men before they were separated. Another carved the roasted meat. Still, I waited.

Then the meal was served, drawing the guards' attention as they jostled for the prime cuts. It was the window I needed. Now, more than ever, I was sure my aim would not fail.

My arrow raced through the air in a perfect arc, slicing through Silas' bindings without so much as leaving a mark. His answering smile was dazzling. Fire danced in his eyes, the most beautiful sight I could have asked for.

He erupted. It was impossible to work out where the flames began, and he ended. He was magnificent, a phoenix rising from the ashes of his captivity, spreading his fiery wings.

An inferno blazed through the camp, a wave of fire that incinerated everything in its path. Most of the guards burned to ash where they sat drinking and laughing. A few reacted quicker and had tried in vain to run screaming from the flames. I put them out of their misery quickly, making the most out of my final two arrows.

Their blood was on my hands, a burden I would carry with me until my last breath, but it was the only way.

My heart thudded wildly as Silas emerged from the blaze. He was vengeance, promising ruin and salvation, and I wanted it all.

The glow of the fire faded until only Silas was left, still smouldering. There was nothing left of the uniformed men, only the charred remains of their camp. I suppressed a shiver.

"Well, aren't you a sight for sore eyes?" he said, wearing his trademark smirk. It didn't quite reach his eyes, but it softened me all the same.

I collided with him, my bow falling from my hand, hugging him tightly and inhaling his smoky scent. He winced at my touch, but grasped me tighter.

"I thought you'd left me," I croaked into his neck. I couldn't believe he was here, and just as relieved to see me as I was to be reunited with him.

"I could never do that. You mean too much to me."

He tilted his head towards mine, but grimaced.

I stopped him with a hand against his chest, easing open the neckline of his shirt. My fingers hovered over the angry bruises that coloured him, the sight of them stealing my breath. "You're hurt. We should wait."

"If I have to wait another moment to kiss you, I'm going to lose my mind."

He claimed my lips with his, a desperate kiss that left me lightheaded. I kissed him back with equal fervour. It didn't feel like enough, too many things left unsaid between us.

Silas rested his head on mine. "I didn't see them coming. I thought they'd whisk me away to Eirel before you realised I was missing."

"They nearly did. It was the scorch marks; I wouldn't have known if it weren't for them." It had been the sign I'd needed, the reassurance that he hadn't left me. "I should never have doubted you."

"They bound my hands, stopping me from wielding my Blessing. It was suffocating. When you freed me, I could barely control the flames. It was like they had a life of their own."

"I'm just glad you're safe." I pressed my lips to his neck. "Silas. I'm so sorry for all those things I said. I should have given you a chance to explain. Will you ever forgive me?"

His hand brushed my cheek, the touch so soft it made me shiver. "You came for me. That's all that matters. You saved me from a fate worse than death. I'm eternally in your debt."

"Let's call it even," I said, finally allowing myself to grin. We had really done it. "Don't you dare leave me again."

"Never."

This kiss was hungrier, the raw need in it causing heat to pool between my thighs. Silas' breath was ragged in my ear, drawing a gasp from me with scorching kisses and a scrape of his teeth on my neck. Burning hands roved over me, settling on my lower back.

I wanted him. It was no longer the curious desire of my growing attraction, a way to release the tension that threatened to boil over. No. I wanted us to be joined together, body and soul, two parts of a whole. I wanted nothing between us, no secrets, no skin left unexplored, no part of him left undiscovered. I wanted to breathe in his scent and let it envelop me. I wanted to claim him with soft kisses and teasing touches and make him mine forever.

But most of all, I wanted him. The easy smiles and the shadows that stole them, the witty retorts and the vulnerabilities they masked, his fierce loyalty and the fears he couldn't face. I wanted all of him.

When we broke apart, it felt too soon.

I plucked an arrow from the body of a guard, returning it to my quiver, before walking over to a second. Two arrows protecting two souls against the dangers of Idrix. We'd faced worse odds. "We should talk. About Us. About the future. No more secrets."

"I'd like nothing more." A cough wracked his body, and he clutched his side in pain. "But later, once we've both had some much needed rest."

"You can say that again," I said, cleaning my arrows on a rag, feeling an ache in my bones that would take weeks to abate. "Now that we're safe, I could sleep for days." The reckoning I would face when I delivered my report could wait that long, at least.

"Safe, for now. The High Council of Eirel won't stop looking for me." I heard Silas say. "They need me in their possession to keep ruling in my name. Those guards will only be the start."

But I was rendered incapable of responding. Strong arms closed around me, their grip holding steady as I fought against them, a sharp object pressed against the sensitive skin of my throat.

"Very perceptive. But it appears we've found you, after all."

Chapter 22

Silas' face distorted into something animalistic. I braced myself for a blast of heat, but when he summoned his flames, they spluttered out weakly, wisps of smoke coiling upward. I shivered. After the demands of the past few days, his magic was drained, and with it, the last of my hope.

The blade against my neck was cold, melting where it met the warmth of my skin. Ice? It didn't make it any less effective, a stinging sensation where it pierced me. Unless I wanted my throat spilled open, I would have to keep completely still, biting my tongue to curb the temptation of speaking my mind.

No hand wielded the blade. Instead, the intruder used his to pin my arms against my side, the deathly-sharp icicle suspended in the air as it threatened me.

The control needed to use a Water Blessing with such pinpoint precision was unheard of, an expert's touch.

Could I melt the weapon? I pressed my skin against it as much as I dared, clenching my jaw as I endured the cold bite of the ice. A single droplet trickled down my neck in response. Not much, but a start.

"I have to commend you. I was convinced we'd find your body in the Valari Woodlands, picked apart by wild animals. Consider me impressed," the voice said. He sounded regal, every word properly enunciated.

"Mirthal. So, the council sent their attack dog?" Silas said, sneering, but his shoulders were stiff, his hand shaking slightly. "Sorry about your guards. They suppressed my Blessing and paid the price."

Mirthal didn't rise to the bait. "It's time for this absurdity to end. Come back to the Isle of Mist where you belong."

"I'm not going anywhere with you," Silas said through clenched teeth.

"So brave to say that with my blade lodged against her throat. It would be easy to kill her, so satisfying to watch it tear you apart while you can only stand by helplessly. But she's your weakness, isn't she? With her in my possession, I bet you'd be an obedient puppet." He realised that his weapon had lost its edge, reforming the ice to a sharp point with a wave of his fingers, scuppering my escape plan.

"Let her go."

"Really now, Silas? This is what you've been reduced to? A pity. I thought you were better than this," Mirthal said.

"If you lay a finger on her, I will burn you alive. Your blood will boil, the skin will melt from your bones, and the last thing you'll do is beg me for the relief of death."

Mirthal chuckled, the movement making the shard of ice graze me, pain licking at my skin. "Glad to see you finally grew a backbone. Who knew you had it in you?"

Silas' eyes found mine, and I was struck by the certainty reflected in them. "I found what I needed all along. Someone who would fight for me."

He deserved so much more than that. He deserved someone who would burn the world for him.

"See, this was always your problem. Ever since you were a boy, you've had a soft heart, and it made you weak. You don't have the guts to do what's necessary for Eirel to prosper. It's a pity we had to take matters into our own hands, but we can't risk our reputation."

"So you locked me away, using me as you needed. But that wasn't enough for you, was it? I discovered your plot. Tell me, were you at least going to wait for the ink to dry on the wedding records before assassinating me?"

I stiffened in a way that had nothing to do with the icicle. Silas had told me his life was in danger, that it had been his reason for running away, but I hadn't realised the extent of it.

"It's regrettable. Death is messy and Eirel's experienced far too much of it. It was Faralt's plan, but he had our unanimous support. You would've made Eirel soft, an easy target for our enemies. We couldn't stand by and let that happen."

"Then I ruined everything by running away. How inconvenient of me." Silas was unrepentant, a dark expression crossing his face.

Mirthal's grip on me tightened. "I admit, the nobility grows weary of our excuses for your absence. Valeria, in particular, has been a colossal pain, questioning your whereabouts at every opportunity."

My mouth twitched at that. The more I heard about Valeria, the more I liked her.

"She'd never allow you to control her. That's what you're worried about, isn't it? I'm the key to your plans. With me, you can rule in my name, passing down the title to a noble family of your choosing. But if Valeria succeeds me, she'd fight you at every turn. You'd lose everything you've worked for."

"Which is exactly why that won't be happening. Now will you come quietly or are you going to make a scene? Because it would bring me great pleasure to slit your little girlfriend's throat."

"If I return to Eirel, it will be on my own terms," Silas said.

"Don't be foolish. Come with me and I'll let your friend go. Otherwise, I'll have no choice but to force your hand, and you know I deliver on my threats."

Silas wavered, the grasslands around us subdued as the words sunk in. "And what will happen if I do? I'll return, the wedding goes ahead, and you kill me off as planned? Hardly a compelling offer."

"Negotiations only work when you have leverage. And right now, I'm the one who holds it all," Mirthal said flatly.

"That's where you're mistaken." The confidence Silas exuded stoked the dying embers of my hope. "Without me, your plan falls apart. I'd consider that to be significant leverage."

For the nobility, perception was power, a balanced scale that could shift at the lightest touch. And right now, Mirthal was using me to weigh Silas down.

I assessed our surroundings, searching for anything that would be advantageous. My eyes fell on my bow, buried in the tall grass, out of reach.

It was now or never.

"Pull the string taut," I rasped, the ice biting into the soft skin of my neck. I winced at the pain, but the precious words had been worth it.

Silas' gaze flitted to the bow, as I hoped it would, two arrows in the quiver resting beside it.

Two arrows were more than enough with the right aim.

Mirthal continued, unaware of our silent exchange. "If that's what you truly believe, come back and negotiate. Besides, I'm sure the rest of the council will be fascinated by the tale of your escape. You would have succeeded if not for your trick with the volcano. We will find many uses for your newly developed powers."

Silas nodded, but the gesture was for me, not Mirthal.

At the signal, I stomped on Mirthal's foot, hard. He was too experienced to do more than slightly loosen his grip, but that didn't matter. I'd known it hadn't been enough to escape his hold, but that wasn't my intent.

My bid for freedom had drawn his attention for a split-second, just long enough for Silas to dive for the bow.

Two arrows sailed through the air in quick succession, finding their mark. As the first pierced Mirthal's left hand, I shifted. The ice blade vanished as his concentration waned, allowing me to free myself in the commotion. The second cut through his right hand, fully neutralising the threat of his Blessing.

Mirthal snarled as arrows protruded from his hands, blood dripping onto the ground as he tried in vain to remove them.

"Forgot to mention, I've had some additional training while I've been out here. Very useful when one's Blessing is taking a short rest," Silas said.

"It was a beautiful shot," I said to him, rushing to his side.

"Thank you. I had a great teacher."

"You're making a terrible mistake," Mirthal growled.

"No. I don't think I am."

"What are we going to do with him?" I whispered to Silas. "We can't leave him here."

He was a loose end, a threat to Silas' very existence. I wanted nothing more than to kill him with my bare hands. But it wasn't up to me. It was his choice and I couldn't make it for him.

I knew little of the political intricacies of Eirel. If I followed my instincts, made one misstep, I could cause him further suffering. So instead, I held my tongue, awaiting Silas' decision.

He drew himself up to his full height, and it was the Lord of Eirel who spoke. "We're in need of a messenger. Make a bargain with us, and we'll spare your life."

I turned to him in surprise.

"And just why would I agree to that?" Mirthal said, looking as confused as I was.

Silas gestured to the grasslands, their vast emptiness unnerving even now. "We could leave you here. How long would it take for your hands to heal enough to regain your Blessing. Hours? Days? You'd never catch up to us, and we'd be the least of your concerns."

"What are you proposing?"

"I'll remove the arrows, on the strict agreement you won't follow us. Instead, you will travel directly to Eirel, taking the slowest route. There, of course, you will inform the High Council of what transpired here, that Silas Stormbook is a force to be reckoned with and won't return without a fight."

"And if I refuse?"

Silas' eyes narrowed. "You're wrong about me. My soft heart doesn't make me weak, it makes me dangerous, because now I have something to lose. You've yet to discover the lengths I'd go to when protecting it."

Mirthal glared daggers at Silas, my partner smirking at him in response.

After a heavy moment, he nodded. "Very well. I accept your terms. This isn't over though. We will come for you."

"I'm counting on it," Silas said.

Threads of light wound around their arms, binding them to the bargain.

Silas removed the arrows, though he did it excruciatingly slowly, relishing Mirthal's agony.

"You'll live to regret this," Mirthal said as he retreated, blood dripping from his open wounds. "Enjoy your freedom while it lasts."

Silas' hand clenched into a fist as he watched him leave.

"Was that wise? Won't they come after you?" I asked Silas, once Mirthal had disappeared into the distance.

"The council needs me for their plans. They'd hunt me regardless of whether Mirthal returned. But this way, they know I'm a threat. They won't risk coming after me until they're confident of success, and by then, we'll be long gone."

"What if there's more of them already out there?"

He shook his head. "There won't be. The High Council is conservative, only taking action when it can't be overtly traced back to them. Mirthal commands Eirel's forces. Sending him here was a huge risk. They'll be monitoring the result."

"In that case, we should get out of here," I said.

"The inn isn't far." He looked at me properly, noticing the condition I was in for the first time. "No offense, but you look like you haven't slept for a week and I'm not faring much better."

With the adrenaline of finding him wearing off, the aches in my body were no longer something I could ignore. I could sleep for days.

It had all been worth it, with Silas by my side, but I couldn't shake the uncertainty of what the future held for us.

I had my mission to complete, bringing the evidence to the Old Keep and facing the consequences of my actions. Silas had the Eirelean High Council to deal with, not to mention his responsibilities as lord. Then there were the remaining terms of our bargain, unbreakable without angering the gods. He had fulfilled his end, helping me with my task, but I was still bound to him for as long as he needed me.

Everything was a mess.

There was also the question of us, together. There was no denying the depths of our feelings, the lengths we'd go to to keep each other safe, but there were practicalities to consider. A scout working for a secret organisation and the Lord of Eirel, one of the most powerful territories in Idrix.

Could we really make it work?

Chapter 23

We moved slowly, Silas leaning his weight on me as we stumbled towards the Traveller's Rest. He winced with every step, my lingering guilt about his captors' fate soon eclipsed by concern about his condition. I needed to examine his injuries properly.

"Never imagined myself as a damsel in distress, but this isn't so bad," he said.

There it was, that enduring ability of his to bring light to the darkest situations. Even now, when he could barely stand, he was trying to cheer me up.

"Does that make me your knight in shining armour?" I replied, helping Silas up the steps to the inn carefully.

He grinned, his laughter swallowed by a hoarse cough. "You can be whatever you'd like. I do enjoy the sound of you in armour, though. We should swing by Gladhaven while we're here."

"Then we must also buy you a beautiful gown, so you may be the damsel of my dreams," I quipped.

Silas' eyes lit up in delight. "You spoil me."

The inn was much quieter than it had been on our last visit. This time, only a handful of tables were occupied, mainly by merchants and a group of excitable adventurers, their chatter echoing around the common room.

I ignored them, heading straight to the bar. The innkeeper paused her work of wiping down the gleaming counter to acknowledge us.

"We need two rooms," I said, more bluntly than I'd intended. She pursed her lips but turned towards the shelf where the keys were hanging up in order, the inn fully vacant.

"No, just the one, please," Silas said, pushing two silvers across the bar.

"That's presumptuous of you," I said, deadpan.

The tips of his ears pinkened as he spluttered. "That's not what I...I didn't-"

The same man had kissed me like he was going to ravage me only a few hours before. Was he worried he'd offended me with the assumption?

I put him out of his misery with a smile. "I know, but it's fun to tease."

"You don't know the half of it." His voice was a dark promise that rekindled the desire he'd stoked earlier. Anticipation coiled through me.

The innkeeper rolled her eyes, pressing a key into Silas' palm before busying herself anywhere else.

We were far from graceful, drawing the attention of everyone in the inn with the racket we made as we manoeuvred up the stairs to our room, Silas still leaning on me for support. His whimpers of pain set my teeth on edge, but putting him through the ordeal was a necessary evil.

When we finally made it, it was all we could do to collapse on the bed. It was a small upgrade to my previous lodgings. The dated interior prevailed, but this room was more spacious, boasting a larger bed, table and chairs, and a bathtub tucked behind a screen.

I blushed when my brain caught up to the fact that I was lying next to Silas, our sweaty bodies pressed together and both of us breathless. I sat up, letting my legs dangle off the edge of the bed. As much as I wanted to follow that train of thought, there were things I needed to take care of first.

"Take off your shirt," I ordered.

"If you want me to strip, you have to ask nicely."

We weren't in any condition to act on those urges, but it didn't prevent me from remembering Silas naked in the pool, my cheeks heating at the memory.

"If I desired it, I wouldn't be asking nicely. You would be begging me to undress you when I was through with you," I said before I could stop myself. He knew exactly how to provoke a response from me.

Heat flared in his eyes.

Focus.

"I need to check your injuries to make sure they can heal," I managed to say.

Silas looked like he wanted to argue, but thought better of it, his arms flexing as he pulled his shirt over his head.

His broad chest was covered in bruises, sending a fresh wave of rage through me. It was a good job his captors were already dead.

I wouldn't have been responsible for my actions if I'd encountered them again.

He whimpered as my fingers brushed over one, tracing the outline. His skin was hot, burning beneath my hesitant touch. Black and blue marks covered his torso, an explosion of sadistic violence that left no part of him unblemished.

I could feel every punch and kick as if I'd been the one beaten.

There were no cuts to clean and dress. They'd been careful to only leave evidence that would heal by the time he returned to Eirel. Their cruelty was cold, calculated, everything I'd come to associate with the Isle of Mist.

I pressed a delicate kiss to the tender skin of his shoulder. "I'm sorry. There isn't anything I can do to ease the pain beyond letting you rest."

"You saved me. You've already done more than enough."

"You saved me too. Not just from Mirthal or the Hightower nobles, but from myself." I grasped his hand, interlocking our fingers together, his steady warmth spreading through me. "Did Mirthal speak the truth? You escaped Eirel because they plotted to assassinate you?"

Silas nodded. "It started when my brother died, the day we both lost everything. I rarely saw my father, and he did the bare minimum to recognise me as his heir. I was never enough. Once, he told me he wished it had been me who was caught in the storm, not my brother."

I had no words for that, squeezing his hand tightly.

"When my father died, the High Council were quick to swoop in, promising support. They convinced me I was too inexperienced to rule, that my decisions would harm Eirel, and I should leave it in their capable hands. After everything, it wasn't hard to believe." Tears glistened at the edge of his eyelids, threatening to spill over. "I became reliant on them, believing I had to follow their guidance if I wanted Eirel to thrive. Valeria set me straight, after months of trying to get through to me, but when I tried to fight back, they imprisoned me in my chambers, only letting me out for superficial functions where I couldn't derail their plans."

"They were wrong about you," I said. "You would be a fair and compassionate ruler."

"I can see that now, with perspective. But when every voice you hear is critical, you internalise it until your own voice becomes just as cutting. I lost faith in myself."

He shuffled on the bed, propping himself up with a pillow. "The night I ran away, Valeria brought me evidence of the plot. I realised they wanted more than a pawn; they wanted everything. I was to be married off to the daughter of one of my advisors, then assassinated when the time was right. Our rules of succession are absolute. So long as the power of her Blessing made her a worthy match, she would succeed me following our wedding. It was meant to be a way to protect the bloodlines, encouraging us to select an equal and produce strong offspring, but the council sought to take advantage of it for their own gain."

"So, you left," I said.

"Without a wedding, everything would stall. I needed to buy time to come up with a better plan. I couldn't let Eirel fall into their hands."

"And you found me."

"The luckiest break of my life," Silas said. "I was fumbling around, struggling to look after myself for the first time. Then *you* appeared. You looked so strong. Capable. I knew I could only do this with your help."

"I shot you." And he'd picked up my arrow like it had been the most precious thing in the world.

He grinned. "I'm sure I deserved it. My attempts to earn your trust were poorly done. I tried using my charm, but that blew up in my face."

"I feared you were just another noble, out to use me for your own entertainment." The ghost of Ithan's betrayal had haunted me, clouding my judgement with suspicion.

"Yet you still gave me a chance. I'm grateful."

I quirked a brow. "So you didn't fall helplessly in love with me the moment we met?"

"I thought you were formidable, that you were someone I wanted in my corner. Then you slowly opened up to me and I realised your kind heart matched my own, that you carried the same pain, but didn't let it hold you back. That's when I knew my feelings had changed."

His lips were soft as they captured mine. I snuggled into him, careful to not put pressure on his chest. We fit together like we were made for each other, two halves of the same heart.

"How can you do it? Smile despite the pain?" Even now, each of my smiles was a hard fought victory, winning against the force of my memories.

He held me tighter against him. "Because it's the only thing I have control over. They've stolen my pride, my purpose, my legacy. I can't let them take my happiness too."

"What are you going to do?" I asked.

"I'm still working on that part."

I tilted my head to look up at him. "You could marry someone else. Their plan hinges on a wedding, after all."

Silas smirked. "Are you proposing?"

"Not me," I said quickly. "I don't meet the conditions about possessing an equal Blessing to you."

"The council would have to sign the contract anyway, so that's out." He tucked a strand of hair behind my ear. "You really think I would marry someone else now I've found you?"

I didn't want to think about it, but it was a grim possibility. "A political marriage, perhaps, if it would benefit your subjects."

"A good ruler doesn't need to barter themselves. They negotiate true alliances, built on mutual interest." His eyes blazed into mine. "I will never let anyone dictate who I marry."

He claimed me with a kiss that made my worries melt away, wincing as we parted.

"You should rest," I said. "Our trials are far from over."

"Can we forget about everything, just for tonight? Right now, you're here and that's enough."

"Of course." My gaze flickered over to the silhouette of the tub visible through the screen. "Reckon you can make it to the bath? I don't want to take any chances with your injuries. If you're clean, they'll stand the best chance of healing well."

"I'm sure I can grin and bear it." He stumbled over, shooing me away when I attempted to help him. "What about you?"

I was in sore need of a bath myself. Ash still coated my hair and skin, and blood stained my neck in a red ring. I'd been surprised when the innkeeper hadn't mentioned it.

"I'll request for the water to be replaced when you're finished. Leave your clothes on the floor and I'll make sure they're washed." My stomach rumbled, and I laughed nervously. "Perhaps arranging a meal should be added to my task list too."

"I could get used to this treatment. Thank you."

He disappeared behind the screen, his clothes sailing past. Water splashed as he slowly climbed into the tub, letting out a whimper. "I'm not going anywhere in a hurry."

I scooped up the garments, closing the door as I headed downstairs. After the scarcity we'd experienced in Threstia, a feast like our last visit would only result in wasted food. Instead, I ordered us a bowl of stew each, knowing it would help restore Silas' strength.

At the sight of our dirty garments, the woman in the laundry room charged me double, providing me with a basic nightgown to dress in, and some linen trousers for Silas, while our clothes dried overnight. Only a few coins remained between us, but the inn's comforts were a justifiable expense.

By the time I'd returned to our room, arms laden with a tray of stew and trailed by a grouchy man who worked for the innkeeper, Silas had left the tub, fast asleep on the bed. He was wrapped in a towel, his damp head resting on the wooden headboard. At the sound of the door closing behind me, his eyes fluttered open.

While I served the meal, placing the food on the table, the man set to work using his Water Blessing to drain Silas' bathwater and fill the tub with clean water once more. He wielded only a fraction of the power Mirthal had, the water trickling from his hands slowly.

"Sorry, must have nodded off," Silas said once the man had left. His movements were stiff as he limped across the room to join me at the table, keeping the towel tightly wrapped around himself. "I'm ravenous. This looks great."

Awkward in the knowledge I'd spent his coin without checking with him, I hesitated. "I used the coins from your pouch. I hope I didn't overstep."

"Of course not. After what you've done for me, I'd gladly give you every coin I have." He ripped apart a bread roll, dunking it in the stew and devouring it. I ate a spoonful, smiling to myself.

The fish stew was rich and salty, settling in my stomach comfortably. We ate in easy silence, polishing off every morsel. When we'd finished, I sagged in my chair, nearly lulled to sleep by my fullness. My body was coming out of survival mode now we were safe and forcing me to recover from the past few days.

Stumbling over to the tub was torture, but I knew it was worth it to wash away the grime of Threstia. My teeth chattered at the chill of the water, but I persevered, submerging myself.

I dug my fingernails into my scalp as I cleaned my hair, determined to dislodge every speck of ash and dirt with the inn's chalky soap, using it to scrub my skin when I was finished.

"Are you asleep?" I called out to Silas.

"No, but before you start, I am resting. It's just a little difficult to drift off knowing that you're naked, with only a screen separating us."

"Am I distracting you?" I said.

He laughed, the delightful sound cut off prematurely by a wince of pain. "I preferred it when I was the one teasing you, and you were the one getting increasingly agitated."

"I can see why. It's highly entertaining to rile you up." Especially when every retort issued a new challenge.

"Willow…" The way he said my name, dripping with longing, dared me to act bold, reckless.

I stood, water dripping from my body as I climbed out of the tub. "I'm no longer in the bath. Problem solved."

Silas groaned.

"Who knew a simple screen could bring the mighty Lord of Eirel to his knees?"

His voice was low, sending a shiver down my spine that had nothing to do with the cool air on my wet skin. "The screen is irrelevant. You're the one playing with my imagination."

His words drew a smile from me as I dried myself with a towel. "How can I resist when you react so eagerly?"

When I was done, I changed into the simple nightgown I'd borrowed, ducking out from behind the screen.

Silas patted the space next to him on the bed, dressed in the linen trousers the inn had provided. His eyes were hooded, glazed over in a way that left no doubt of where his imagination had taken him. "Sleep here. I promise I'll keep my wandering hands to myself, since you were so concerned about that before."

I snorted. After all, I had been the one with wandering hands as we'd shared a bedroll. It felt like an age ago. I looked longingly at the bed, remembering how well I'd slept last time at the inn. His healing took priority, but there was room for both of us.

"Very well," I said. "But for future reference, wandering hands wouldn't be so bad."

He chuckled, the sound low and dark. "I'll bear that in mind."

I climbed in next to Silas, acutely aware of his proximity. but he was injured, and I sorely needed rest. I rolled over, staying as far away from him as I could. It still wasn't far enough. I was conscious of every breath he took, the warmth of him under the blanket, and every movement he made, no matter how slight, as he found a comfortable sleeping position. It was torture.

The last thing I remembered before I succumbed to sleep was Silas murmuring something too quietly for me to hear.

Chapter 24

Sunlight streamed into the room through a gap in the hastily drawn curtains, stirring me from my slumber. It had been a dreamless sleep, the type where exhaustion demanded that rest took priority, and it took a moment for me to remember where I was.

And who was with me.

Waking up next to Silas felt like the most natural thing in the world. He was already awake, stroking my head softly where it rested against his bare chest. During the night we'd drifted together, Silas holding me against him like he would never let me go. I cuddled into him, wanting to enjoy the moment of bliss for a little longer before facing reality.

He felt like home.

His bruises had faded significantly overnight to a yellow-green colour. They still marked his skin enough for me to want to march to Eirel on his behalf, but it was a rapid improvement from the previous evening. His healing was already underway, amplified by the returning power of his Blessing.

The worst was over.

When he noticed I was awake, his hand stilled. Our gazes locked, and I found myself drowning in the beauty of his emerald eyes, seeing into the depths of my soul without flinching.

"Have you been awake for long?" I asked. He brushed a strand of hair off my forehead, his touch sending shivers ghosting over my skin.

"I didn't want to disturb you. You needed the rest," he said.

"I did, but I feel better now." I was almost back to normal, aside from a few lingering aches.

His hand trailed down my cheek, caressing it softly. My breath hitched.

Was he aware of the power he possessed over me, eliciting pleasure with the simplest of touches? Was it the same for him?

I traced one of his bruises with my finger, enjoying the relaxed smile it drew from him. My gentle exploration continued along his forearm, Silas' eyes fluttering shut in response.

"I feared this had all been a dream, that I would wake up still a prisoner. I don't know what I've done to deserve this slice of happiness with you, but I'm grateful for it all the same."

I nuzzled into his neck, his scent washing over me. How did he make the inn's cheap soap smell so good?

"You believed in me, even when I didn't believe in myself," I murmured against him. "You made me feel safe enough to trust again."

"That will never change, I promise." That mischievous hand of his blazed a trail across my collarbone, raising goosebumps in its wake.

His touch was intoxicating, the anticipation of where he would tease next making heat rush to my skin. By the way his eyes burned as they followed the movement, the feeling was mutual.

My fingers flexed as they resisted the urge to touch him again, but I feared if I moved, the magic would break and this would all fall apart.

"I'll always be here for you," he murmured, his lips brushing my cheek.

I turned my head, greedy, wanting his mouth on mine. He groaned, deepening the kiss, his hand fisting in my hair.

The intensity of my feelings for him boiled over. I wanted to feel him anywhere, everywhere, all at once. Discover what he liked and what made him lose control. Watch, enraptured, as he entered me, finally joining us together as one.

I moaned. As my lips parted, Silas seized the opportunity to explore my mouth with his tongue, his teasing strokes making me melt against him.

His kiss tasted sweeter than moon wine and was far more addictive.

He devoured me as I clung to him, held captive by the sensations.

"Do you know how long I've been dreaming of this moment?" His thumb brushed my lip, his gaze fixated on my mouth. "I wanted you to be mine since the day you dragged a tree across half the forest to rescue me. I knew then I didn't stand a chance."

"You'll have to try harder than that to have any claim over me," I said, goading him.

I straddled him, pinning his body to the bed, careful to avoid the worst of his bruises. My nightgown rode up daringly to reveal my skin.

He grinned as if this had been his plan all along, gripping my hips.

"You already have my heart, but I will spend every day of my existence earning yours if I have to."

I kissed him feverishly, my hands splayed on his warm chest. The growing hardness between his thighs pressed against me insistently, temptingly close. I was bare beneath my clothes and only the material of his trousers stood between us, the friction stoking my need until it was unbearable.

"And you already know I'm incredibly skilled," he continued once his mouth was unoccupied.

I swatted him playfully. His fingers unravelled the fastenings of my nightgown until it was loose on my chest, exploring the cleavage that he'd exposed with tantalising caresses. I shivered, arching into his touch and grinding down onto him.

He moaned, the sound rumbling through me. "Fuck, Willow."

His responsiveness only encouraged me, driving me to discover what other sounds I could elicit from him. I grinned, moving my hips again until he bucked against me, his thick length unyielding where our bodies met.

Silas' eyes darkened, a dangerous expression on his face that made me want to push him further. "I didn't realise we were playing dirty. That changes things."

He flipped us, roughly ripping my nightgown over my head in a single move, drinking in every inch of exposed skin.

"You're exquisite," he said, not fire in his eyes this time, but pure longing.

Without warning, he took a nipple into his mouth, sucking and teasing me until I was incoherent with need. I couldn't move, his body pressing me to the bed as he subjected me to his torment.

I felt every lick of his tongue like it was between my legs, wetness pooling there.

He was single-minded in his focus, determined to bring me pleasure like I'd never experienced before. I let out a sigh as his fingers toyed with my other breast, at his mercy. He took his sweet time, savouring me, in no hurry to take things further.

By his smirk, he knew exactly what effect he was having on me.

I squirmed against his hold, needing more than the excruciatingly slow torture.

"Patience," he chastised. "I've had many sleepless nights envisioning what I'd do to you if I ever had the chance. Indulge my fantasies for a moment, won't you?"

"Please," I whimpered. My need was a powerful force that had me spinning out of control, twisting beneath him, desperate for friction, for any sense of relief. It did little to help, heightening my desire until it became overwhelming.

"Silas, I can't take much more of this," I panted as his mouth moved from my breast to nip at my neck.

"Good," he said with a hint of smugness.

I wrestled for control over my mind, one thought cutting through the haze. I wanted to make him feel as wild and helpless as I did.

Resisting his attempts to keep me where I was, I cupped his cock through his trousers, giving it a light squeeze where it filled my hand. His fist clenched the bedsheets.

I smiled at him savagely. This was going to be fun.

"I already regret teasing you," Silas said, his breath laboured.

My touch was feather light as I hooked my fingers into his waistband, rolling the trousers down his thighs. His impressive length jutted out proudly, a bead of pre-cum visible on the tip that I would've tasted if not for my desire to bring him to his knees.

I wanted him whimpering underneath me and begging for my touch, lost to pleasure as I had been. Removing his trousers completely, I trailed my hands up his toned legs, slowly, his skin hot beneath my fingers. As my thumbs kneaded his inner thighs, he groaned, the sound spurring me on.

My desire was unbearable. I wished for nothing more than for him to sink into me, filling me and satisfying my aching core, but I needed to bide my time. I traced teasing, light touches around him, deftly avoiding his attempts to push into my hands with a laugh. He was panting already, his body taut and shaking with need.

He was beautiful.

Silas' hair was a mess, and the rest of him wasn't much better. His cheeks were flushed, his eyes lidded with lust, and beads of sweat ran down his heaving chest. At every caress of my fingers on his skin, his head dropped back, his face contorted like he was in pain. But then his cock would twitch, his ruinous smile igniting me.

When my hand finally grasped him, hot and hard, he thrust into it involuntarily with a shudder of relief, moaning my name. I worked him mercilessly with fast strokes, swallowing his moans with a kiss that was all need.

He was getting close. There was no trace of the confident fae I knew left, only a writhing mess beneath me.

"Please," he panted. "I need you so much."

I'd been patient so far, but my iron resolve was breaking.

I hesitated, suddenly nervous. I'd been physically intimate before, but this was different. With Silas, it would change everything.

His eyes searched mine. "We can stop here if you need to."

I shook my head. I didn't think I could stop if I tried. "No, I want this. It's just...I've never felt anything like this before."

It was exhilarating and terrifying, everything I craved and feared at once.

"Me neither. I want forever with you, Willow. If you'll have me," Silas said with an intensity that matched my own.

It was another leap of faith, just like the one I'd taken with our bargain, but this time I leapt off the ledge, feet first.

"I want it all with you. Please."

He pushed inside me at last, filling me in a way that would ruin me for anyone else. I moaned into his chest, my thighs wrapping around him as he fucked me. I was molten, surrendering myself completely to the need. Every stroke of him nearly undid me, too much and not enough, Silas pouring weeks of tension and longing into his thrusts.

We were united as one, claimed by each other.

His lips captured mine again, the kiss burning with his passion. I clawed his back desperately, and his pace only intensified until all I could do was hang on, lost to the pleasure.

Silas' cock hit a spot inside me that made me see stars. I cried out, clenching around him. He laughed at the noises that came out of my mouth, finding that spot again and redoubling his efforts until I was trembling.

If I thought he would take pity on me, I was sorely mistaken.

He withdrew from me, leaving me feeling empty. The sensation was short-lived. He helped me to my knees until I was braced on all fours.

"Don't you dare go easy on me," I said, my voice husky.

"The thought never crossed my mind. I know you can handle it." His hand stroked the curve of my rear as his cock teased my entrance.

He slammed into me, giving me no time to recover before he did it again. I gave myself over to the ecstasy, pushing back against him to meet every thrust. He was true to his word, giving me all he had, pounding me into oblivion, the bed squeaking beneath us.

I was burning alive, sure I would erupt if he kept up his relentless rhythm. His fingers dug into my hips, guiding my movements as he drove into me, my legs shaking.

When I couldn't stand it any longer, Silas reached a hand between us, massaging my clit with an expert touch. I shattered, my climax crashing into me, pressing my face into my arm to muffle the sound of my scream. My body convulsed with the power of it, shockwaves of pleasure thrumming through me.

He gave me no respite, continuing to fuck me with slow, deep thrusts as I pulsed around him. It was a bliss like I'd never felt, and a sob came out of me.

When the sensations finally ceased, I wiggled out from underneath him, rolling so I could face Silas as his cock claimed me. He was devastatingly handsome, his eyes dazed and his lips swollen from kissing me.

This time when he pushed into me, it didn't take long before I was close to the edge again, brought nearer by his ragged breath in my ear as I took him deeper, lifting my hips from the bed.

His thumb drew a circle around my clit, the extra pressure enough to destroy me.

I gasped with the force of my orgasm, Silas wearing a wicked grin as he watched me come apart on his cock.

"You are more beautiful than words can describe when you come for me. I can't wait to watch you do it again and again until you beg for mercy."

Soon, his movements became jerkier. I tilted his head towards me, the raw desperation in his gaze utterly captivating. As his eyes met mine, he groaned, his cock jerking as his release joined with mine.

Afterwards, I rested my head against his, content to stay there, but Silas had other ideas. He brushed my aching clit, and he plunged two fingers into me. I bucked against his touch, every sensation amplified by my sensitivity.

"I meant what I said," he murmured, curving them inside me as he increased the pressure. "I could spend all day watching you come, but this will have to suffice."

My release had me arching off the bed, Silas' arms steadying me.

I could think of worse ways to spend the day.

Chapter 25

Hours later, when we were completely spent, Silas requested fresh water for the bathtub. I cocooned myself under the blankets of the warm bed while we waited for it to be filled, dozing off several times. My body ached in the best kind of way, and I stretched, satisfied for the moment.

Once we were alone, I emerged, intending to take full advantage of the tub, but Silas held up a finger, motioning for me to wait. Before I could protest, he plunged a hand into the water, steam rising as it heated.

"You can do that?" I asked, my mouth hanging open.

"Now that my Blessing has recovered? Of course," he said.

I rushed to his side, hugging him tightly, tears in my eyes. Soaking in hot water was a luxury I had never experienced. The bathing pools at the Old Keep were lukewarm at best, and on missions, I had to rely on whatever streams and rivers I could find. All of them had been freezing cold and downright unpleasant.

"Thank you," I said into his chest.

"It's not entirely selfless. I intend to share it with you this time," he said, a twinkle in his eye.

"Then what are we waiting for?"

I sank into the steaming bathtub, relishing the heavenly heat that soaked into me. Silas climbed in behind me as I made room. I settled between his thighs, leaning back against him, a sigh of contentment escaping me. Strong hands massaged my shoulders.

"I've been missing out. There are certainly perks for keeping a Blessed fae around," I said.

He chuckled. "I'm sure we can find some *creative* uses for my magic."

With the warmth of the bath caressing me, and Silas' firm body supporting mine, I found the courage to voice my vulnerabilities. "I'll never understand what you saw in me when I was so harsh to you. I don't know if I deserve you."

His hands froze, and I worried I'd exposed too much to him. But then he wrapped his arms around me, pulling me against him, reassuringly steady.

His voice was low in my ear. "You never once tried to impress me, even after discovering my Blessing. And you never hesitated to tell me exactly what you thought about me. Do you know how rare that is? In Eirel, the nobility attempted to sway me with false flattery, but no one dared speak their mind. Until you."

"I was awful to you. I'll regret it until the end of my days."

"You were protecting yourself. Who could blame you for that? I can't say I wouldn't have done the same in your shoes. I like every part of you, even the dark parts you're scared to acknowledge. Because without those, you wouldn't be you."

His lips brushed the soft skin of my neck, tender and sweet. "Do you know what kept me going when I was captured? The thought of you razing the world to save me. There's no one I'd rather have by my side."

I tilted my head to kiss him, this extraordinary man who by some miracle had fallen for me. I would spend forever making sure he knew just how much I appreciated him.

We soaked in the tub together until our skin pruned and the water cooled. Silas insisted on drying me, an endeavour that nearly resulted in us falling back into bed for another round, but our future still loomed over us, and we wouldn't be able to find peace until it was resolved.

"We've denied our problems long enough. Any thoughts on where to go from here?" he said, as we dressed in our freshly laundered clothes. I couldn't remember the last time I'd felt so clean. It restored me, feeding the flames of my confidence.

Neither of us wanted to leave the other, our connection undeniable, but we both had our obligations.

The only path I could accept was to face them, together.

"I have an idea, but it could be dangerous." That was the understatement of the century.

"Tell me," Silas said, lacing his black trousers before pulling on his shirt.

"Remember in Threstia when we fought, and I told you about the bargain I'm bound to?" It pained me to ask him to revisit that day, but I needed him to understand the cost of what I offered him.

"Briefly. You said you search for information to protect Idrix. Something to do with the curse."

I nodded. "I know someone who may be able to help us, but I'm not exactly on their good side. I could be putting both of us at risk."

Silas studied me cautiously. "But you think there's a chance?"

"A slim one," I said, threading my arms into the sleeves of my shirt.

"Would I need to make a bargain too?" He didn't look enthused at the prospect. My stomach twinged. Was I pushing him too far?

"I don't know for sure," I admitted, "but it's highly likely. Without it, I can't tell you the full truth."

He frowned. "I can't abandon my subjects. They're my responsibility. I'll never forgive myself for leaving them at the mercy of the council. I need to fight for them, even if returning alone is a death sentence."

I took a deep breath. This was it. "What if you weren't alone?"

The question lingered in the stale air of the inn.

"Where are you going with this?" Silas asked, sitting on the edge of the bed to put on his boots.

"With your influence and Blessing, you'd be a formidable ally. You'd have leverage, as Mirthal called it," I said.

"You think your contact would be willing to negotiate? Help me win back Eirel?" His voice was bursting with optimism, and I only hoped it was warranted.

"It's worth a shot. But it requires a leap of faith, far greater than anything I've asked of you before." I met his gaze. "You should know the odds are stacked against us. I hurt someone important in the process of saving you. I won't be welcomed with open arms, but it's the best chance we have. You'll need allies to stop the council."

"And you're sure about this?"

"No." I said. "But we have information they need. That should be enough to hear us out. After that, let's hope you can earn their trust, just like you did with me."

I fastened my cloak before retrieving my pack and bow.

"And this way, you could stay with me?" Silas asked, picking up his remaining belongings where they were haphazardly scattered around the room.

I softened. "It's the only way without breaking my bargain."

I refused to let this be the end. We deserved our opportunity for a future together, and the Night Ravens could provide that, even with its limitations. I would fight for whatever I could get if it meant he was with me.

His features set in determination. "Then it's decided."

We left the inn hand in hand, acting as sickening as newlyweds. Even the drizzling rain couldn't sour our happiness. Instead of seeking shelter, Silas took my hand and led me around the grasslands like it was our dancefloor. Afterwards, when it had subsided, he'd bathed us in a warm glow, drying the water and kissing our numb skin with heat.

The days blended together as we swiftly progressed north, our tight partnership helping us to travel with ease. We pushed ourselves during the day, Silas fully healed and eager to match my pace, then by night we made love under the stars, unrushed as we treasured each other.

Before long, we reached the Blossom Sea. It remained as breathtaking as ever, sunlight cascading over the blooming meadows. I laid on a canopy of flowers, their soft petals tickling my bare flesh, as Silas took me to the brink of release, holding me there for an agonising moment, before coaxing me over the abyss with a command I was more than willing to obey.

The next day, the charming scenery of Valtarra appeared over the horizon, looking as inviting as ever.

"Should we stop by? Visit your friend?" Silas asked. The travel had taken a toll, his appearance becoming increasingly dishevelled, but he'd kept his complaints to a minimum. Still, I didn't miss the way he looked longingly at the village.

"No. Without a cure, we would be a burden to them. Better to come back with positive news. I just hope Dorea can hold on until then."

On the fifth day, I breathed a sigh of relief as we crossed into the Yewdew Forest. It hummed with life, from the raglaw singing in the treetops to the plants that grasped towards the sunlight. Returning with Silas felt right, like the pieces of my soul were reunited at last. The forest was the same as ever, but I was different. We both were. So much had changed since we'd first met.

"This feels familiar. You're not going to shoot me this time, are you?" he said when we'd stopped for a rest, roasting a few raglaw over a campfire. Their rich, savoury scent filled the air, and my stomach groaned.

"That depends," I responded, appreciating his handiwork. It had taken a few attempts for him to hit them with our two remaining arrows, dashing back and forth to retrieve them when he'd failed, but it was worth the wait to watch his confidence grow.

"On what?" He raised an eyebrow.

"How distracting you plan to be."

Silas tackled me to the ground, kissing me while I laughed, eventually succeeding in batting him away. I took his hand in mine as we watched the fire hiss and crackle.

He grinned smugly. "How was that?"

"Not bad, but I hope that was only the beginning."

"Just wait for nightfall," he promised, a glint in his eye.

We ate quickly and smothered the campfire when we were done, wanting to travel further while we had daylight. The Old Keep was only a day away. I was nervous to accept the consequences of attacking Norwyn and delaying my return to the Night Ravens, but with Silas by my side, it didn't feel so overwhelming. And I had to confront my fears for Dorea's sake, to secure her the help she needed.

If I wasn't too late.

Every time he noticed me quieten or my smile fade, Silas reassured me he wanted this. That we could face whatever greeted me together.

With him, I felt stronger than ever.

Nearly a week after we'd left the inn, we reached the fortress, yet again masked by the wards that protected it.

"I never ventured this deep into the forest last time," Silas said.

"Good. That was our intent."

"Why? What are you hiding out here?" He strode ahead, so distracted he neglected to notice his surroundings, not that it would've mattered.

I called out to him in alarm. "Watch out!"

But he didn't hear me, colliding with the solid barrier of the wards and bouncing off it, falling to the ground.

"What the fuck was that?" he said, cradling his arm where he'd landed on it.

"An excellent reason to listen to me."

I felt for the telltale ripple of the glamoured wards hiding the Old Keep's existence. They resisted me at first, as if realising Silas wasn't meant to be there.

"He's with me," I said to them. "I can vouch for him."

"Who are you talking to?" Silas said, his head darting from side to side.

"You'll see."

The wards seemed to consider me for a moment, the magic tickling as it brushed across my skin. Silas tensed, as if he could feel it too. Then they hummed, melting away at my touch without further complaint, the forest distorting as it transformed around us.

We'd passed the first test.

He let out a low whistle at the sight of the ruined castle, thousands of years of neglect eroding its walls. I had almost forgotten the awe I'd felt seeing it with Reuben as a new recruit. I'd looked at the crumbling stones and seen something broken, yet beautiful. A symbol of hope.

His eyes widened as he took in the sheer scale of what we'd concealed for centuries, and his grin made my heart soar.

"Welcome to the Old Keep," I said.

Chapter 26

A familiar silhouette stood at the gatehouse, resolute as they guarded the entrance alone. Wielding her longsword, Sal's brown eyes swept over us, a guardian of fury protecting the Old Keep. None of her usual softness peeked through her armour. It was the Head of the Watch that greeted us, the first point of defence for the castle, and she wouldn't be swayed by pleasantries.

"Stay back!" she shouted, but we didn't falter as we climbed the stone steps. "You know I can't let you in."

I persisted. Failure wasn't an option. "I've returned from my mission. We found something. It's urgent."

"Willow..." she growled, but wavered, if only for a moment. It gave me the glimpse of hope I needed.

"I swear I haven't betrayed the Night Ravens. I'll explain everything. Please give me a chance," I pleaded.

Sal's sword dropped almost imperceptibly, but I would take every inch as a victory. Her gaze shifted to Silas, sizing him up. "And him? You can't just walk in here with a stranger."

Silas beamed at her like he didn't have a weapon pointed at him.

I gave it to her straight, as Sal had always respected. "This is Silas. He's the Lord of Eirel."

He took that as his cue to bow. "Charmed to make your acquaintance."

Confusion flashed across her face. "I must have misheard. I thought I heard you say he's the Lord of Eirel."

I stared up at her. "He is. It's a long story."

"Gods have mercy," Sal said, keeping her sword levelled at us. "And what, pray tell, was the reason you decided to reveal our existence to a ruler of Idrix?"

"We need him, just like he needs us," I said.

Her eyes narrowed. "He'll destroy everything we've worked for."

I knew that wasn't true. "The wards allowed him inside. That has to count for something." If they sensed a threat, they wouldn't yield easily. Silas making it this far bolstered our case significantly.

Sal raked her fingers through her short, blonde hair, conflicted.

"If I may," Silas said, clearing his throat. "Would this vouch for my intentions?"

He retrieved a familiar aurabloom from his pocket, wilted but alive. The sight of it made warmth spread through my body.

"You still have that?" I asked in disbelief.

"Of course I do. It's a precious memento from the time you started to trust me." It had been the first step on our path to friendship.

As he held it, the petals changed into a parade of joyous colour. A few muted ones signalled his fears for Eirel, but they were outweighed by the vibrancy of the rest. Life seemed to flood back into the aurabloom as Silas grasped it in his fingertips.

"See. I'm an open book," he said.

Sal finally lowered her sword, resting it on the ground in front of us. She studied the flower in his hand, her gaze lingering on a vivid pink petal in interest. "He's fond of you."

"The feeling's mutual," I said. Silas nudged me affectionately.

I took a step towards Sal, my confidence growing. "All we're asking is for you to hear us out. We discovered something deep in Threstia. Reuben will want to know."

Sal grimaced. "He won't like this."

"I know."

She looked between the two of us and the aurabloom and sighed. "We'll need to isolate you until you've been questioned. I must treat this seriously."

"Thank you," I said, relief coating my voice.

"You owe me. Don't forget it." She beckoned for us to follow her. "I'm partial to mead, but open to surprises."

The rusty portcullis squealed in protest as it lifted, and we took our first steps inside. Silas absorbed every detail with unrestrained amazement, from the plants that grew from the stone, to what remained of the curtain wall.

As we passed the sentry who had opened the gate, Sal spoke to him. "Take over the front sentry position. I'll send someone to relieve you shortly."

The man nodded, squeezing past us towards the gatehouse.

Rather than taking us into the main castle, Sal led us down a dark staircase into the old dungeons, ignoring the inquisitive glances the other sentries threw our way. "I must say, I'm curious why the Lord of Eirel has granted us the honour of his presence."

"It's quite the tale," Silas said.

"I wonder if you'll feel the same after you've repeated it for the tenth time."

The dungeons were a miserable place, even more damp than the rest of the ruined castle. It smelt revolting, like something had crawled into the walls and died, the scent stubbornly clinging to the stone. The only fresh air came from a grate on the ceiling, too high for anyone to reach.

Silas didn't balk as he followed closely behind Sal's intimidating form. A row of five cells was built into the north wall. I hadn't seen them since the day I'd stepped foot into the castle, my first memory. Sat in the cell, alone with my thoughts and unsure of what I'd got myself into, doubts had crept in about my decision to take up Reuben's offer.

"A precaution," Sal said to Silas. "You'll be confined here until we're satisfied you will keep our secrets."

"And me?" I asked, dreading the answer.

"You too, until you've explained yourself sufficiently for Reuben to clear you."

I sighed. Convincing Sal had only been the beginning.

She unlocked the door of the nearest cell, the metal creaking on its hinges. "This one's for you, Lord of Eirel. Not as fancy as you're used to, I imagine."

Silas took in the small cot that furnished the dark space, a candle providing the only source of light. "I've stayed in nicer conditions with much crueller captors. I vastly prefer it this way." He perched on the bed, giving me a good-natured wave.

Sal addressed me. "You're in the next block. I'll let you say your goodbyes."

I supposed it had been unrealistic to hope we'd be kept in neighbouring cells.

"Thank you, Sal."

Sal turned her back to us, giving us a moment. I wrapped Silas in a hug, kissing him fiercely, providing him whatever comfort I could. His eyes shone with uncertainty.

"You can do this," I assured him. "You'll do great."

"What happens now?" he asked.

"Initiation. They'll interrogate you, asking every question you could possibly think of to determine if you're trustworthy. Don't hold anything back. It's better to be upfront and honest. If you pass, they'll move onto the bargain. That's your opportunity to bring up your terms."

Vetting recruits was the domain of the sentries, part of their duties of keeping the Night Ravens safe. It eased my mind to know that Sal would be involved in the process, but I desperately wished I could be there with him.

"Will they hurt me?" His voice went weak.

"No." I held him tightly against me. "I would never bring you here if that was a possibility. They just want to protect this place."

"Time to move along." Sal clapped a hand on my shoulder. "If you've been honest with me, you'll see each other again in a few hours."

I pressed a gentle kiss to Silas' forehead. "I'll see you soon, I promise. Show them what you're made of."

Once Silas was securely locked in his cell, Sal led me through a wooden door to the next room, closing it behind us.

"You're in a lot of trouble, you know," she said, once Silas couldn't overhear us. "Norwyn was furious when he returned. He was in with

Reuben for hours, apparently. There's never been an instance of a scout attacking another."

"I had to do what was necessary to save Silas. I'm ready to face the punishment for my actions."

"That's very noble of you, but I hope you understand the severity of this. Reuben is expected to make a decision on your fate once he's heard your side of the story. They could kick you out for this."

I swallowed thickly. "Let's hope it doesn't come to that."

"You should be careful. Reuben's been in a foul mood since he received your letter. You'll find him more obstinate than usual, so don't test his patience," she said.

Sal shut me inside a similar cell to the one Silas was imprisoned in before excusing herself to return to her duties. I made myself as comfortable as I could, dozing off before the sound of a key in the lock disturbed me.

Reuben had joined me, lingering by the door, his face as unreadable as ever.

My palms became clammy, my mind going blank. I couldn't remember the last time I felt so nervous. It wasn't just my own interests I needed to look out for, but Silas' too.

"Have you betrayed us?" Reuben asked plainly, his steely eyes searching mine.

"No. I'm loyal to the Night Ravens." I took a deep breath. "I returned to brief you on the evidence I've found and will submit to whatever punishment you deem necessary."

He didn't let up on his scrutiny, crossing his arms where he stood. "Then explain yourself. Why did you disobey my orders?"

"It was the only way."

I told him everything, beginning with what I'd discovered in the bookshop, Dorea's mysterious illness, and how it had stemmed from her work with the researchers. Reuben listened in silence, his brow furrowed. I explained my chance encounter with Silas, how I'd pushed him away, and how despite that, he'd proven himself a useful ally, and a trusted partner. That he'd protected me against the threat of the Hightower nobles, Reuben himself witnessing the condition they'd left me in once before. How he'd helped me infiltrate the research camp and saved us from the aftermath, revealing himself to be the runaway Lord of Eirel. When I made it clear that my behaviour towards Norwyn had only been to ensure Silas' safety, Reuben still didn't say a word, so I continued.

"The researchers had a vast operation in Threstia, taking soil samples and cataloguing them. That's what Dorea had been doing when she was injured. They said they were searching for traces of ancient magic and portals. At the heart of the camp was a map of locations they'd tried already. Threstia was their focus due to the forest that was once there."

I removed the scrolls of parchment from my pack. "I stole these from their camp. It's results from previous sites."

Reuben took them, reviewing the contents with a frown.

"Do you think they're onto something?"

He ignored the question. I felt tiny, cowered by his looming presence as I waited for him to say something, anything, to temper my worries.

All he did was open the door, leaving me alone again.

Panic overwhelmed me, its weight settling over my chest, making it difficult to breathe. Had I doomed us both? What if I'd brought Silas here, condemning him to life in a cell while his subjects suffered his absence?

It was the seeking stone that pulled me from its clutches, the amulet growing warm and projecting Silas' heartbeat over mine. He was here with me, even with the thick walls separating us.

We could do this.

Sal returned shortly afterwards, swinging the loop of dungeon keys around her finger.

"What's going on?" I asked, sick of being kept in the dark.

"Following your debrief, Reuben concluded that you didn't betray the Night Ravens." I felt dizzy with relief. "But your attack on Norwyn needs to be punished. You'll be removed from scout duty and contained to the castle for a month, working overtime to support the other divisions. I suggest you keep your head down and out of trouble. The scholars are expecting you. Eldon said something about crafting a cure?"

My shoulders sagged as the tension left them. It was a far more lenient punishment than I'd expected. I would've volunteered to help Eldon, the Head Scholar, work on a way to save Dorea.

"Why isn't he telling me this?"

"You'd have to ask him that."

"And Silas?"

"He handled his initiation well. Didn't choke once. Since he's clean, we can proceed with the bargain. He's requested that you're present for it. I'll take you there now." She helped me out of my cell. "Reuben will want a word with him once he's settled in."

"Why?" I tensed at the thought of Silas exposed to Reuben's questioning.

"Why would the scout leader want to talk to the most powerful fae that's visited the Old Keep in its history? One with intimate knowledge of the nobility and their inner workings?"

"I suppose that makes sense." It didn't mean I liked it.

"He won't be the only one with questions. You'll have an uphill battle to win everyone's trust. I suggest you comply with whatever Reuben wants if this is your plan."

Silas was sprawled on the bed as we approached his cell, looking as exhausted as I felt. He sipped water from a goblet, some spilling on his chest in his haste to sit up when he noticed us.

"Are you ready?" Sal asked him through the bars.

"I have two conditions before I agree to your bargain." His words were edged with a quiet confidence. How had the council made him doubt his abilities when negotiation came this naturally to him?

"State your terms," Sal said.

"I seek aid for Eirel. It's currently under the malignant influence of its High Council. If you protect Idrix, as I've been led to believe, then you will find my subjects very much in need of your services."

Sal snorted. "Look around. We hardly have resources to spare."

"I don't need resources. I need her," Silas' gaze found mine, "and others with her skills. My preference is to avoid bloodshed and to take a more considered approach to regain control. I understand that's a strength of this group."

"Be as it may, that's still a significant request."

"I appreciate that. Therefore, in return, once my affairs are settled and I'm satisfied Eirel is in safe hands, I will swear my full allegiance and serve you faithfully."

"Silas!" I exclaimed. "You can't."

Eirel was everything to him.

"My duty is to the fae of Eirel. If this is the best thing for them, then it's a sacrifice I'm willing to make."

"You would abdicate your position and join us permanently?" Sal clarified.

"Yes, but only once Eirel is safe and ruled by a worthy leader. I would supervise the transition of power, then make a discreet exit."

"You would be giving up everything. Are you sure it's what you want?" I asked him.

Silas exhaled a slow breath. "If this will free Eirel from the council's clutches, then what I want doesn't matter."

"Dare I ask what your other condition is?" Sal interjected.

Silas pointed to me. "Her." The world came to a standstill around me. "Whatever you ask of me, it will be with Willow by my side. I understand assignments may part us temporarily, but my second requirement is that we are stationed together."

Of everything he could request, that was what he wanted?

He grinned. "You didn't think I'd let you go that easily, did you? I told you. We'll face the world together."

Sal considered us thoughtfully. "This is beyond the scope of what we'd usually accept. I will need to discuss it with the other leaders for approval."

"Take your time," Silas said. "I'm not going anywhere in a hurry."

Chapter 27

D ays passed with no news. I was free to roam the Old Keep again, though with word spreading of my eventful return and the stares that followed me wherever I went, I chose to spend my pitiful amount of leisure time sat outside Silas' cell. The sentries kept us under strict supervision, moving from their usual position of guarding the dungeon's entrance to monitor our conversations.

While I wasn't permitted to discuss my work, or any other official business with him until he'd taken the bargain, we found plenty of ways to while away the hours. We took meals together, sharing tales of our childhoods, and after discovering Silas had been an avid reader in his youth, I brought books from the scholars' library to occupy him in my absence.

"I hate that you're trapped in here," I said, passing new reading material through the bars of his cell. Hopefully, 'A Brief History of

Wards and Their Uses' would be a stimulating read for him. "I don't know what's taking them so long."

Silas shrugged. "Why? I get to sleep and read all day while you're working yourself to the bone. I wish I could trade places so you could rest."

He was right. My daily routine had become gruelling to meet the conditions of my punishment. I woke before sunrise, preparing breakfast with the stewards and cleaning up afterwards, then worked my guard shift, stuck with the positions none of the sentries wanted. After a short break to dine with Silas, I'd spend my evenings with the scholars, working long into the night. They bombarded me with questions about the research camp, hoping I'd unlock something in their quest to find a cure. So far, there had been no breakthrough.

I reached between the bars, taking his hand in mine. "You don't have to put on a brave face for me. I know firsthand how isolating it is in here, how there's nothing to anchor you to reality."

"You're my anchor," Silas said, intertwining our fingers. "I've had plenty of experience with confinement. Luckily, I'm a fascinating individual, and haven't tired of my own company yet."

"Silas, it's me. You don't have to pretend everything is fine."

A shudder went through him. "I have nightmares that I never escaped, that I'm trapped doing the council's bidding."

The thought of him isolated for years in Eirel, just to end up locked up again broke my heart. I loathed myself for bringing him here.

"I won't let that happen."

"I know, but still..."

"Being imprisoned here takes you back to that time," I finished. "It smothers you, extinguishing your spark. You deserve better than this."

"It was my choice."

"But I was the one who proposed it." I sighed. "I wish we were back in the inn. Everything was so much simpler without all this." I gestured to the dungeons surrounding us.

"Me too. It was our own little world, shielding us from the responsibilities of our positions."

"And now we must face them."

He rested his weight on the cell door with a look of mischief that made my skin heat, speaking lower so the sentries couldn't eavesdrop. "It's not all bad. I've become rather adept at entertaining myself. When I'm alone at night, I close my eyes and remember how well you took my cock."

"Silas," I hissed, shooting an alarmed glance at the sentries. They showed no signs of hearing him.

"Don't pretend you haven't thought about it." His thumb brushed my palm before circling my wrist, his touch as silken as his murmured words. "I picture that day a lot. The tiny shifts in your expression that hinted you were close to falling apart, the way your eyes widened, and finally, the soft noise of satisfaction you made as you gave yourself over to the pleasure, clenching around me as I drew it out for you. It's a knock to my ego how quickly it makes me finish, but it pales in comparison to the memory of you. I crave you with every fibre of my being."

"You're cruel." A wave of desire flooded me as my body recalled exactly how good he had felt inside me, how he'd anticipated what I'd needed before I could voice it. "Since you have so much free time, I'm sure you'll have plenty of inspiration when we do find some privacy."

"It would take centuries to try everything on my list. I'd start with-
"

"Stop whispering over there," a sentry called out.

"Pity. You'll have to wait, I suppose," Silas said.

"Anticipation is half the fun." I bowed my head to his ear. "And you're not the only one with a filthy imagination."

Silas' hungry expression brought a delighted smile to my face.

Whilst torturing ourselves wasn't the worst way to spend an afternoon, I had more serious topics in mind. I ran my fingers along the rusted metal of the cell door. "I've been meaning to ask, why did you decide to step down as lord? Was it just because of the negotiation?"

The guilt would never leave me if it was.

"No, though that gave me the push to do it." His hands tightened around the bars. "Travelling with you made me realise life could be different. I've spent so long battling to fit in, to be what others demanded of me, but with you, I discovered who I truly am, what I'm capable of. I found myself along the way."

"You were so desperate to fight for your subjects. I can't help but worry that I'm the cause of your change of heart."

"Not for the reason you think. I never once considered I could be the problem, not the solution. The High Council felt emboldened to make their plans because of me. My weakness. Eirel needs a ruler that will break down the barriers between the common fae and the nobility to make a better world. With my history, I could never garner the support to do that, especially with the High Council standing in my way. The bargain provided an opportunity to kill two birds with one stone."

What was he saying?

"Eirel needs Valeria," he said, noticing my confusion.

"You want to make her Lady of Eirel?" From what he'd told me, his cousin was tenacious enough to forge a new path forward.

He nodded. "With me at the helm, the cycle will never end. Taking down the High Council will be for naught if others, even more conniving, take their place. But if I can clear the way for Valeria to succeed me, they will have no choice but to swear their fealty. She shares my compassion but is strong enough to face opposition without yielding, and her Blessing is just as powerful as mine. I have no doubt Eirel would thrive under her rule, and my obligations would be met."

"I take it it's not as simple as going to the Isle of Mist and abdicating your position?"

"When has anything on this journey been easy? On my death, control would automatically pass to her, but if I step down, there would be a free-for-all, every noble vying for their chance. I'd probably wind up dead either way." He swept his dirty hair from his face. "That's why I need the scouts. Deep within the Isle of Mist, there's a secret chamber. The archives contain records of every Eirelean ruler's ascent to power. I'm betting on at least one of them being sneaky enough to discover a loophole. The only problem is the knowledge of its location has been lost to time. I've heard whispers that its entrance lies deep beneath the lake and accessing it without inside help will be near impossible."

"Slightly more challenging than a research camp."

"Indeed."

My brow furrowed. "And you truly want this? You would give up your power and privilege for a lumpy mattress in a damp castle?"

"From what I've seen so far, this place is more hospitable than my gilded cage was, and here, my Blessing will make a huge difference. We achieved so much working together. Imagine what we could do for the rest of our lives."

Hope bloomed in my chest. "I'm not the easiest partner."

Silas grinned, his fingers closing around mine on the bar. "This wouldn't be half as entertaining if you were."

I sighed. "Just promise me you'll consider it further before completing the bargain. It's for life. When the novelty wears off, you'll still be bound to the terms, even if your desires change."

"I promise, though I assure you, my mind is made up."

A week went by with no sign of Silas being released from the dungeons. His conditions may have been unusual, but so was he. He should've received an answer either way.

I lost my patience, storming into Reuben's office without knocking. He was unfazed, not bothering to look up from the scrolls that cluttered his desk.

"Why haven't you made a decision yet?" I demanded.

"The leaders are still reviewing the evidence," he said, matter of fact.

"I know you're the one dragging your feet." Sal had told me as much, though she hadn't needed to.

"I'm merely applying the appropriate level of caution. It wouldn't be the first time you misplaced your trust."

My mouth went dry, my pulse roaring in my ears. This was because of me and my poor judgement with Ithan?

"You're doing this because of a mistake I made nearly a century ago? I'm no longer a naïve girl who falls for sweet promises. Silas would never betray me. I'm certain of that," I said, though my voice wobbled.

"That may be the case, but you can't blame my hesitation." He returned to his documents, stacking them in a neat pile. "Will that be all?"

"No." I straightened. Something had bothered me since our last conversation in my cell. "You never chastised me for failing to return immediately from Valtarra, even though you'd given me specific orders to do so."

Reuben finally looked at me. "No, I did not."

The realisation struck like a slap to the face. "You knew. You knew I'd take one look at Dorea and wouldn't be able to walk away," I said, my voice barely a whisper. His earlier words echoed in my mind. He needed someone who could think on their feet. He'd even brought up the curse to hook me in.

Reuben always had been three steps ahead of me.

"I was counting on it. Cassandra was more than a friend to me, once. Long ago. But we didn't end on the best terms. I knew if she was reaching out to me, she was truly desperate." A smile briefly graced his face, twisting his stern features.

"But you're the one who told me to never intervene, that we were only meant to be silent observers. That it was our duty and our burden as a scout." He'd laboured the point so often that it was his voice I heard inside my head, urging me to forget about the victims, the helpless, those Idrix had broken. His fault that I was wracked with guilt at leaving them to their fate. Countless innocents, as Aster had been, becoming collateral damage to Idrix's treachery. "I trusted you. I stood by when I could've helped, but all this time you've been using me for your own motives."

He didn't flinch at my accusatory tone. "I had to be sure you were ready. That when faced with a choice you were unprepared for, you would make the right one."

"So, I passed your little test. What now? Are you going to tell me what a good scout I am? Dangle the next carrot in front of me?"

"Don't be unreasonable."

"Unreasonable? You're lucky I'm doing you the respect of holding this conversation. You know how sacred trust is to me, yet you didn't spare a thought for how I would feel about this."

"There are greater forces at work here that you don't understand," Reuben said.

"How convenient." I laughed bitterly.

He stood, squaring up to me, but I refused to back away. Somewhere along my journey, I'd unlocked a new power within myself, a fire that blazed through my veins filling me with its strength.

"Do you know why the Night Ravens were founded?" Reuben asked, catching me off guard. Where was he going with this?

"To protect Idrix from those who would harm the realm." From the scouts scattered across it, to the scholars compiling our information, to the sentries who guarded the Old Keep and the stewards who kept it running, all were united by that one purpose.

"Then why the need for secrecy? Why not make our presence known so no one dared prey on the weak? Why hold back?"

"I..." I had no answer for him, the room spinning around me in a sickening way. I'd never questioned it. From the moment I'd learned about the bargain, I'd taken it for granted that we remained hidden because it was the best way to protect Idrix.

Reuben seized upon my uncertainty, assaulting me with questions. "What happens to the evidence the scouts gather? What have we used it to achieve?"

I couldn't breathe. What had it all been for?

When I'd washed up on the shores of the mainland, throwing up the water I'd swallowed thanks to the wave, it hadn't taken long to realise I was the only survivor. I'd screamed and cried and cursed the gods, but nothing brought me solace.

It was then I'd made my promise. I vowed to live a life worthy of all those I'd lost, a life that would make them proud. I had to make something of myself to earn the second chance I'd been granted.

It had been difficult to stick to it when survival was all I could manage. But then, Reuben had found me clinging to life after Ithan's betrayal, and offered me new hope. A new purpose.

A way to fulfil my last promise.

And it had all been for nothing. Every mission I'd toiled over to bring peace to Idrix had been an illusion, a glamour Reuben had tricked me with.

I felt hollow inside, the numbness spreading through me and turning my blood to ice.

"There are two sides to the Night Ravens. You've only known the first, but with what you uncovered in Threstia, you've unwittingly stumbled into the second. There's no turning back now." He grimaced. "It's time you met the founder."

"What?" I couldn't hide my shock. No one had met the founder. I'd long suspected them to be a myth, a means of giving us hope that we weren't alone in our fight.

"Only a select few have been granted an audience, usually those that have proven themselves with centuries of service, but with everything that's come to light, the founder agreed to make an exception in your case." He wrenched open the door of his office, light spilling into the dark space. "There are certain things that I'm not at liberty to discuss with you. If you want answers, this is your chance."

I glowered at him, but he knew my curiosity would win over my anger. "Fine, I'll go with you, but let me make one thing clear. If the founder confirms what you've said and all this has been justified, I will accept it, but I will never trust you again. You've broken something that can't be fixed."

Reuben only held open the door, waiting for me to pass.

Chapter 28

I followed Reuben down uneven steps to a hallway I didn't know had existed. Flaming torches lit the way through the long passage, a single door waiting for us at the end. The stone walls were well-preserved, untouched by the cracks that plagued the castle.

"Where are we going?" I asked, my tone icy. I doubted there was anything Reuben could show me that would justify his actions, but I couldn't pass up the opportunity to learn the Night Ravens' apparent secrets.

"To the inner sanctum. The founder hasn't left their chambers in years."

I laughed darkly. "And suddenly I'm worthy of being trusted with something so important?"

"It wasn't my decision to make." His voice was pained. "I made a bargain. I'm only allowed to bring you here now because the founder authorised it. You can't tell a soul about what you witness, even if your new friend joins as a member."

"Partner," I corrected. With everything Silas had done for me, it was the least I could do to proudly assert what we were. "And you have some nerve asking me to withhold anything from him when he just became the only fae I trust."

He shook his head, his loose blond hair spilling over his shoulders. "You'll see for yourself soon enough."

Reuben unlocked the door with an old, rusty key, stooping down to pass through it as it creaked open.

I coughed as I inhaled dust, noticing the cobwebs that clung to the corners. "I suppose the stewards are also prevented from entering without permission?"

"Except for Paxton, and only for important meetings. Believe me, it bothers him more than you. Last time he tried to smuggle a broom down here with him. Sal confiscated it before he could do anything." Paxton was the long-suffering Head Steward, often found chasing after new recruits with their forgotten messes asking if they'd been raised by animals.

The chamber we entered was huge, rivalling the size of the dining hall. On one side, ten chairs stood in a circle. Beside them, mounted to the wall, was a map of Idrix, several pins embedded in the parchment. The rest of the room was bare except for what looked to be modest living quarters. There was a small bed tucked away in the corner, a round table with three stools and a velvet armchair.

There, flanked by two robed attendants, sat a beautiful woman. Her vivid amber hair fell to her hips, framing her freckled face and full lips. She wore a simple blue dress, its hem skirting the floor, the bodice fitted snugly to her chest.

The founder. She wasn't what I'd pictured.

"Welcome. I've been expecting you." Eyes so dark they were nearly black studied me as intently as I studied her until a flicker appeared near her forehead.

"You're glamoured." It was unmistakable.

"A requirement of my position, I'm afraid. It's as much for your protection as it is for mine. Few have seen my true appearance, and fewer yet know my name. Wearing a glamour ensures you don't bear the burden of unnecessary secrets."

"She changes her appearance often," Reuben said, bowing his head in acknowledgement to the founder. "If someone asked for a physical description, I wouldn't be able to provide one."

"I can scarcely remember what my true face is anymore. One day, I hope to meet it again." She crossed her legs, leaning forward in the chair. "I assume you're wondering why you're here?"

"Yes," I replied. "Reuben mentioned it's an honour usually reserved for those with more experience."

"Not quite. Experience often goes hand in hand with entitlement. I need to get the measure of someone before I know I can trust them, and that requires a delicate balance of time and insight. I wonder, are my instincts right about you?"

It would be unwise to answer without knowing her true purpose for revealing herself. "That depends on what you're referring to."

She gave me an approving smile. "Don't let my concealment fool you. Nothing happens in this castle without my knowledge. You're Willow Duskril, one hundred and twenty-six years old, born on the Tigal Isles. You've served faithfully as a scout for ninety years. You're known to be stubborn, reckless and difficult to work with, but have an otherwise impeccable record. When faced with a new challenge, you rose to the occasion and returned with more evidence than any of us had anticipated. You also earned the favour of a bloodline heir,

Lord to Eirel, who is now proposing an alliance." She cocked her head. "Well, have I forgotten anything?"

"I suppose that's an accurate summary," I managed to say.

She fixed me with a steady look. "Not a whisper of what I'm about to tell you is to leave this room. Do you understand?"

I nodded.

"The Night Ravens have existed for centuries without discovery because of how we're organised. Information is tightly controlled, kept strictly to those who need it to fulfil their orders. As a scout, you only have the context of your mission and are forbidden to share it with others. Reuben acts as a conduit, collating reports from across our scouting operations and distributing them where they're needed. When further research is required, he liaises with Eldon. If it pertains to our security, he informs Sal. They, in turn, keep me notified of their work. Hiding myself away ensures I protect that information."

She waved a hand at Reuben, who had been conspicuously quiet up until that point.

"The limitations of this approach are becoming increasingly apparent. Gathering intelligence and bringing it back to the Old Keep is no longer enough. By the time we've analysed it and decided what to do, it's too late," he said.

"We need a new class of scout, trusted resources in the field who are able to act on what they find without our guidance," the founder continued. "Norwyn and Calliste were our initial recruits, but we need greater numbers. I think you could be exactly what we're looking for."

My head felt dizzy with the revelations. "I don't understand. What do you need me to do?"

"For now, I want you to tell me, in your own words, everything you witnessed in Threstia." She crossed over to the circle of chairs, gesturing for me to take one of the seats. Reuben sat next to me.

I recounted the events of the research camp in as much detail as possible, leaving nothing out aside from the first kiss I'd shared with Silas. That memory was mine alone.

The founder made me repeat what I'd overheard several times, pursing her lips when I was finished.

After a moment of thought, she spoke. "Reuben, bring her up to speed."

"All of it?"

She nodded. "All of it."

Reuben approached my chair, grasping my hands in his. I tried not to stiffen in response, but I was fighting a losing battle, my body repulsed by his presence.

"Do you swear to never breathe a word of what you witness here to anyone else, unless permitted by the founder?" he said.

"I swear it." The bargain shimmered, winding itself around our arms.

He backed away, taking a seat opposite me. "While it's true that the Night Ravens were formed to protect Idrix, there's more to it than that. During our quest to find a way to break the curse, we realised there were plenty of fae with vested interests who benefit from it remaining unbroken, who would go to any lengths to stop us."

"But why? The curse destroys magic." Everyone wanted it stopped, didn't they?

"When a resource becomes scarce, there's profit to be made, power to be gained. Evil has infested every corner of Idrix, from the nobility in their castles to the villagers in their cottages, ensuring the curse isn't broken. We moved our work underground, keeping tabs on those we deemed suspicious. That's when we made our discovery."

The founder gestured for him to continue.

"Pockets of ancient magic still exist in Idrix today, despite the best efforts of the curse. You already know about enchanted artefacts and the fragment they contain, but there's more. Reserves that have yet to be discovered. Useless by themselves, they are echoes of the gods' power that once saturated Idrix. No one has learned of their existence until now."

He let out a tense breath. "We've identified a group of fae with a concerning interest in the remnants of ancient magic and whether it can be revived. The research site you uncovered appears to be one of their operations. There's also reports of artefacts going missing."

"That's why you sent me to the Amber City."

"I sent scouts to investigate every rumour," Reuben confirmed. "I'd hoped to gain a lead to follow up, or at least uncover an artefact we could use as bait to draw them out."

I bit my tongue about the one hanging around my neck, the seeking stone snugly hidden beneath my shirt. If Reuben hadn't sensed it, its existence was my secret to share. A bargaining chip I didn't want to play just yet.

"What do they want?"

"We're still trying to establish that. They appear to be an independent entity, unaffiliated with any of the districts."

The founder's eyes found mine, surprisingly vulnerable. "Ancient magic differed to Blessings. It wasn't an ability to wield, a gift from the gods, but their raw power, wild with a mind of its own. If it were to fall into the wrong hands, the curse would be the least of our worries. Anyone who could learn to harness it would be as powerful as the gods themselves."

A shiver ran through me.

"What about the portals the researchers were looking for? Are they real too?" It was a startling thought.

"They were once, before the curse destroyed them too," the founder said.

"Then other worlds exist?"

"Perhaps, though I wouldn't dwell on that. The portals existed in a different time, where magic was abundant. Even if someone did revive ancient magic, who's to say there would be enough to activate them?"

I took it all in, keeping my breathing even. There had been so much I hadn't been aware of, right beneath my nose. The world I thought I'd inhabited no longer existed. It was enough to overwhelm anyone.

But my newfound courage spread its reassuring warmth through me. I'd passed every test thrown at me, faced my worst fears in the process. I could handle this.

"What are my orders?"

The founder nodded at Reuben.

"For now, continue your work with the scholars. Their research on a cure for Dorea may also prove beneficial to our understanding of ancient magic. After that, we can talk about your next assignment."

That I could do. "And what about Silas? Will you accept his conditions?"

I needed him by my side more than ever.

The founder's mouth set in a firm line. "We don't interfere with politics. We must stay neutral."

"Please," I said, setting aside my pride. "He's sacrificed so much to come here."

She studied me. "Reuben believes him to be a liability," she said.

"It's not true." I rose to my feet. "I thought that too, once, but Silas has proven himself to be loyal, intelligent, and courageous. He was instrumental in infiltrating the research camp. I wouldn't have succeeded without him."

"Yet he refuses to join unless his conditions are met." Her tone was abrupt.

"Selfless conditions. He seeks reassurance that his subjects won't suffer due to his absence." I said. "Don't you see? We all want the same thing, to stop Idrix from being exploited by those with selfish ambitions. How long have you been trying to make a better world? How much progress have you made?"

I stalked towards Reuben. "I saw what it was like there. The common fae lived under constant threat of what the guards will do to them, and from what Silas has told me, the nobility isn't safe either. Nothing will change without our help. We might not be able to save the whole of Idrix tomorrow, but we could save one district."

"And what do you say?" the founder asked Reuben.

"It's a waste of our limited resources. We can't detract from our purpose to meddle in the affairs of the nobility."

I was losing control.

"How many members of the Night Ravens have a Blessing?" I countered.

"Nine." The founder sat forward in her chair.

"And how many could maintain a blackout for over an hour in an area vastly larger than the Old Keep? How many could raise a volcano beneath their feet? He's the most valuable asset you could have. Don't let him slip through your fingers."

"It's too risky." Reuben's voice was raised.

The founder looked between us, conflicted, the weight of Reuben's influence a powerful argument. I said the one thing I knew would sway him.

"There's something else. He's in possession of an artefact. A powerful one. As a sworn member, I'm sure he'd be more than happy to lend it to you."

It was the final push I'd needed to swing things in my favour. Reuben's surprise was palpable, rendering him speechless.

At his silence, the founder spoke. "Give the lord what he wants."

"But…"

She cut him off with a glare. "One mission, in exchange for the use of an artefact and a powerful Blessing? You won't find a better deal. Make the arrangements."

She rose to her feet, returning to the comfort of her armchair. "Next time, you will bring him with you. I want to see this power of his for myself."

Chapter 29

"How I've missed the sweet taste of freedom," Silas said, tilting his head towards the sky. He'd made just one request as Sal had unlocked his cell door, to feel the sun on his skin again. I was only too happy to oblige, sitting next to him on a stone bench in the Old Keep's courtyard, allowing myself a moment of peace. Reuben had released me from my duties for the day to help him settle in, a kindness I was certain I owed to the founder.

Making the bargain had been a formality once we'd secured her approval. Silas had been taken to Reuben's office, who looked less than thrilled at the prospect, the white light of the magic binding him and the four leaders of the Night Ravens together. When it was done, I'd flung myself at Silas, nearly tackling him to the floor.

The courtyard was a hive of activity. It fulfilled a dual purpose, a training space for the sentries and somewhere everyone could enjoy the outdoors without leaving the safety of the wards. Silas' gaze was fixed on the keep and the twisted tree that stubbornly grew through it, his jaw set. His hand rested on my thigh, absent-mindedly rubbing it through the material of my trousers.

I motioned to a group of sentries, their bare chests on full display as they grappled. A suspicious number of young women loitered nearby, eyeing their bouts intently. "Can I tempt you to join them?"

His dimples protruded as he smiled, his mood lifting as I'd hoped it would. "Are you sure you could control your jealousy? I'd attract quite the crowd."

"I believe I could tolerate it if it meant being blessed with such a striking view," I said.

His eyes burned into me. "Rest assured, that view is for your eyes only."

A steward interrupted us, handing Silas a pile of clothes identical to my own. He thanked them, rifling through them and holding the creased shirt up to the light. Warmth settled over me at the sight. It was real. He wasn't going anywhere.

"What do you reckon? Will the colour suit me?" he asked.

"It's not quite the gown I promised you, but it will do in the meantime." I stood, pulling him to his feet. "Are you ready for the grand tour?"

"Does it include the dormitory?" His gaze roved over me hungrily, leaving no doubt of his intentions.

"It does, but before you get too excited, you should know we're sharing a room with thirty others."

His expression soured. "I wasn't planning on an audience."

"There's a bright side to my punishment. I now have intimate knowledge of the castle." I trailed a finger down his chest, Silas shivering in response. "I know where the sentries don't patrol, and the location of every forgotten store cupboard. Once you're settled in, I think we should investigate further."

His hand caught mine, stopping it from travelling dangerously low. "Then we'd better get the necessities out of the way, because I won't stop until we've crossed off at least three things from my list."

With that to look forward to, I started the tour with the bathing chambers. Private stalls in the cellar held large, sunken pools, maintained by a handful of Water-Blessed fae. Where the dungeons were dark and dingy, here, sunlight peeked through gaps in the stone, reflecting off the calm waters. I led Silas into the nearest room, turning to leave.

"Aren't you joining me?" he said, lingering by the doorway.

"Not if we want to achieve anything today. Wash quickly, then get changed."

"You're no fun."

The breath rushed out of me when he emerged after several minutes. His damp hair was brushed back, a few rebellious strands falling onto his face. The cheap shirt fit him snugly, doing nothing to disguise the lean muscle underneath, and he'd left it open at the collar, exposing an indecent amount of skin. Thankfully, his trousers were loose, otherwise there wouldn't have been a soul in the Old Keep that could keep their eyes off him.

"Careful now. Look at me like that for much longer and I'll have no choice but to abandon this tour," he teased, catching me red-handed as I ogled him.

"Don't you dare distract me from my important work," I said, but my lip curved up in a grin.

The dormitories were up several staircases on the third floor of the keep. Silas' mouth hung open at the bunks crammed inside. How we practically slept on top of each other. It was the worst part of being a Night Raven.

"This one's mine." I gestured to a barely used bunk. I only stayed here on the odd night I wasn't on a mission, a rare occurrence, yet all scouts had their own bed allocated to them, a precious comfort to help us rest. "We can share until you're assigned one. It could take a while. They're still trying to make some rooms habitable."

"If you want to cuddle, you just need to ask," he said. "But if you insist on sharing a bunk, I suppose I'll go along with it."

Once he'd packed away his meagre belongings, he joined me on the familiar walk to Reuben's office. We returned downstairs, cutting through the empty dining hall, and out into the courtyard to reach the east wing. I taught him where to step to avoid the worst of the damaged staircases and cracked hallway. The last thing I wanted was for Silas to require a visit to the healers.

"Aren't we going inside?" he asked, watching me carefully as we hovered outside Reuben's door.

The truth was that I didn't want to. Reuben's betrayal was a raw wound, festering as time went on. Facing him would poison Silas' first day when it was the lift to our spirits we sorely needed.

"I'll spare you that particular ordeal for now," I finally said. "Reuben will request your presence soon enough."

If I had my way, he never would, but there was no doubt Silas would join the scouts. I hoped Reuben wouldn't be too tough on him.

I continued the tour, showing Silas where he could pick up supplies, and how to handle Barrett; and the medical room where healers patched up our more serious injuries. Finally, we ducked inside the library to introduce him to the scholars.

It was just as cluttered as Reuben's office, but with old books lining the walls instead of scrolls. A series of desks took up the floor space where scholars were hard at work, studying texts and making copious notes. Over the course of my punishment, I'd joined them, sometimes waking up hunched over a desk after a particularly late night.

Eldon greeted us with a smile. He was short and bald, with beady eyes that never missed a thing. His second in command, Idina, who also happened to be his wife, waved at us from her desk. He wasn't traditionally handsome, but whenever he looked at her, it was with such warmth that his whole face lit up, bringing out the radiance that lurked within.

"So, this is who was reading all those books you borrowed?" Eldon asked, studying Silas with a fascinated gleam in his eyes.

"Guilty as charged," Silas said.

"The pursuit of knowledge will always be an admirable quality. We are fortunate to have you. I've heard you have quite the Blessing." Silas beamed as Eldon turned to me. "I know you're not scheduled to join us this evening, but there's something I'd like to test. Would you come along at the usual time, both of you?"

"What is it?" I asked, curious. Eldon was a man of theories. If he wanted to test something, it was promising.

"I tasked Carmelia with studying rock compositions, among other lines of inquiry. For a while, it appeared to be a lost cause, but yesterday, in a tome that's seen better years, she found references to a type of rock that could absorb magic and inherit its abilities."

My eyes widened. "You think that's what Dorea touched?"

"It's possible." For Eldon, that was a grand statement.

"Why do you need me?" Silas interjected.

Eldon lowered his voice so only we could hear. "You're a powerful source of magic. From what little we understand, ancient magic is fickle. It seeks power, craves it. If my suspicions are correct and Dorea was exposed to it as an Unblessed, it's possible that it's draining her life in the absence of any higher power. If I can find a way to isolate your Blessing, and contain it in something she can ingest, we may be able to free her from its influence."

It could work.

Silas nodded. "I'll give you whatever you need."

"Thank you," I said, looking at them both.

"Don't thank me yet. This is just the beginning, but it's progress in the right direction."

"I hope so." Time wasn't on our side. With every failed attempt, the chances of saving Dorea were further out of my reach.

When our hunger became impossible to deny, we made our way to the dining hall. It was worse than I'd imagined. Hundreds of heads turned toward us, voices falling silent as we took a slice of pie and sat down. No one found the courage to join us as we perched on the end of a bench, Silas nearly finishing his meal before I'd taken a bite, but my skin prickled with awareness.

On the other side of the room, Norwyn ate, glaring at us. There were no visible injuries on his head and he'd managed to procure a new pair of spectacles, but the damage to our working relationship had been far deeper than that.

I jolted at the sound of a bowl being placed on the table. Calliste slid onto the bench opposite us. Long braids neatly framed her heart-shaped face. Her umber skin glowed in the candlelight, her brown eyes alight with curiosity.

"So, you're the one who brought a lord into the lion's den. Bold move, I like it." Her gaze travelled to Silas. "And you must be the lord in question."

Silas winked at her. "You can call me Silas."

My gaze strayed to Norwyn again, his hand shaking as he held his fork.

Calliste turned to see what had caught my attention. "Don't worry about him. He's just annoyed you bested him. Leave him to lick his wounds for a few days."

"I don't know if he'll be so quick to forgive and forget," I said.

"Take it from someone who's known him a long time. He will once his ego's recovered. Just be prepared for him to ice you out in the meantime." She leant towards us conspiringly. "I heard you broke into a hostile camp and stole evidence. Is it true?"

"For a secret order, everyone sure is terrible at keeping secrets," I muttered under my breath.

"It's true," Silas said, wearing a proud smile. "We took out a dozen guards in the process."

She raised an eyebrow. "Consider me impressed."

Reuben joined Norwyn's table, both of them shooting furtive glances in my direction.

Calliste sighed. "I don't know what happened between you two, but Reuben means well, even if he does a poor job of showing it."

"He betrayed my trust," I bit out.

"Have you known him to do anything without good reason? You have every right to be pissed off, I'm sure, but don't let it ruin this opportunity for you. You've earned it."

We were interrupted by a squeal of delight.

"Cal, when did you get back?" Sal strode over to our table, engulfing Calliste in a bear hug.

"Late last night," she answered, her voice muffled.

Sal jabbed a finger at Silas. "I wasn't at the gatehouse to greet you because of the trouble this one caused."

"I'll have you know I'm a delight." Silas said, indignant.

"And I've waited months for this."

Calliste patted her arm. "I have a gift for you. Remind me later."

"This is why you're my favourite scout." Sal gave me an apologetic look. "No offense."

"None taken," I replied.

Leaving them to their reunion, I finished Silas' tour outside the Old Keep, leading him through the Yewdew Forest until we'd passed through the wards. Reuben had insisted that Silas remained within the confines of the forest while the council was still looking for him, at least until there was a plan in place for the mission. Silas had reluctantly agreed, but I could tell being stuck here weighed on him.

"I have something for you," I said, removing the bow and quiver from my shoulder and handing it to him.

"You're giving me your bow?"

"No. Mine's still tucked away in the dormitory. This one's yours."

Silas gazed at me in disbelief. "You bought me a bow?"

"I had it made especially by one of the Earth-Blessed fae, though I think I may have scared him a little. I remembered how much you enjoyed using mine on our journey, and I thought you could practise while you're stuck here."

"Thank you, I'll treasure it." He pressed a kiss to my forehead.

"You don't have to thank me. You've given up everything to be here with me. I want to make it as easy on you as I can."

"So, what's next?" He smirked. "Another boring lecture for me?"

I glared at him. "They weren't boring, they were informative. It was thanks to my lessons that you know how to use that bow."

"And I'm eternally grateful." His lips brushed the tip of my ear as he spoke into it. "Why don't we find one of those cupboards you mentioned?"

If he thought it would be that easy, he was mistaken. "You'll have to catch me first."

Chapter 30

I didn't give Silas a chance to react, dashing through the forest at full speed. My blood heated at the sound of his footsteps behind me, hot on my tail.

"You're playing a dangerous game," he said as he chased me. "Are you sure you're ready for the consequences?"

A thrill went through me. "I'll take my chances."

I had the home advantage, knowing the Yewdew Forest as well as I did, but I'd underestimated his tenacity as he pursued me, weaving through the trees with ease.

Hopping the steps up to the gatehouse two at a time, I passed the sentry in Sal's usual position, shouting my apologies as I rushed past, Silas following close behind.

"Getting tired yet?" he said between breaths.

"You'll need to try harder than that to wear me out."

"I'm planning on it."

We crossed the courtyard, the sentries pausing their sparring to watch us, but I didn't slow down, knowing exactly where I was leading him.

I ducked into what remained of the north tower from its isolated position at the farthest reaches of the castle grounds. The roof had caved in long before it had become home to the Night Ravens, and it had been deemed unusable. Some even claimed it was haunted, but I'd learned the truth during my punishment. A sentry used his Air Blessing to make the wailing noises when he was bored on the night shift.

I jumped over a gap in the staircase, hearing Silas land behind me, soon reaching the circular room halfway up the tower that was as high as I could go.

"You've made a fatal error," he said, catching his breath.

"Perhaps I wanted to be caught."

He prowled towards me, cold stone meeting my skin as I backed into the wall. He braced his arms on either side of me, trapping me in his embrace. "Then I'd better make it worth your while."

His lips were scorching as they met mine, setting my blood on fire. I didn't hold back, tearing at his clothes as he kissed me vehemently, every moment in his embrace making me crave him more. I would never get enough.

When we broke apart, I leant in, desperate for more. Silas stopped me, his body hard against me as he pinned my arms above my head. "Keep them on the wall."

I bristled at the order, immediately disregarding it and dropping my hands.

A wicked grin crossed his face as he caught me by the wrist, restraining me with more force this time. "Don't move."

"Why?" I asked, struggling against him.

"Because I want to test how long you can last without touching me."

His words stoked the flames of my desire, my core already aching and wet for him. "You'll be waiting a long time."

"Then you underestimate me." He released my hands to untie my trousers, agonisingly slow as he rolled them down my hips. I held onto the cold metal of the unlit torch for support, curious to see what he would do next.

"I won't hold back," he said, his voice thick with lust.

"I'd be disappointed if you did."

He unlaced my boots one foot at a time, freeing my legs and tossing my trousers to one side, baring my bottom half. I didn't know what to expect, but it certainly wasn't Silas lifting me, bracing my thighs onto his shoulders.

"Hands," he growled, as they slipped from the torch in surprise, lowering his head between my legs once I'd complied. At the delicate brush of his tongue against me, I ignited.

"What? Fuck!" I said, hitting the wall as my back arched.

Silas didn't stop, his tongue whisper light as it circled my clit. I nearly lost the challenge immediately, wanting to grab onto him as I writhed against him, but my pride refused to let him master me so easily.

Still, I wouldn't last long, even with Silas drawing it out. I had never let anyone do this before, afraid it would feel too intimate, which I'd apparently been right about. All things considered; I was hanging on admirably well until I locked eyes with Silas. He smirked, pushing my thighs open wider.

A loud moan escaped me as he finally put me out of my misery, his hot mouth exactly where I needed it. My hands slid down the wall, scrambling to grip onto something as he feasted on me, his tongue feeling like it was everywhere, all at once.

I lost control of myself somewhere along the way, overtaken by my need, my fingers sinking into his hair, my body convulsing as he kept up his relentless rhythm.

My heart swelled with the intensity of my feelings for him. Silas wasn't just someone I would trust unquestionably, my closest confidante, but a bright flame to chase away the darkness in my soul.

He shifted and then his fingers plunged into me, each stroke bringing me closer to release as his tongue continued to tease my clit.

I came apart with a sob of pleasure, nearly crushing him with the power of my climax. Rather than showing any sign of discomfort, slowly, deliberately, he tasted me, looking downright obscene as satisfaction flashed in his eyes.

He would be the death of me.

"I need you," I said, the words as shaky as my legs.

"I'll never tire of hearing you say that," he replied, lowering me to the ground, keeping a firm grip on me until he was satisfied I could support my weight.

Neither of us messed around, the time for games over. Silas removed his cloak, laying it on the dusty floor in a chivalrous gesture, but otherwise didn't bother to undress. I freed his cock from his trousers, hiking up my shirt so I could watch him enter me.

"Better than the memory?" I couldn't resist asking.

"There's no comparison. A memory could never do you justice," he said, breathless.

His thrusts were unhurried, savouring the sensation of us finally being able to enjoy each other again. I trailed my hand down his cheek, caressing it with the tenderness he brought out in me. "I can't believe you're real."

"You're one to talk. Let me worship you like you deserve."

His cock pushed into me harder, coaxing a sigh from my lips, but still he continued his slow pace. I lifted my hips, allowing him deeper, rewarded by Silas' sharp intake of breath.

His hand travelled under my shirt, cupping my breast, but when his thumb brushed my nipple, it was hot. I jerked at the unexpected sensation, in surprise, not pain.

"Last time, we didn't have the opportunity to explore my Blessing. It would be a shame for you to miss out again."

His other hand joined it, Silas drinking in every reaction as he toyed with me, varying the levels of heat from his fingers, the contrast a cruel tease. All the while, he fucked me with his unrushed pace.

I was close, Silas sensing it and finally unleashing himself. He grabbed my hips, anchoring himself as he pounded into me, my thighs slick from his teasing.

"Together," he urged, reaching to where our bodies joined, heat kissing my clit. I shattered, losing all sense of reality, only aware of his teeth grazing my neck as his release claimed him.

We laid on his cloak panting for a while, not wanting to part, but then I shivered and he slipped out of me.

The light had faded around us, the room barely visible in the growing darkness. "We should get ready. It'll be time to head to the library soon."

"Duty calls. I promise to behave if you'll share the bathing pool with me." His gaze softened. "I don't want to be apart from you just yet."

"Fine, but we can't be late."

At nightfall, Eldon waited alone for us in a small room adjoining the library. It was occupied by a long bench; several glass tubes evenly spaced along its surface. I clasped Silas' hand as he took it all in.

"I hope you don't mind the change of scenery. I thought it wise to conduct this experiment away from the books. In my experience, they don't fare well under direct flame," Eldon said.

"How will this work?" Silas asked hesitantly.

"I've filled these vials with oil extracted from palai, a root found in Drei possessing the unique quality to preserve something in its current state permanently. It should contain Silas' magic if we can determine the right method of infusing it. We're going to test three variables that our research suggests would have the highest chance of success." Eldon walked behind the bench, standing behind the first vial. "Igniting the oil directly." He moved to the next. "Slowly heating it to its boiling point." His steps took him to the end of the bench, where he held up a scrap of parchment. "And finally, burning something before combining it."

"How will you know if it worked?" I said.

"We won't, for certain, though I'm hoping Silas here will be able to sense any remaining traces of his Blessing. We'd need to administer it directly for confirmation."

"I'm ready when you are," Silas said, resolute in his determination.

Eldon nodded, guiding me by the shoulders to the edge of the room. "We should stand back."

Silas pointed, his brow furrowed in concentration. Inside the tube, the oil caught fire, blue flames licking at the glass.

"Keep it going," Eldon said, watching intently.

Silas' eyes narrowed as he maintained his focus, his hand steady. The flames danced before burning out, a thin line of smoke rising from the liquid. He didn't falter, moving onto the second vial, until the contents bubbled and steamed, only half of it remaining afterwards. Finally, for the third, he burned the parchment while he held it, following Eldon's instructions before submerging it in the oil.

When the glass had cooled, Eldon poured them into three potion bottles, beckoning Silas over.

"Can you sense anything?" he asked.

Silas closed his eyes, his fingers brushing against each one. "I don't know what I'm looking for. There's maybe something, though it's weak."

"Can you identify which one?"

Silas shook his head. Hope died in my chest. We were so close. We had to be.

I couldn't fail Dorea after everything we'd been through. I would never forgive myself. "What if I took all three to Valtarra? Would there be any harm if she ingested them?"

Eldon frowned. "We wouldn't learn which worked. The results would be inconclusive."

"Dorea doesn't have the luxury of time. I'm sure Silas would support future experiments, but right now, all that matters is helping her." Tears danced in my eyes. "Please let me do this for her."

I braced myself for the dreaded words. *We can't save everyone.*

Eldon rubbed his head. "There's a chance it won't heal her," he said, "but I'm willing to let you try."

I ran to him, engulfing him in a relieved hug. Silas laughed as Eldon broke free, brushing down his clothing and staring at me in horror.

"Never do that again," Eldon said. "I must insist."

"It's my influence, I'm afraid." Silas explained. "I've softened up those hard edges of hers."

I took the potions from Eldon, carefully tucking them into my pack. All that remained was convincing Reuben to let me be the one to deliver them to Dorea.

I only hoped we'd done enough.

Chapter 31

Valtarra looked identical to how I'd left it. Even its blooming flowerbeds were the same height as before, evidently the pride and joy of an Earth-Blessed resident with a gift for precision. I strode confidently down the cobbled path, not caring what anyone thought of me.

There was a blemish on the immaculate appearance of the village, one which caused my chest to tighten. Shutters covered the bookshop's windows, a closed sign hung on the door. Window boxes that had once overflowed with peculiar plants had wilted and wasted away. It appeared abandoned, a mere ghost of the place where I'd first met Dorea and her mother.

Unease unfurled through me, holding me in its icy grip. Was I too late?

I'd brought the three vials of magic-infused palai oil to Reuben, knowing he was the key to securing my passage to Valtarra. He'd refused immediately, informing me someone else would deliver the possible cure to Dorea. It had taken me hours to convince him that the only fae Cassandra would trust with this would be me or him, and he couldn't leave without impacting every scout. In the end, he'd begrudgingly agreed I could go, but told me to be on my best behaviour.

Silas had waved me off, a flicker of envy crossing his face before he could hide it. Leaving him behind felt like losing a limb, but it was the safest course of action with the High Council searching for him. I was counting down the days until we could send a team to Eirel to free him for good.

Surprisingly, the bookshop's door was unlocked, creaking open with the slightest pressure. A thick layer of dust coated the inside, tickling the back of my throat. I spluttered, no doubt announcing my arrival if there was anyone left to hear it. The shop had been frozen in time, books cluttering the floor like someone was interrupted while shelving them.

"Hello?" I called out in a hoarse voice, climbing over the disturbed stacks as I navigated the room. It hadn't seen a customer in weeks, that much was apparent. My uncertainty at what I might find intensified.

The ceiling groaned before the sound of footsteps reverberated down the stairs, signalling someone's approach. I straightened, preparing myself. The door at the back burst open.

"We're closed. Please leave."

Cassandra looked like she'd aged a decade since I'd last seen her. Dark circles betrayed her lack of sleep, lines of worry etched into her forehead. She appeared smaller than before, a shadow of the woman I'd met the previous month.

"You...you came back." The glimmer of hope in her voice nearly broke me. I only hoped the antidote hadn't come too late to make a difference, if it even worked.

"I have something that may help Dorea. Where is she?" I asked, peering around. The shop was too quiet without her chaotic presence.

"She's resting upstairs. Did you find what you were looking for?"

I retrieved the vials from my pack, holding them up so they were visible in the dim room. "I hope so."

She gave me a heartbreaking smile. "Come with me."

I followed her up a winding staircase, so steep that I needed to use the handrail to help me climb. A storeroom awaited us at the top of the stairs, filled with piles of books as tall as the low ceiling. We wove through them to reach a room on the other side.

Only the barest of essentials furnished the sparse space. A bed, where Dorea lay unmoving, a table next to it, and a wooden chair, its backrest splintering away from the rest of it. Cassandra took a seat, body tense as she returned to her vigil.

The black veins now covered every inch of Dorea, her pale skin tinged with grey as the life leeched from it. Her hair had become brittle and lost most of its colour, her pillow coated in loose hairs that had already fallen out. Dread filled me until her chest moved with a shallow, rattling breath. She had survived, but the end was near. That much was obvious.

"We believe we've figured out the cause of her affliction, though I'm not permitted to tell you." If Cassandra was surprised by my statement, she didn't show it. I continued. "I'm afraid there are no guarantees, but one of these three vials may contain a cure."

I removed the stopper from the first vial, taking great care not to spill a drop. Eldon had been clear with his instructions. Dorea must drink the entire vial for the antidote to take effect, regardless of which, if any, held the true cure.

"Can you help Dorea sit upright on the bed and make sure her mouth stays open?" I asked Cassandra. She nodded and carefully arranged Dorea in a comfortable position on her pillows.

I tipped the oil down Dorea's throat, one bottle at a time, tilting her chin to make sure she swallowed without choking. For a moment, nothing happened, and I worried that we'd failed.

Then, so slowly I had to blink to confirm my eyes weren't tricking me, the tendrils started to recede. Colour returned to Dorea's greying skin, her cheeks becoming rosier and her hair regaining some of its shine.

The cure was working.

Cassandra sobbed in relief, collapsing back into the rickety chair next to the bed. The veins had disappeared from Dorea's face and neck, and were withdrawing from her chest.

Her eyes blinked open weakly. "Mother," she said, her voice hoarse from misuse.

"Thank the gods. I've been so worried." Cassandra turned to me, her eyes shining with tears.

"How are you feeling?" I asked Dorea, making sure the improvements weren't superficial.

"The pain. It's gone." She smiled, the movement weak, but victory roared in my chest.

Cassandra sobbed, reaching for my hand. I grasped it gladly. "I don't know how we'll ever repay you," she said.

"There's no need. Your information led to a major breakthrough. You've done a lot of good."

The Night Ravens had dispatched a team to investigate Threstia based on mine and Silas' reports. Although all traces of the research camp had disappeared, they'd brought back soil samples from areas where the ground had been disturbed. Whatever they'd found had thrown the Old Keep into a frenzy, and Reuben had spent more and more time tied up with the founder.

Despite the relief of finding a working antidote, their suffering was far from over. Cassandra and Dorea looked like a strong gust of wind would knock them over.

I handed Dorea my canteen of water, which she accepted gratefully with shaky hands. But that wasn't enough.

"I'll be back soon. Make sure you get some rest." I gave a meaningful look to Dorea's mother. "Both of you."

They needed to prioritise their recovery and they couldn't do that if they weren't sure where their next meal was coming from. I decided to set them up with a hot meal and enough supplies to get back on their feet before I returned for my next orders.

My quest began in the kitchen, emptying my newly procured sack of raglaw onto the counter where I plucked and trimmed the meat before coating it in salt and packing it away. I kept one aside, chopping it into small pieces.

When I finished, I spent what remained in my coin purse to stock their pantry from Valtarra's market, including vegetables to complement the raglaw. The merchants initially balked at my attempts to barter on cost, but relented when I explained who it was for.

Cooking was not my forte. But that mattered little, so long as the result was edible and contained enough sustenance to nurse Cassandra and Dorea back to health. In the end, I gave up navigating the bookshop's tiny kitchen, instead bringing a heavy pot to the outskirts of Valtarra and building a campfire. Lighting it posed no challenge, not when I could ask for help from the villagers, who were more than happy to lend a hand.

I carried a steaming tray of raglaw soup up to the bedroom where Dorea rested. Cassandra was hunched over the bed, asleep on her arms, whilst Dorea slept soundly. I cleared my throat, both of them stirring.

"I've left some food in the pantry. It should keep you going for a while. But this should help in the meantime."

Cassandra smiled weakly at me as I placed the tray beside the bed. "Thank you. For everything."

She retrieved a dusty book from a shelf behind her. "This is for you. A small token of our appreciation."

"I told you before, you don't owe me anything," I insisted.

"I know. But I want you to have this. It's a tome covering Idrixian history passed down through my family. I believe you'll find it insightful."

"Thank you." The gesture didn't go unappreciated, but I rarely had enough free time to read. Still, I was sure it would make a worthy addition to Eldon's ever-growing library. "I must leave now, but will you be able to hang in there?"

"Of course. We have everything we need." Her gaze was on Dorea as she ate a dainty mouthful of the soup.

"Oh, I nearly forgot. There's something else. Reuben asked me to give this to you." I retrieved a sealed scroll from my pocket, passing it to Cassandra. She examined it with interest.

"He enjoys his letters." She smiled wistfully. "Do stop by, if you're ever in the area. There will always be a hot cup of tea waiting for you here."

Warmth surrounded me at the thought. Friendship had felt out of reach for so long, an honour reserved for those free of my burdens, but now I was fortunate to have several friends dear to my heart.

I would treasure them.

A few days later, I arrived at the Old Keep, unable to wipe the smile from my face. Silas wasn't in the dormitory like I'd expected, or the weapons store or dining hall. I ducked my head into other places, flushing at the inquisitive looks sent in my direction. Adjusting to the attention that now followed me would require some time. I'd always taken my anonymity for granted, wielding it as a quiet weapon. The spotlight exposed me, giving me nowhere to hide.

A commotion in the inner courtyard drew my curiosity. The Old Keep offered little in the way of diversions, everyone too busy working on their assignments for much else. Mealtimes provided an opportunity to bond, but even then, talk rarely strayed beyond our duties.

My eyes took a moment to adapt to the sunlight as I left the dimly lit hallway and went outside. A flaming bird flew past me, not unlike a raglaw in size. I jumped back on instinct. Silas soaked up the attention of his audience like a performer on a stage, showing off by sending more birds soaring around a crowd of delighted children who giggled and chased after them.

"Don't feed his ego," I said as they marvelled at the display. "If his head grows any bigger, he'll struggle to stay upright."

"And there was me thinking you were rather fond of my appearance. I must have been mistaken." His eyes twinkled in challenge and the barest hint of unrestrained longing. "Show's over for today."

A chorus of protests met his words, the group surrounding him and demanding his attention.

"Will you come back tomorrow?" one child asked. "I want to see a dragon!"

The children squealed in excitement.

"Fine, I will, but only if you listen to your parents. Especially you, Kairos. I've heard all about how much trouble you've caused."

"But if we behave, you'll come back?"

"Yes, I promise." A sly smirk crept across his face, causing my skin to prickle with awareness. He dismissed the children with a wave. "Now run along. I have important business to attend to."

As the crowd cleared, I made my way towards him. "You've assembled quite the fan club."

"Can you blame them? Look at me." He twirled, gesturing at himself. He wore the standard issue clothing all Night Ravens recruits were provided with, yet the garments looked like they'd been made for him. "Besides, you're the founding member."

"I am?"

"You were singing my praises the other day. Do you need a reminder?"

I let my gaze settle on his mouth. "I believe I will, at least once I've recovered from the mission."

Silas' arm snaked around my waist, pulling me against him. He murmured in my ear, in a low, seductive tone, "who says I haven't considered that in my plans for you? I intend to take great care of you."

I shivered in anticipation, earning a dark chuckle. His hand found mine, leading me back inside the keep, and down to the bathing pools. He stayed true to his word, heating the water until it was blissfully hot. Delicately, he removed my clothes, neatly folding them, before doing the same for himself. Stepping into the pool, he helped me down the steps until we were both submerged in its warm embrace.

I expected him to stir my need with teasing touches and burning kisses. But he surprised me, reaching for a jug and using it to dampen my hair. His deft fingers lathered it into my scalp, sighs of contentment falling from my lips.

"That feels divine," I said, leaning into his touch.

"I thought you refused to feed my ego?" He massaged the soap into my skin, working out a knot that had formed in my shoulders during the mission.

"I'm making an exception." I closed my eyes, savouring the warmth of the water as it lapped against my body. "What have you been up to in my absence?"

"Nothing much. They're not sure what to do with me. I tried joining the novice scouts in training, but you already taught me the basics. My boredom led to me distracting the class, so they scrapped that idea. I'm hunting a lot, as you saw, and keeping the children entertained, but that's it."

I turned to face him, running my hand down his cheek. "We'll fix it, I promise."

"I know." He laughed, but the smile didn't quite reach his eyes. "Who knew I'd miss sleeping outside on the ground?"

I kissed his forehead. "Maybe you don't have to miss it."

We finished bathing and dressed quickly. I pressed a finger to my lips, beckoning Silas to the shadows. He rose to the challenge, sneaking around the keep by my side like a seasoned scout. We reached a supply cupboard without detection, but instead of occupying it, we merely swiped some bedrolls and a few blankets.

Sal crossed her arms as we exited the gatehouse, fixing us with a stern look from her position guarding the castle. I plastered on my best pleading smile, hoping she'd understand how much Silas needed a break.

She sighed, but a grin broke through the facade. "Fine, it's none of my business, anyway. Just don't do anything stupid."

We fell into our old routine, setting up our camp in a secluded part of the forest. It wasn't long before two raglaw were roasting on the fire as we huddled together, sharing the blankets beneath the stars.

"I never asked. Why did you decide to brave the Yewdew Forest the day we met?" I said.

Silas smiled sadly. "My brother told me that the forest always provides. In hindsight, that was probably more rooted in his Earth Blessing than survival skills, but when I succeeded in my escape and needed somewhere to go, it stuck with me. What better place to lie low than a forest no one wants to visit? But when I got here, I quickly realised I was out of my depth. Luckily for me, a beautiful, fierce woman, with a talent for hunting raglaw crossed my path."

"And then promptly told you where to go," I finished, removing the birds from the campfire and serving them. We'd eaten them before they'd had a chance to fully cool down.

"I should've known I was a goner then."

"All it took was a few bottles of moon wine and some well-timed kisses."

Silas grinned. "What can I say? I'm a romantic at heart."

I nestled closer to him, the warmth of his skin caressing me. "Thank you for teaching me to trust again. I couldn't have done this without you."

"I doubt that, but I'll happily take the credit." He played with a strand of my hair, twisting it around his fingers. "So, it was my kisses that won your heart?"

"Amongst other things. But I'll need a reminder to be sure of it."

I melted into Silas, enjoying the sensation of him, demanding and confident, as he captured my lower lip between his teeth. I tugged at his shirt, wanting to feel his warm skin. He obliged, raising his arms to allow me to undress him. My hands greedily roved over him, the muscles of his chest flexing at my soft caresses. He was amusingly responsive, responding with enthusiasm to my touch.

Silas slipped his hand inside my trousers, finding the thin layer of my underwear already damp with need. His lips latched onto the sensitive skin of my collarbone as he teased me through the fabric, sending sparks of pleasure through me.

"More," I moaned, desperate for there to be nothing between us.

"Anything for you."

Silas undressed me slowly, leaving me bared for him. I was glad for our secluded spot, far enough from the Old Keep for there to be little chance of us being discovered. He made to resume his teasing, but I held up a hand to stop him.

"Not until you lose the clothes."

His eyes burned with an intensity that stole my breath. Then he straightened, a slow smile spreading on his face. "Very well."

Excruciatingly slowly, every second stoking my anticipation, Silas undid the fastenings of his trousers. They fell to the floor, revealing his hard length, where he stepped out of them and closed the distance between us.

I reached for him, covering his lips with mine. He pushed me down on my bedroll, nudging my legs open with his knee. His fingers, warmed with the heat of his Blessing, trailed up my thighs to where they joined, dragging through the wetness he found there.

The touch was slow, tormenting my unrelenting need for him. I was burning up, driven by the urgency of my desire. He smiled, as if reading my mind.

I pushed him away, covering his body with my own when he fell backwards. My tongue swirled seductive patterns down his chest, drawing satisfaction from the way he tensed in response, his chest heaving. Eyes dazed with pleasure watched me intensely as I reached his groin, pressing a soft kiss to the tip of his cock.

Silas shuddered, his eyes flickering closed. He was a work of art, as handsome within as he was on the outside. I couldn't help but enjoy his every reaction, the way his jaw clenched at the feel of my breath on him, his hand fisting the blankets as my tongue lightly traced his length, the whimper that escaped when I finally wrapped my mouth around him. I craved more of the subtle salty taste of him. His low moans as I took him deeper set me aflame, and I needed him to completely unravel at my hands.

A firm grip on my shoulder made me pause.

"It's too good. I need a moment," he said, taking the opportunity to catch his breath.

"Struggling to keep up with me?" I teased.

His eyes flashed. "Is that a challenge?"

"Do you want it to be?" I crawled to him with a boldness I didn't know I possessed, settling on top of him with his cock pressing insistently against my entrance.

His voice was dark and dangerous, my blood surging in response. "The last one to find their release is the victor."

My mouth widened in surprise at his wicked proposal, curving into an amused smile. "You're on."

I sank down on him without warning, biting back a moan. The challenge would be more difficult than I'd anticipated, but I wasn't one to back down. Silas grasped my waist, guiding the movement of my hips, grinding me against him with wild, frantic need.

Every stroke brought me closer to my ruin. I sucked in a breath, staving off the pleasure. Silas watched with rapt attention, his eyes glazed over in sinful rapture.

I ground against him with reckless abandon. He let out a strangled noise, his grip tightening on my hips.

"Willow," he pleaded, thrusting to match my rhythm. It all suddenly became too much, and I lost control.

I trembled, coming undone with a cry. Silas groaned, joining me in oblivion, controlling our movements as we melded together in perfect harmony, riding out our pleasure.

"Who won?" I asked later, snuggling up against him under the blankets.

Silas shot me a wolfish grin. "It was too close to call. Guess we'll need a rematch."

"Same time tomorrow?"

"Naturally." His smile faded. "It's good to have you back. Watching you leave cleaved my heart in two, but it's worth every second to welcome you home again."

I held onto him tightly, never wanting to let go. "You are my home. And next time, you won't have a chance to miss me."

He sat up with a jolt. "What do you mean?"

My joy was bright enough to light the whole forest. "Reuben summoned me just before I came to find you. I'm going to Eirel and you're coming with me."

Author's Note

Thank you so much for reading The Archer & The Flame. I hope you enjoyed your adventures in Idrix as much as I enjoyed writing this book. Willow and Silas' story will conclude in book two of the Whispers of the Night Ravens duology, and further details will be announced soon.

It would mean the world to me if you left a review on your preferred platform. As a new author, every single review makes a difference and is massively appreciated.

If you'd like to keep up with the latest updates and receive bonus chapters from Silas' POV, you can join my newsletter at marievioletauthor.com.

Acknowledgements

To *Andrew*, my partner, and real-life romantic hero. Thanks for your endless patience and belief in me. And thank you in advance for all the spreadsheets I'll be requesting you make to aid my author journey!

To my sister, *Claire*, the only person I can trust with my KU history — I did it! You've always shown me what a strong woman is capable of, and I am so lucky to have you in my life.

To *Ana* and *Victoria*, my character artists, you are incredible! Seeing your interpretations of these characters who are so close to my heart has been a real highlight of this process, and I loved working with you so much.

To my incredible beta readers (in no particular order): *Paulina Grenda, Lauren, Frankie, Viktorija Severgina, Kirsten, FromTheFae, Kirsty (thebookdragon), Amber Kira Sky Mcloughlin, Brittany, Nora Nyberg, Kaylea, Bookgirly68, Catherine Brown, Kath Jacks, Charlotte, Shelby Crosier, Clarissa Stark, Hayley Kent, A.J. Charlotte, JHughes, K. M. Burns, Aaliyah, Courtney C, Pippa,* and *Emsy Lynch*. This book wouldn't exist without you and I don't say that lightly. It takes a special kind of person to not only give a debut author a chance, but read an early draft and give thoughtful, insightful feedback. I hope you can see how your hard work has helped shape this story, and I cannot thank you enough.

To the Bookstagrammers and Booktokers who stumbled across one of my posts and have rooted for me ever since. Your support has been the thing that kept me going on the hard days and each one of you is special to me.

And finally, to you, my readers. Thank you for spending your precious free time with me. Without you, this dream wouldn't be possible.

www.ingramcontent.com/pod-product-compliance
Lightning Source LLC
Chambersburg PA
CBHW030937120726
47906CB00002B/603